# DEATH SONG

# MICHAEL McGARRITY

# DEATH SONG

## A KEVIN KERNEY NOVEL

DUTTON

DUTTON
Published by Penguin Group (USA) Inc.
375 Hudson Street, New York, New York 10014, U.S.A.
Penguin Group (Canada), 90 Eglinton Avenue East, Suite 700, Toronto, Ontario M4P 2Y3, Canada (a
division of Pearson Penguin Canada Inc.); Penguin Books Ltd, 80 Strand, London WC2R 0RL, England;
Penguin Ireland, 25 St Stephen's Green, Dublin 2, Ireland (a division of Penguin Books Ltd); Penguin
Group (Australia), 250 Camberwell Road, Camberwell, Victoria 3124, Australia (a division of Pearson
Australia Group Pty Ltd); Penguin Books India Pvt Ltd, 11 Community Centre, Panchsheel Park, New
Delhi—110 017, India; Penguin Group (NZ), 67 Apollo Drive, Rosedale, North Shore 0632,
New Zealand (a division of Pearson New Zealand Ltd); Penguin Books (South Africa) (Pty) Ltd,
24 Sturdee Avenue, Rosebank, Johannesburg 2196, South Africa

Penguin Books Ltd, Registered Offices: 80 Strand, London WC2R 0RL, England

Published by Dutton, a member of Penguin Group (USA) Inc.

First printing, January 2008
1   3   5   7   9   10   8   6   4   2

⬛ REGISTERED TRADEMARK—MARCA REGISTRADA

LIBRARY OF CONGRESS CATALOGING-IN-PUBLICATION DATA
McGarrity, Michael.
Death song: a Kevin Kerney novel / Michael McGarrity.
p.    cm.
ISBN 978-0-525-95036-3
1. Kerney, Kevin (Fictitious character)—Fiction.   2. Police—New Mexico—Santa Fe—Fiction.
3. Police chiefs—Fiction.   4. Santa Fe (N.M.)—Fiction.   I. Title.
PS3563.C36359D43 2008
813'.54—dc22      2007026642

Printed in the United States of America
Set in Sabon

## PUBLISHER'S NOTE

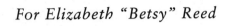

*For Elizabeth "Betsy" Reed*

Thanks go to James and Lynda Sanchez of Lincoln, New Mexico; Peter Rogers and Carol Hurd Rogers of San Patricio, New Mexico; former Capitan police chief Robert Bird; former Capitan mayor Steve Sederwall; Capitan municipal judge J. D. Roehrig; and retired Lincoln County sheriff Tom Sullivan.

# Chapter**One**

The week had been a long grind for Sergeant Clayton Istee. On paper he'd been scheduled to pull four ten-hour shifts, but the demands of the job had turned his workweek into five twelve-hour days.

In small, underfunded, undermanned law enforcement agencies, officers routinely carried out multiple assignments that required constant juggling of their time and priorities. The Lincoln County Sheriff's Office was no different, and while Clayton's primary duties consisted of supervising patrol deputies and serving as lead investigator for all major felony cases, he'd recently taken on the additional responsibility of training supervisor for the department. As a result, he'd been forced to work overtime and put in an extra day on the job to get a newly hired deputy up to speed.

In general, Clayton enjoyed the variety that came with his job and had no complaints, other than he didn't get to see his family enough. From a professional standpoint, the time he'd spent with the Lincoln County S.O. had been much more satisfying and rewarding than the years he'd worked as an officer with the Mescalero Apache Tribal Police. But five twelve-hour days in a row was pushing it even for Clayton, and he was eager to end the week and get home at a reasonable hour.

The new deputy, Tim Riley, a certified police officer with six years' experience, had spent most of the week in Clayton's company learning the ropes. Clayton had toured Riley through the back roads and out-of-the-way places in the county, introduced him to criminal justice and law enforcement personnel, walked him through the county jail, and showed him some of the best places to run radar.

He coached Riley on department protocols and procedures, watched him conduct traffic stops, had him handle a report of a gas skip at a convenience store, and showed him where some of the badass felons and sexual predators on parole from the state pen lived. Now the only thing that stood in the way of turning Riley loose on his own was getting him certified with his department-issued firearms.

On Friday afternoon Clayton drove Riley to the range the S.O. used for weapons recertification, where a state police firearms instructor from Roswell was standing by to test Riley's proficiency with a .45 semiautomatic and a pump-action shotgun.

A quiet man in his mid-forties, Riley was more than ten years older than Clayton, but the differences in their rank and age didn't appear to be a problem. Riley had a low-key, pleasant personality, wasn't bothered by long periods of silence, and rarely made small talk. By the end of the week, Clayton knew very little about the man other than he was married, had a grown son from a prior marriage, and was a retired air force master sergeant.

Riley's five foot, ten inch frame matched Clayton's height, and although he carried a few extra pounds around his gut, he looked to be in good physical shape. He had brown eyes and a long narrow face that gave him a somewhat serious look that was offset by an easy smile.

At the firing range, Clayton turned Riley over to the instructor, and watched from his unit to avoid the swirling, chilly March wind. First the instructor went over the range protocols and walked Riley through the outdoor combat pistol range, showing Riley what to expect on the course. Just as Riley was about to start a dry-fire practice run with the pop-up targets hidden from view, the wind kicked up a dust devil that obscured him from Clayton's sight. When the wind subsided and the dust settled, Riley ran the course with ease, holstering his weapon while moving from one concealment point to the next, assuming a proper shooting stance at each firing station.

Riley returned to the starting line, where he donned protective eyewear, loaded his weapon with live ammo, put extra magazine clips in the pouches on his belt, and waited for the instructor's signal to go. When it came, Clayton tracked Riley's progress with binoculars. After Riley finished, the instructor inspected the targets, tallied the score, and gave Clayton a thumbs-up sign. Then he moved Riley over to the adjacent stationary target range and tested him with the shotgun. Once live firing ceased, Clayton joined the instructor behind the firing line while Riley went downrange on the handgun course to pick up his spent brass.

"Good shooting," the state cop said, handing Clayton the paperwork. Riley had qualified as an expert marksman with both his department-issued 45-caliber semiautomatic and the twelve-gauge pump shotgun.

"Excellent," Clayton said as he slipped the signed paperwork into Riley's training file, went downrange, and gave his new deputy the good news.

Riley smiled slightly as he dumped his spent brass into a rusty coffee can. "I thought I did okay."

Clayton nodded. "More than okay. Let's head back to the office. Sheriff Hewitt will want to talk to you."

Riley feigned a worried look. "Am I in trouble already?"

Clayton laughed and shook his head. "No, he just wants to give you his traditional pep talk before he cuts you loose on patrol."

"The new guy speech?" Riley asked as he slipped a fresh magazine into his .45.

"Exactly."

Riley holstered his weapon. "Thanks for your help this week."

"Not a problem. Welcome to the Lincoln County S.O. I think you'll do just fine."

Riley laughed. "Believe me, I'm glad to be here."

On the drive to the sheriff's office in Carrizozo, the county seat, Clayton glanced at the dashboard clock. It looked like he would actually keep his promise to Grace to get home on time, so he could look after Wendell and Hannah while she attended an evening meeting of the Mescalero Apache Tribal Council.

Grace ran the child development center on the reservation and was scheduled to give her annual report and submit a budget request for additional funding. She'd been working hard on the project all week long.

In Carrizozo, Clayton took Riley into Sheriff Paul Hewitt's den of an office and sat quietly while Hewitt gave the new deputy his spiel about teamwork, the importance of the chain of command, his vision of community policing, and other weighty matters. The meeting ended with Riley amiably agreeing to work a double that evening to cover for an officer who'd called in sick.

Hewitt held Clayton back after Riley left. In his fifties, Hewitt was serving his last term as sheriff and would retire when it expired. He sat behind his big desk, kicked back in his chair with his cowboy boots up on the desk, rubbed his chin, and shot Clayton one of his patented "give it to me straight" looks.

"You've had Riley under your wing for a week. What do you think of him?"

"He's solid, levelheaded, and intelligent," Clayton said. "Takes direction and supervision well. The only question I have is why he never made any rank at his old job."

"Did you ask him about it?"

"Yeah. He said he likes patrol duty, likes being on the street, doesn't care much about moving up the chain of command, especially after being a top sergeant in the military."

"Do you buy it?" Hewitt asked.

Clayton shrugged. "Why not? Don't you?"

"It's possible," Hewitt said as he paged through the training report Clayton had assembled on Riley and the personnel records that his previous employer, the Santa Fe County Sheriff's Office, had sent down. "He got solid performance evaluations in his old job and was promoted to deputy three, which is equivalent to a corporal's rank."

"Did you talk to the Santa Fe County sheriff about Riley?" Clayton asked.

Hewitt closed the paperwork and got to his feet. "Yep, and he reassured me that I wasn't getting a reject or a screwup from his department. Said he was sorry to lose him. So let's hope Riley works out, likes it here, and stays with us."

"That would be nice," Clayton said.

"Don't you need to get home so Grace can go to an important meeting or some such?"

"Affirmative," Clayton said, rising to his feet.

Hewitt grinned. "Well, then, get the hell out of here, Sergeant, so I don't have to pay you any more overtime this week. Enjoy your days off."

Clayton threw Hewitt a quick salute on his way out the door, dumped his files into his desk drawer, locked it, went to his unit, and started home to the Rez.

After an unusually wet summer and fall, winter in New Mexico had failed to materialize. From December on, the days had been unseasonably warm and no measurable moisture had fallen. The mountains were bare of snow, and last summer's lush grasslands were now straw-colored tinder fields ready to explode into raging wildfires caused by a lightning strike, a careless smoker, or campfire embers kicked up by the wind.

Clayton took his favorite route home, driving the road that crossed the river by the old stone stables of Fort Stanton, an authentic nineteenth-century U.S. Army fort where General Blackjack Pershing had once served as a young officer. He passed the maritime cemetery where some World War Two German POWs were buried, and navigated a series of curves to the top of the mesa, where two dark and heavily forested mountain ranges filled the horizon east and west, sharp against a clear, cloudless sky.

A regional airport on the mesa served mainly private planes. Most of the rest of the tabletop land was state and federal, which kept the real estate developers at bay. But in the grassland valleys, vacation homes and five-acre ranchettes dotted the landscape, and on the private land near the town of Ruidoso, high-end gated communities with homes on million-dollar-view lots peppered the mesa.

Touted by the local politicos as evidence of a growing local economy, more subdivisions to serve the upscale vacation home market were in the planning stage. But Clayton didn't think that building second and third houses for very rich boomers benefited the area in any meaningful way.

The sun, bright in a cloudless sky, hovered at the tip of the Sierra Blanca Mountains. Clayton lowered the visor to cut the intense glare and reached for his sunglasses. When he glanced up, a deer attempting to hurdle the hood of his unit slammed into his windshield.

Clayton stomped hard on the brakes as the animal's front legs shattered the glass. The impact bounced the deer onto the roof, and Clayton heard the emergency light bar rip free and clatter to the pavement. Through the rearview mirror Clayton saw the deer thud onto the highway.

He peered as best he could through the shattered windshield, veered back into his lane, and ground to a stop at the side of the road, thankful that there had been no oncoming traffic. Shaken, he got out and walked to the animal. It was a buck with large ears and a white tail tipped with black that identified it as a mule deer. Clayton guessed it weighed about 350 pounds. It was mortally wounded: Blood streamed from its ears and mouth, and bone splinters jutted through the torn muscle and ligaments of its legs. The buck tried to lift its head, and the effort made it convulse in spasms.

Clayton stepped back, unholstered his .45 semiautomatic, chambered a round, and steadied his weapon. The animal's eyes blinked rapidly at Clayton just before he put it down with a bullet in the head.

Back at his unit, he assessed the damage to his vehicle. The hood and roof were caved in, the windshield and emergency light bar were destroyed, and a mangled right front fender had chewed up and shredded the tire right down to the rim.

He got some emergency road flares, put them on the highway to warn oncoming traffic, and called dispatch on his handheld radio to report the incident.

Paul Hewitt broke in on the transmission before dispatch could respond. "Clayton, are you all right?"

"Ten-four, Sheriff," Clayton responded. "But I'll need a tow truck at this location."

"Affirmative," Hewitt replied. "We've got personnel rolling to your twenty."

"I'm standing by," Clayton said as he disconnected. The sun had dropped behind the western mountains, and dusk had started to deepen. He went to his unit, got more flares, put them out, and then stood by the deer carcass with a flashlight to guide the occasional car around the scene.

Department policy required the state police to investigate any accidents involving on-duty sheriff's personnel, and Clayton knew it would take a good amount of time for the officer to conduct the investigation once he was on the scene. It didn't matter that it was clearly a no-fault incident; every detail would be done by the book because it involved another cop.

Clayton glanced at his watch. Even under the best of circumstances it would be several hours before he could get home. There was no way he'd be there in time to look after the children while Grace attended the tribal council meeting. He called her on his cell phone, explained what had happened, reassured her that he was unhurt, and gave her the bad news.

"Don't worry," Grace said. "I'll find someone to look after the children."

"Call my mother," Clayton said.

"I'm sure she'll be glad to help out. Are you certain you're not hurt?"

With his flashlight Clayton waved a slow-moving car around the deer carcass. "Not a scratch, but my unit is a mess and I'm gonna have to hitch a ride home."

"How did you manage to run into a deer?" Grace asked.

"You've got it reversed," Clayton replied. "The deer ran into me."

"Still, you killed Bambi's father," Grace whispered in mock seriousness.

Clayton laughed. "Please don't tell the children."

"Never," Grace replied. "I'll see you when you get home."

"Good luck with the tribal council."

"Thanks. Your dinner will be warming in the oven."

Clayton disconnected. He could see flashing emergency lights approaching from both directions. From the west, a volunteer fire department EMT unit slowed and stopped on the shoulder of the road, and two men hurried toward him. From the east, two S.O. units ground to a halt. Paul Hewitt and Tim Riley dismounted their vehicles and moved quickly in his direction.

There were more flashing lights coming down the highway

from Ruidoso, probably the state cop and the tow truck. Or a state game-and-fish officer. Or whoever, Clayton thought as he groaned inwardly. For the next several hours he would be on the receiving end of a police investigation, which was never a happy prospect, especially for a cop.

Clayton apologized to the dead buck before Sheriff Hewitt and Tim Riley drew near. He was truly sorry the animal had died for no good reason.

It was a hell of a way to start the weekend.


After making sure with his own eyes that Clayton was unhurt, Paul Hewitt stayed at the scene with his sergeant until the state police officer's investigation had been wrapped up, the dead buck had been removed from the roadway, all other emergency personnel had departed, and the tow truck operator had winched the disabled unit onto the flatbed and driven away.

In the back of Hewitt's vehicle, a 4×4 Explorer, Clayton had stowed all of his personal gear and the department-issued equipment he'd cleaned out of his unit. The two men sat in the Explorer and watched the blue flashing emergency lights of the tow truck fade down the highway into the night.

"Have you had enough excitement for one day?" Paul Hewitt asked as he cranked the engine to his unit. "If that buck had come through your windshield, chances are good that I would be on my way to tell your wife that she had just become a widow."

"That scared the bejesus out of me," Clayton replied.

Hewitt laughed and put his unit in gear. "Me too, and I wasn't even here. Let's get you home."

"Yeah," Clayton said. "Good idea."

On the drive, the two men fell silent. Weary from all the explaining he'd done at the crash scene, Clayton appreciated the quiet. Hewitt came to a stop in front of Clayton's house—a house that the sheriff had helped to rebuild some years back after a killer with a vendetta had blown it up in an attempt to murder Clayton and his family. It sat on a wooded lot a good ways in from the highway that ran through the reservation, but not too far from the village of Mescalero.

"The place is looking good," Hewitt said, eyeing the single-story house with a pitched roof that now sported a covered porch he hadn't seen before.

"It's coming along," Clayton said as the porch lights came on.

"I like the new porch," Hewitt said.

"It took a bunch of my days off to finish it," Clayton replied.

"Do you need a hand with your gear?" Hewitt asked.

Clayton opened the passenger door. "No, I've got it."

Hewitt nodded.

"Thanks for the ride, Sheriff," Clayton said.

Hewitt nodded again. "Not a problem."

Clayton gathered up his gear and carried it to the house. The front door opened and Grace stepped outside with Clayton's mother, Isabel. Clayton put his gear down and embraced the two women. The children, Wendell and Hannah, both in their pajamas, scooted out the front door and joined the family hug.

Paul Hewitt honked the horn once and drove away, happy—considering the alternative—to have been able to deliver Sergeant Clayton Istee home safe to his family.

Covering 4,859 square miles, Lincoln County was almost three thousand square miles larger than Santa Fe County, where Tim Riley had served as a deputy sheriff for six years. He was glad the population difference between the two counties was even more staggering. Home to about fifteen thousand permanent residents, Lincoln County had roughly one tenth the population of Santa Fe County and a much lower crime rate. Riley liked the idea of living and working in a place where folks were mostly law-abiding and the pace of life was a good deal slower.

When Tim had broached the subject of applying for the Lincoln County S.O. job to his wife, Denise, he'd expected her to dig in her heels and say no. Born and bred in Santa Fe, she loved living close to her siblings and her nieces and nephews. But surprisingly, Denise had backed Tim's decision all the way, asking only that they return to live in Santa Fe sometime in the not-too-distant future.

Encouraged by Denise's support, Tim immediately turned in his application and paperwork to the Lincoln County S.O. and interviewed with Sheriff Paul Hewitt and his chief deputy, Anthony Baca, as soon as he could. When the position was offered to him, Tim accepted on the spot and gave his two weeks' notice. Now he was working the new job, pulling his first solo patrol, and staying in a one-room cabin in Capitan, while Denise remained at home in their double-wide trailer until Tim found a place for them to live that would accept the two horses they owned.

The Santa Fe double-wide sat on twenty acres in Cañoncito, about ten miles outside of the city limits. Tim had paid cash for the land after a messy divorce from his first wife, who had walked away with half his air force retirement pension and almost everything else.

What was left over from the settlement, Tim had used as a sizable down payment on the double-wide, which was now paid off. But he wasn't about to sell the property. Land values had skyrocketed in Santa Fe County and would probably continue to rise, and Tim's dream was to someday build an honest-to-goodness real house on the acreage, throw up a good barn, and start a wilderness outfitting business.

Since coming to Lincoln County, Tim had used his free time trying to find a decent place to rent where he and Denise could keep their horses. Several of the locals warned him that finding such a place wouldn't be easy. After looking at a couple of run-down trailers on barren, fenced acreage and a ramshackle cottage that came with a collapsed two-stall horse barn, Tim had begun to agree with them.

He'd called Denise every night after work to give her an up-date on the job, which he liked, and his house hunting, which wasn't going well, although he tried to stay positive about it. Prospects had remained dim until Sheriff Hewitt hooked him up with a rancher who was willing to exchange free rent for a part-time caretaker.

Last night on the telephone with Denise, Tim had avoided saying anything about the offer until he met with the rancher and looked the place over. Early in the morning, he'd visited the ranch before starting work, met with the owner, and toured a really nice adobe cottage that was within shouting distance of a rambling, hacienda-style ranch house surrounded by a thicket of trees.

The rancher, George Staley, a friend of Sheriff Hewitt's, liked the prospect of having a sworn law enforcement officer living on the spread. Tim's sole duties would consist of keeping an eye on the ranch headquarters when Staley was away at his Texas ranch or looking after his other properties. All the cowboying and wrangling chores were the responsibility of a ranch manager and some hired hands.

It was a perfect arrangement, and Tim couldn't wait to tell Denise, but it wasn't until long after Clayton Istee's collision with the mule deer that he had a chance to call her. The first few times he tried, he got a busy signal and didn't think anything of it. But as more time passed, he continued to get a busy signal and it began to bother him. Denise didn't know he'd agreed to work a double and was expecting him to drive home to Santa Fe tonight. In fact, his arrival was overdue.

Even if she was having one of her marathon chats with one of her sisters, she could at least interrupt the phone conversation and answer the call waiting. He wondered if there was some family emergency happening with one of her siblings.

Although Tim's first night on solo patrol as a Lincoln County deputy had been quiet so far, he stayed focused on the job. It wasn't unheard of for supervisors to shadow and observe new officers on patrol. The sheriff, his chief deputy, or even Clayton Istee, for that matter, could be out there under the cover of darkness watching him, and Tim didn't want to get caught making any dumb mistakes.

While cruising through some of the small settlements along the Hondo Valley, patrolling two rural neighborhoods where recent burglaries had occurred, Tim continued to try calling home, each time getting a busy signal. Back on the main highway north of Carrizozo, he stopped on the shoulder of the road and clocked vehicles on his radar just to get a feel for the traffic flow. None of the big-rig truckers on the two-lane highway that ran from El Paso up to the Interstate paid any attention to the speed limit. But as soon as they spotted Tim's unit, brake lights flashed and the trucks slowed. A voice crackled over the police radio.

"What's your twenty?" Chief Craig Bolt of the Capitan Police Department asked.

"Highway 54 just north of Carrizozo," Tim answered.

"Are you ready for a cup of coffee?" Bolt asked.

"Affirmative," Tim replied. He'd met the chief earlier in the week and liked the man's straightforward style.

"The pot's on. Come on over to my office."

"Ten-four. ETA twenty minutes."

He put the unit in gear, headed toward Capitan, and cruised into the village where a prominent billboard on the west end of town proclaimed, "JESUS IS LORD OVER CAPITAN."

Earlier in the week, as they'd driven through the village, Clayton Istee had asked Tim what he thought about the message on the billboard.

"It's a bit too much for my taste," Tim said, caught off guard by the question.

"You've got that right," Clayton replied with a laugh. "The way I see it, gods come and go depending on what tribe rules the land, not who lives in the heavens."

"That's very philosophical," Tim said.

"You think so?" Clayton asked, shooting Tim a sharp look.

"Why not?" Tim said with a shrug. "Organized religion isn't a big deal to me."

Clayton nodded in agreement and grinned. "Hallelujah, brother."

Tim pulled to a stop at the Capitan Police Department, which shared space with other village agencies in a prefabricated metal building fronting Smokey Bear Boulevard, the main drag through town. Chief Craig Bolt's white Ford 4x4 with Smokey Bear's image on the door was parked next to the blue entrance, which also bore the bear's likeness.

Over fifty years ago, after a devastating forest fire in the nearby mountains, a young bear cub had been found alive clinging to the trunk of a burned tree. As Smokey Bear, the cub had gone on to become the most famous icon for forest fire prevention in the world. Because Capitan was the place where the legend had been born, Smokey Bear's name and image was now an indelible part of the town's identity. Capitan sported a Smokey Bear Historical Park, a Smokey Bear Museum, various businesses that bore Smokey's name, and the town hosted an annual Smokey Bear Festival and Smokey Bear rodeo.

Smokey's presence permeated the village, right down to the two life-size carved wooden bears, one black, one brown, that guarded the entrance to the town hall. Although Smokey did draw a fair number of travelers to the village, most stopped for a quick look on their way to somewhere else, and thus Capitan remained a quiet, pleasant, thriving ranching community and not an international tourist destination.

Tim stepped through the door and greeted the chief, who poured him a mug of hot coffee, held it out, and motioned to an empty chair.

About fifty years of age, Bolt was a stocky man five-eight in height with a broad upper body, gray hair cut short, and huge hands that hung down from chunky arms. He had the look of a former weightlifter who'd thickened up a bit but hadn't gone to seed. According to Clayton, Bolt had put in his twenty with the Las Cruces P.D. before retiring as a lieutenant and taking over the Capitan department.

"Thanks," Tim said, as he took the mug and settled into a squeaky chair behind a gray, government-surplus metal desk.

Bolt nodded as he raised his cup. "When you work late nights, the only fresh coffee you're gonna find in Capitan is right here in this office. If the lights are on, the pot is on. Come by for a cup anytime."

"That's good to know."

The Capitan police headquarters consisted of one fairly large room where Tim and the chief sat and two small offices. It was just adequate for Bolt and the two sworn officers who manned the department with him.

"Do you really have a lightning bolt tattooed on your arm?" Tim inquired.

Bolt chuckled. "Who told you to ask?"

"Clayton Istee, Sheriff Hewitt, Chief Deputy Baca, and just about everybody else who mentions your name."

Bolt rolled up his sleeve and held out his forearm. "Well, there it is. I got it when I was in the army serving with the Twenty-fifth Infantry Division."

Tim recognized the unit patch insignia. "Impressive."

"I'm gonna use it as part of my election campaign when I run for county sheriff next year," Bolt said. "My name, the lightning bolt. Get it?"

Tim nodded. "The chief deputy isn't going to run?" he asked. In New Mexico, sheriffs had to stand down after two consecutive four-year terms. Usually, the chief deputy would get elected and the two top cops would simply switch jobs for the next eight years. At least, that's the way it had been up in Santa Fe County during the time Riley had worked there.

"Anthony Baca is also retiring," Bolt said, showing his gums in a toothy smile. "Both Paul and Anthony are going to support me. So the chances are, if you're still with the S.O. by then, I'll be your new boss."

"That gives me something to look forward to," Tim said straight-faced.

Bolt huffed in a joking way and raised his eyebrows. "Are you being sarcastic with me, Deputy Riley?"

Tim laughed. "If I am, I better do it now before you get elected."

Bolt slapped his leg and smiled. "I like your style, Riley. So help me out here, I'm trying to come up with a catchy campaign slogan to go with my name. How does 'Zap the criminals. Elect Craig Bolt Sheriff of Lincoln County' sound to you?"

"That's good," Tim said, faking some enthusiasm.

"I don't like it either," Bolt said with a grimace. "It's too heavy-handed."

Tim nodded in agreement. "How about using 'Bolt the door on criminals in Lincoln County.'"

Bolt's eyes widened. He whistled and repeated the slogan. "I like that a lot better than what I came up with, a whole lot better. I think I'd like to run it by my campaign manager."

"Who's that?" Tim asked.

"My wife," Bolt said with a laugh.

"Speaking of wives, I've been trying to call my wife up in Santa Fe on my cell phone and haven't been able to get through. Mind if I make a quick call to her on your office phone?"

Bolt waved at the desk phone next to Riley's elbow. "Have at it. Do you need some privacy?"

Tim shook his head, dialed the number, got a busy signal, and hung up. "No luck," he said. He finished his coffee, got to his feet, and shrugged. "It can wait. I'll see her tomorrow when I get back to Santa Fe. Thanks for the coffee, Chief."

"The pot is always on. Next time you stop by I'll fill you in on some of the local Capitan characters you need to know about."

"I'll look forward to that," Riley replied as he headed out the door.

Bolt waited until he heard Riley drive away before dialing Paul Hewitt's cell phone number. "Where are you?" he asked after Hewitt answered.

"Sitting in my truck watching my new deputy drive out of town. So far, he's doing okay. Goes where he says, does what he says, isn't slacking off. Now that you've had a sit-down with him, what do you think?"

"I think he's a good one," Bolt said. "Are we still on for breakfast in the morning?"

"You bet," Hewitt replied.

"You going home now?"

"You bet," Hewitt said again.

"Me too." Bolt hung up, turned out the lights, locked the door, and went home.

In a troubled frame of mind, Deputy Tim Riley resumed patrol. He decided that something was wrong in Santa Fe. Denise should be calling him by now, wanting to know why he was late getting home. A few miles outside of Carrizozo he pulled off to the side of the highway, called the dispatcher, gave her his Santa Fe home phone number, and asked her to contact the phone company and have them check the number. Within minutes, the dispatcher reported that the phone was off the hook at Tim's Santa Fe residence.

"Okay," Riley said with a sense of relief, "that explains it. Thanks."

"Do you want me to ask the state police to send a uniform to check on her?" the dispatcher asked.

"Negative," Tim said. "Thanks anyway." He dropped the microphone on the seat and dialed his sister-in-law's number on his cell phone. When Helen answered, he explained the situation.

"She probably didn't hang up the phone properly," Helen said.

"I know," Tim replied. "But I'd feel better about it if you went out and checked on her."

"Of course."

"Have her call me right away."

"I will. She's going to be upset that she worried you unnecessarily."

"Tell her not to be. Thanks, Helen."

Tim disconnected and listened to incoming traffic on his radio. A Carrizozo police officer was en route to a fight in the parking lot of a local bar. Riley turned on his emergency lights, put his unit in gear, accelerated, and alerted the officer that he was on his way to assist.


In the eastside Santa Fe home her grandfather had built eighty years ago, now surrounded by millionaires' mansions, Helen Muiz found her husband sleeping in his favorite chair in the den with the television turned down low. She shook him awake and told him to put on his shoes and drive her to Cañoncito right away.

"What's the problem?" Ruben asked grouchily as he laced up his shoes.

"Probably nothing," Helen replied. "But Tim's worried because he can't reach Denise, and the phone company says it's because the phone is off the hook."

Ruben shook his head. "It's pretty late in the evening to go joyriding out to Cañoncito and back."

"Don't be such a grump, Ruben. You're retired, remember? So it's not like you have to get up in the morning and go to work. Besides, she's my baby sister and I'm worried about her."

Ruben knew better than to argue with Helen about her five sisters and one brother, all younger than she was. She was about to turn sixty and had been mother hen to all of them since their parents had died. Denise, the youngest by twenty-one years, was her favorite.

He went to the hall closest, got his jacket, put it on, and held out Helen's coat. She slipped her arms into the sleeves, turned around, and kissed him on the cheek. "I wish she wasn't moving to Lincoln County."

Ruben shrugged. "A wife goes with her husband."

"Chauvinist."

"I prefer the term traditionalist," Ruben replied.

"That may be, but you're still a chauvinist," Helen said, patting her husband on the arm. "There's no earthly reason for Tim to take Denise away to Lincoln County. He could have easily gotten a job with the Santa Fe Police Department."

Ruben opened the front door and stood aside to let his wife pass. "Yes, he could have. But I don't think he wanted that."

Helen looked sternly at Ruben. "Has he talked to you? Do you know why he's so set on moving away?"

Ruben shook his head. His wife had done her best to change Tim's mind about the job in Lincoln County. Helen had spent thirty-eight years working for the Santa Fe Police Department. She and her boss, Chief Kevin Kerney, a man she'd known since his first day on the job, were both retiring at the end of the month. She'd spoken to Kerney about Tim, who'd encouraged Helen to have him apply for a transfer to the SFPD. But Tim would have none of it.

"Some people thrive on change and variety," Ruben said. "Tim spent twenty years in the air force and lived all over the world. Maybe it's just in his blood."

Helen sighed and marched down the walkway toward the car. "Well, since her return to Santa Fe, it's certainly *not* in Denise's blood. I think she should come stay with us until Tim finds a place to rent in Lincoln County. I don't like the idea of her being out in Cañoncito by herself."

"I'm sure you'll tell her that when you see her," Ruben said as he opened the passenger door to the car.

Helen settled into her seat and grimaced at her husband. "I hate the idea of her moving away."

"I know you do," Ruben said, gazing at his lovely wife, who didn't look a day over fifty and had a figure that still earned admiring glances from strangers. "But they're only going to be living three hours away by car. We can easily visit."

Ruben got behind the wheel and Helen gave him a smooch. "You're always so logical," she said.

"Only when I'm not being chauvinistic." Ruben buckled his seat belt and cranked the engine. "Okay, let's go on this rescue mission so we can tell Denise to hang up her telephone."

A five-minute drive on empty city streets got them to the Old Las Vegas Highway, once part of the original Route 66 and now a frontage road that paralleled I-25. On the map, Cañoncito was a settlement where the pavement dead-ended at a small chapel. But in fact, houses, trailers, and double-wides were sprinkled through-out foothills and mesas all the way to the mainline railroad tracks that followed the Galisteo Creek south toward Albuquerque.

Tim and Denise lived up a small canyon near the creek, on a mixture of pasture and woodland, their double-wide tucked under some trees near a rock outcropping. Helen and Ruben arrived to find Denise's car parked outside, lights on inside the residence, and the front door ajar.

As soon as Helen saw her sister's car keys and purse on the kitchen counter and the wall phone dangling from the cord, she started to panic. In a loud voice she called out to Denise, only to be greeted by silence. Nothing appeared to be out of order in the front room, but it was unlike Denise to be gone from her home at such a late hour. Helen hurried through the rest of the house searching for her sister with Ruben at her heels.

"Something's wrong," she said when they returned to the front room. Her heart was racing and she patted her chest to catch her breath.

Ruben handed Helen his cell phone. "You call your sisters and brother, and I'll check the stable."

"She would have heard us if she was with the horses."

"Maybe not," Ruben replied calmly, trying to hide his own growing anxiety. "If I don't find her, I'll knock on the neighbor's front door. She could be just visiting nearby."

"I didn't see any lights on in that house when we drove by," Helen said.

"I'll check anyway. Call your sisters and brother. They might know where Denise is."

Helen speed-dialed a number. "Don't be long."

"I won't," Ruben said. Outside, he took a flashlight from the glove box of his car and walked to the corral and stable. Tim and Denise's two prize quarter horses were in their stalls. Ruben found the light switch. Both stalls were dirty and stinky from the smell of urine and manure. No feed or fresh water had been put out and the horses were restless, snorting in displeasure.

Ruben released the animals into the corral and walked around the stable. The horse trailer was parked in its usual place next to the old pickup truck Tim used to haul hay and supplies. He made a circle around the double-wide, shining his flashlight on the ground and behind the trees, thinking that maybe Denise had met with some accident. Finding nothing, he hiked down the driveway to the nearest neighbor and pounded on the front door. The porch light came on and a sleepy-eyed man in his fifties opened the door a crack and looked out.

"I've got a pistol," he growled. "What do you want?"

Ruben raised his hands. "I'm not a crook. I'm Denise Riley's brother-in-law. My wife and I are looking for her."

The man opened the door. His hair was matted against his forehead, and he had a very large pistol in his hand. "I haven't seen her drive by recently."

"Do you speak to her frequently?" Ruben asked.

"No, usually we just wave at each other."

"Could she be visiting some other neighbors?"

The man shrugged. "This time of night? I doubt it."

"Okay," Ruben said. "Thanks."

"Has she run off?" the man asked.

"We don't know," Ruben replied. Back at the house he found Helen standing outside on the deck, about to dial the cell phone.

"Did you learn anything?" she asked, snapping the cell phone closed.

Ruben shook his head. "You?"

Helen grimaced. "Nobody in the family has seen or talked to Denise in the past two days."

"The neighbor I spoke to asked me if she'd run off," Ruben said.

"Run off? That's absurd." Helen flipped open the cell phone.

"Are you calling Tim?"

Helen shook her head. "Not yet. I don't want to upset him any more than he already is. I'm calling Chief Kerney."

By the time Tim Riley arrived at the parking lot outside the Carrizozo bar, the fight had turned into a brawl. Six men and two women were mixing it up big-time. Fists were flying, kicks were landing, and the women were especially hard at it, pulling hair and gouging each other with their fingernails. It took some scuffling with the brawlers by Tim and the Carrizozo cop to settle things down, but eventually pepper spray did the trick. They made arrests, called for EMTs to treat the injuries sustained by the combatants, and took witness statements.

According to all concerned, brawlers and onlookers alike, the fight had started inside the bar when the two women began arguing about who had dibs to play the next game of pool. In all his years as a cop and as a career military criminal investigator, Tim had yet to hear a rational explanation for a bar fight given by drunks. Plausible excuses, perhaps, but never rational reasons.

Tim's shift had ended by the time the suspects in custody were transported and booked into the county jail. He finished the booking paperwork, went to the sheriff's department, and put his completed shift reports in the tray on the chief deputy's desk.

In the silence of the empty offices—there would be no deputies on duty until the morning shift—Tim again tried calling home on a landline, only to get another irritating busy signal. Why hadn't Denise called him? Or Helen for that matter?

Tim decided he couldn't wait for a phone call to find out what in the hell was going on at home. He'd go to his rented cabin, change into his civvies, and hit the road for Santa Fe. At this time of night, if he pushed it hard he could make it in under three hours.

In Capitan he rolled to a stop in front of the cabin. The street was dark and there were no lights on in any of the adjacent houses. Before he reported himself home and off duty, Tim searched the backseat of his unit. It was something he always did after transporting perps or prisoners. Experience had taught him that even when cuffed, people would hide items from the cops in police vehicles that had been overlooked in pat-down searches. Over the years, he'd found things like knives, drugs, needles, money, condoms, and wallets stuffed behind cushions and under the seat.

This night he found nothing, signed off with dispatch, locked his unit, and headed for the front door.

Behind him a familiar-sounding voice whispered, "Hey."

Startled, Tim turned, and the last thing he saw was the flash of a shotgun blast that hit him full force in the face.

# Chapter Two

The shotgun blast woke up nearby residents, and in the silence that followed, several nervous but curious neighbors left the warmth and safety of their homes to investigate. Separately they converged on Tim Riley's body lying in a pool of blood and called 911 to report it, their voices cracking with alarm. Within minutes, Craig Bolt and Paul Hewitt arrived at the scene. After a quick look to confirm that Riley was dead, they covered the body, cordoned off the area, and ordered every available officer under their commands back on duty ASAP.

A number of officers and some emergency personnel had gathered by the time Clayton pulled up to a police barrier on the street to Riley's rented cabin. In the numbingly cold night, a small crowd of citizens stood quietly gazing at the flashing lights of the police vehicles parked in front of the crime scene.

The deputy manning the barrier waved Clayton through. As he drove slowly down the street, he saw Craig Bolt's officers interviewing people outside their homes. On the sidewalk in front of Riley's rented cabin, two male civilians dressed in pajamas, slippers, and winter coats were giving statements to deputies.

Clayton parked his pickup truck next to Paul Hewitt's vehicle and spotted the sheriff standing near a tree in the front yard talking to his chief deputy and Chief Bolt. Crime scene tape had been strung from the cabin's front porch, wrapped around the rearview mirror and bumper of Riley's unit, and tied off on the antenna of a pickup truck parked close by. It formed a triangle that enclosed a body covered by a tarp, illuminated by the headlights of Craig Bolt's police vehicle.

Deputy Sheriff Bennie Anaya guarded the crime scene. Approaching sixty and close to retirement, Bennie was a jovial, roly-poly man who wasn't the smartest cop on the street by a long shot, but who did a barely adequate job of transporting prisoners to and from court.

"Who has inspected the body?" Clayton asked as he approached Anaya.

"Just the sheriff and Chief Bolt," Anaya replied. He held out his clipboard with a crime scene log-in sheet attached.

Clayton noted the time on the form and signed it. "Did you take a look, Bennie?"

Bennie nodded. "It's not a pretty sight."

Clayton handed him the clipboard. "Sign yourself in."

Bennie did as he was told.

"Has anyone been inside the cabin?" Clayton asked.

"I don't think so," Bennie replied. He paused and reconsidered his answer. "Maybe, before I got here. But the sheriff didn't say."

"Nobody enters the crime scene or the cabin without my permission," Clayton said, nodding in the direction of Hewitt, Bolt, and Baca. "That includes the top brass who are over there by that tree jawboning."

"Affirmative," Bennie replied.

"Do you know who else will be joining us?" Clayton asked.

"The DA and the medical investigator are on the way," Anaya said, "and state police are sending a mobile crime lab and some techs up from Las Cruces. Every law enforcement agency in the region has offered to help out."

Clayton ducked under the tape and put on a pair of gloves. "Do we have anything for them to do?"

Bennie snorted. "We don't have squat. Not yet, anyway."

"That could change," Clayton said as he walked to Riley's body, bent down, and pulled back the tarp. From the looks of it, a rifled shotgun slug fired at close range had almost obliterated Riley's face. A massive amount of blood from the large entry wound had saturated the ground under Riley's head. On his forehead, above what was left of his nose and eyes, gray brain matter dripped down like coagulated gobs of cooked pasta.

For a moment Clayton found it hard to remember what Riley had looked like before he'd been murdered. He forced his gaze away, composed himself, and rapped a knuckle on Riley's chest. As he suspected, Riley had been wearing his body armor. Did the murderer know that and take the head shot to be sure of the kill?

Clayton raised his eyes back to Riley's mangled face. Earlier, he had apologized to the deer for its needless death. Now he wondered what circumstance had gotten Riley killed. It surely wasn't a random act. From the position of the body, he guessed that Riley had turned to face his killer. Perhaps a sound had alerted him. He inspected the soles of Riley's boots, fished out a flashlight from his equipment bag, and went looking for footprints. The ground was too frozen to show fresh impressions, but on the porch he located two partials. One matched the tread on Riley's boot and the other did not.

Clayton dropped down for a closer look. Riley's footprint showed him leaving the cabin. Wind had obliterated part of the tread, and Clayton judged it to be the older of the two partials. The second, smaller footprint was fresher and pointed in the direction of the front door. There was nothing on the porch to suggest Riley had entered the cabin prior to the shooting. The presence of the second partial suggested the possibility that the killer had arrived before Riley and been lying in wait.

Clayton unzipped his equipment bag, pulled out his camera, and took photographs of the footprints, his thoughts focused on trying to figure out the sequence of events in the last few minutes of Tim Riley's life.

He walked to Riley's unit, studied the ground, and saw what appeared to be a small indentation of a boot tread on a crushed leaf near the rear of the vehicle. By the passenger-side rear door there was a partially broken twig that might have been caused by the weight of a step. In the flashlight beam he saw a crumpled-up piece of paper lodged against the rear tire. He picked it up and smoothed it out. It was a month-old Lincoln County credit card receipt for two new windshield wipers that had been purchased by another deputy.

Clayton wondered if Riley inspected his vehicle at the end of his shift. It was common practice among seasoned officers to do so. He imagined the scene. Riley would have been exposed and vulnerable while checking for contraband or cleaning out trash inside the unit. He would have been bent over with his back exposed. Why wait for a frontal shot when a slug to the back of the head would do the job just as well? Did the killer want Riley to see it coming?

Although there were no defensive wounds on Riley's hands, Clayton looked around for any sign of a struggle. Nothing on the ground or near Riley's unit pointed to an altercation.

The doors to Riley's unit were locked. If he had been on his way to the cabin, chances were good he would have had his keys in his hand. Clayton went back to the body. He searched around the corpse and emptied Riley's pockets. He rolled Riley carefully onto his side and looked for the keys on the ground under the body.

The exit wound was gruesome. He lowered Riley and glanced over at Deputy Anaya, who watched with interest. "Bennie, did you find Riley's keys?" Clayton called out.

Bennie smiled and patted his pants pocket. "Yeah, I secured them so that they wouldn't get lost."

Clayton forced a smile at Anaya. "Where exactly did you find them?"

"They were in his hand."

"Which hand?"

Bennie pulled the keys out of his pocket. "His right hand."

"Give them to me," Clayton said as he walked over to Anaya.

Bennie dropped the keys into Clayton's palm. Rather than chew out Anaya in public for being stupid, Clayton turned on his heel and went back to the body. Riley was right-handed. Clayton looked at his holstered sidearm. It was strapped down, which meant Riley hadn't anticipated any danger. Was that because the shooter was known to him, or simply because he'd been caught off guard?

"What have you got, Sergeant?" Paul Hewitt called out from behind the crime scene tape.

Clayton covered the body with the tarp and approached his boss. "I think the killer surveilled the cabin and waited for Riley to show up. There is a partial footprint on the porch which may belong to the perp. I've photographed it. I also believe that Riley either knew his attacker or was caught unawares. He had his keys in his hand and was walking toward the cabin just before he was killed. The head shot tells me that this was a deliberate murder carried out by someone who knew what he was doing. I believe he surmised Riley would be wearing body armor. Otherwise he would have aimed for the chest."

"A professional?" Hewitt asked.

"Not necessarily. I think the shooter wanted Riley to see him. A professional would have simply taken his first clean shot."

"You're saying it's revenge? A grudge? Something personal?"

"I'm doing a lot of guessing here, Sheriff," Clayton replied, "but maybe."

"You spent most of the week with Riley," Hewitt said. "Did he mention any personal or family problems?"

Clayton shook his head. "Nothing like that. Did you or Chief Bolt go anywhere near the cabin?"

"Negative," Hewitt answered as he walked Clayton away from Bennie Anaya. "Chief Bolt and I want you to take the lead on this case. We'll give you whatever you need."

"Ten-four."

"I don't even know Riley's wife's name," Hewitt said, sounding peeved at himself.

"Delores or Diana," Clayton replied. "Something like that."

"I'll look it up in his file."

"It's Denise," Clayton said as he pulled the name to the forefront of his mind. "Are you going to call her?"

Hewitt shook his head. "Not yet." He looked over his shoulder at Bennie Anaya. "What was the exchange you had with Anaya all about?"

"Bennie thought it best to secure Riley's keys from his lifeless hand so they wouldn't go missing from the crime scene."

Hewitt groaned and rolled his eyes. "Unbelievable. I'll deal with it. Thankfully, in three more months he retires. I want this cop killer caught, Sergeant."

Clayton nodded. "I may be wrong, but I don't think Riley was in Lincoln County long enough to make any enemies."

"Agreed. Unless we come up with a suspect fast, you're going to need to make inquiries in Santa Fe about Riley's professional, personal, and family life."

Clayton turned toward the sound of an engine drawing near on the street. The mobile state police crime lab from Las Cruces had arrived. "Excuse me, Sheriff. I need to get the lab techs started taking prints."

"It's your show, Sergeant," Hewitt said as he watched Clayton walk away.

Years ago, long before he'd returned home to Lincoln County to run for sheriff, Paul Hewitt had seen his best friend and partner get blown away in a narco bust gone bad. He would take that image to his grave along with the sight of Tim Riley's mangled face.

Riley had been with the department for only a week, but he'd been killed on Hewitt's watch. Paul had never lost an officer under his command before, and although he knew it wasn't so, he felt responsible. Somehow he'd failed Riley. It left an angry feeling in his gut.

He wondered about a "what if?" What if he got the chance to face down Riley's murderer? Would he violate every rule of law he was sworn to uphold and kill the son of a bitch himself? Hewitt didn't have an answer.


Helen Muiz's phone call persuaded Kerney there was sufficient reason to call out the troops and start a search for Denise Riley. Because Cañoncito was outside his jurisdiction, he asked dispatch to notify the sheriff's office and state police and request officers be sent to Helen's location.

He hung up and tiptoed into the den, where Sara was sleeping restlessly on the couch. She was twitching and mumbling through a clenched jaw. Kerney figured she was caught up in another Iraq bad dream. They had been plaguing her almost every night since her release last month from the army hospital.

Frequently over the past few weeks, Kerney had woken up late at night to find Sara in the den, sitting mute, wide-eyed, and shaking, staring into the darkness. He sat quietly with her until the episodes passed and she was ready to return to bed.

As an ex-infantry lieutenant with a Vietnam combat tour under his belt, Kerney knew about flashbacks that made you remember events you wanted to forget, nightmares that woke you up in a cold sweat, panic attacks triggered by nothing more than strange random sounds, and temper tantrums that came out of nowhere. He also knew there wasn't much he could do ease to Sara's journey back from the insanity of combat other than be there for her.

He reached over and turned on the table lamp. Sara sat bolt upright and gave him a fierce look. "What is it?" she demanded, blinking rapidly.

He explained what he knew about Helen Muiz's missing kid sister. "According to Helen, who doesn't overdramatize, it's completely out of character for Denise. I have sheriff's deputies and state police on the way, but I told her I'd personally come by."

Sara nodded. "Of course, you must go and help out." Unconsciously she rubbed her right arm where a piece of shrapnel from an improvised explosive device had gouged an inch of muscle from her triceps. The army doctors had done a wonderful job of repairing the damage, but Sara found the scar ugly.

"I won't be long," Kerney said, eyeing the half bottle of wine and the glass on the end table next to the couch. "Will you be okay?"

Sara followed Kerney's gaze. "I'm not going to sit here and get drunk while you're gone, if that's what you're worried about," she snapped.

"I wasn't thinking that you would," Kerney said gently. He tried to kiss her on the lips, but she turned her face away. He gave her a peck on the cheek instead. "I'll be back soon," he said.

Sara nodded and said nothing, her gaze fixed on the black night sky outside the den window.

In his unmarked police cruiser Kerney's thoughts remained with Sara as he drove toward Cañoncito. She'd become the first female officer in Iraq to receive the Silver Star for bravery under fire. After being wounded by an IED, Sara had repelled an insurgent attack, single-handedly killing several enemy fighters who were advancing on seriously injured U.S. Army personnel. The wounded soldiers credited Sara with saving their lives.

Along with the Silver Star, Sara had been decorated with the Purple Heart, given a meritorious promotion to full colonel, and, after her release from the hospital, placed on extended convalescent leave.

She had been sent to Iraq by her former superior officer, a chickenshit Pentagon one-star general with political connections who was willing to sacrifice Sara's career, even her life, to advance his own ambitions. Instead, Sara had returned stateside a newly minted full-bird colonel with a citation for valor and a clean slate.

When her convalescent leave ended in two months, she had orders to ship out as a military attaché to the United States Embassy at the Court of St. James's, which meant that soon the family would be moving to London. Kerney had willingly signed on for the duration, but their son, Patrick, had been voicing serious reservations about leaving the Santa Fe ranch and his Welsh pony, Pablito.

Using directions Helen had supplied, Kerney arrived at the Cañoncito double-wide to find a small cluster of police officers surrounding Helen and Ruben on the wooden deck to the house. One of the cops was the Santa Fe County chief deputy, Leonard Jessup, who introduced Kerney to the uniforms when he joined the group.

"We were just about to start a search of the property," Jessup said.

Kerney nodded and smiled at Helen and Ruben, who looked back at him with worried expressions. "Good deal. What else?"

"One of my deputies will go door-to-door to every house in the area and interview the neighbors," Jessup answered.

Kerney nodded again and spoke to Helen. "I know you've already checked with the entire family, but do you have a list of Denise's friends and coworkers we can call?"

"No," Helen said. "But I found an address book in her purse."

"Great," Kerney said with a reassuring smile. "Let's start with that while the officers do the property search."

"She could be hurt or dead out there," Helen said, her voice cracking.

"Stay calm, Helen," Kerney said. "Searching is just a precaution. You're right to be a little concerned about your sister, but this could be nothing more than a false alarm."

"I know, I know," Helen said without conviction, looking beyond the porch light into the black night.

Kerney gave Ruben a heads-up nod of his chin. "Why don't the three of us go in the house and start making those calls?"

Ruben smiled in agreement, and with Kerney close behind he guided a reluctant Helen by the elbow into the double-wide.

Late-night telephone calls to the people in Denise's address book yielded no helpful information about her whereabouts. Kerney quizzed Helen about her sister's place of employment and learned that until recently Denise had worked as an office manager for an insurance agent. She'd quit her job to prepare for the move to Lincoln County.

Kerney called the insurance agent at home, on the off chance that he might know where Denise was, and got the man's voice mail. He left a call-back message, disconnected, and asked Ruben to see if he could access the e-mail accounts on the desktop and laptop computers in a spare bedroom that served as a home office. After a few minutes Ruben returned and reported that both computers were password protected.

Kerney phoned Detective Matt Chacon at home and woke him up. Over the past two years, Chacon had taken specialized law enforcement training in computer technology and was now the in-house expert on computer crimes for the department. Kerney explained the situation and asked him to come out to Cañoncito. While they waited for his arrival, Kerney had Helen give him some background on her baby sister.

"Denise was the rebel in the family," Helen said as she paced across the room. "Always at odds with our parents, especially our father. She left Santa Fe as soon as she graduated high school and didn't come home for years."

Kerney pulled out a chair at the dining room table and invited Helen to sit with him. "What was she doing during those years?" Kerney asked once she had settled into a chair.

"She worked as a waitress and a bartender and traveled a lot. I would get postcards from her when she moved to a different city. Miami; Honolulu; Brisbane, Australia; Toronto—she even spent six months living in London."

"She had a wild streak when she was young," Ruben said as he joined them at the table. "Especially when it came to boys."

Helen shook her head in opposition. "She never deserved that reputation."

"How many years was she gone?" Kerney asked.

"Twelve," Helen replied. "She left when she was eighteen and didn't return to Santa Fe until she was thirty."

"Not even to visit?" Kerney asked.

Helen shook her head.

"She always took the last name of whatever man she happened to be living with," Ruben added. "We must have gotten postcards and letters from her with at least five or six different surnames."

"Boyfriends, not husbands?" Kerney asked.

"Her marriage to Tim is her first, as far as we know," Helen said.

"Did any of those old boyfriends ever come to visit?"

"Not that I know about," Helen said.

"Tell me about Denise's relationship with Tim."

Before Helen could respond, Leonard Jessup stepped through the door.

Helen jumped to her feet. "Have you found something?"

"Nothing yet," he replied, casting a quick look at Kerney. "Can I have a minute of your time, Chief?"

Kerney nodded and stood.

"Why do you need to speak privately with Chief Kerney?" Helen demanded as she stepped up to Jessup. "If something is wrong, tell me now."

Jessup shot Kerney a questioning look.

"Tell her," Kerney said.

Jessup took a deep breath. "I just got off the phone with the Lincoln County sheriff," he said. "Tim Riley was killed earlier tonight."

Helen gasped and her hand flew to her mouth.

The news out of Santa Fe that Tim Riley's wife was missing complicated Clayton's investigation. The sketchy information he'd received—her purse, wallet, car keys, and vehicle had been found at the family residence—suggested an abduction or worse. But with so few facts available, Clayton didn't know if Riley's wife should be considered a potential homicide suspect or a possible double homicide victim.

The neighborhood canvass was over and nobody interviewed had seen or heard anything until the sound of the shotgun blast had broken the silence of the night. A three-block radius around the crime scene had been searched for any sign left behind by the perpetrator, and nothing had been found. A fresh search would be done in daylight, but Clayton had little hope that any valuable evidence would materialize.

The state police crime scene techs had collected at least a dozen different fingerprints from the exterior and interior surfaces of Riley's cabin, which quite probably belonged to Riley and everyone else who had rented the place as a vacation retreat over the last six months. Although there were no signs of a forced entry, Clayton had the techs bag and tag every piece of personal property belonging to Riley, along with the bedding, bathroom towels, and the dishes in the sink that were supplied to renters by the owner of the cabin. When that was accomplished, he had the techs vacuum the floors before turning them loose on Riley's police vehicle. It was a scatter-gun approach to evidence collection, but Clayton knew that every homicide left a trace, and if one blot, smudge, stain, scratch, fiber, or speck was overlooked, the killer could get away with murder.

Dawn came with a stiff wind that blew dust, tumbleweeds, and brown, brittle cottonwood leaves across streets, sidewalks, and lawns. Clayton assembled a group of officers, including Sheriff Hewitt and Chief Bolt, and carried out another three-block search for evidence. Every piece of loose trash and litter that hadn't been blown away by the wind was bagged and tagged, every tire track and skid mark was photographed, and every parked vehicle was inspected and run through Motor Vehicles.

When the officers returned to the cabin, EMTs were rolling Riley's body on a gurney to an ambulance that would transport his remains to Albuquerque for an autopsy to determine the cause of death, which in this case would be a formality. All night long Clayton had wondered what had become of the rifled shotgun slug that had taken Tim Riley's life.

He stood facing the cabin about six feet from where Tim Riley's body had fallen. The slug had caught Riley in the head straight on, but from the position of the body on the ground it was impossible to tell if Tim's head had been turned or if he'd faced his killer squarely.

If Riley had faced his killer straight on, the slug would have missed the front of the cabin by a good ten feet. If the killer had fired from a slight angle to the right, the spent slug should be lodged somewhere in the front of the cabin. It wasn't. If the killer had fired from the left, the slug could be buried in a tree trunk or the back porch of a neighboring house. It wasn't.

Clayton scanned the cabin, wondering where the spent slug might be. Because he didn't have the murder weapon, didn't know the gauge of the shotgun, and could only estimate how close the shooter had been to the victim, it was mostly guesswork.

"What are you studying, Sergeant?" Paul Hewitt asked as he walked up.

Clayton looked at the sheriff. "Angles." He shuffled through the Polaroid photographs he'd taken of Tim's body. The entry wound at the front of Riley's head looked slightly lower than the exit wound at the back of his skull. Clayton noted the difference to Hewitt. "I think the killer may have been shorter than Riley. Either that, or he just raised his weapon at an angle and fired from the hip."

"Wouldn't that make it a lucky shot?" Hewitt asked.

"Not from such a close distance," Clayton replied, returning the photographs to his shirt pocket. "A typical shotgun has a twenty-four- to twenty-eight-inch barrel. If you're firing a long-barreled weapon from a distance of four to six feet, muzzle end to target, it would be pretty hard to miss what you're shooting at. And there might not be any powder residue on the victim. Personally, I think the killer deliberately took the head shot. Riley was my height, five feet ten. I make his killer to be two, maybe tree inches shorter. I wonder how tall Riley's wife is."

"You think she's the shooter?"

"I don't know enough about this crime to exclude her as a suspect."

Hewitt looked at the cottonwood tree, at the cabin, at the neighboring house, and then at Clayton. "So where's the spent slug?" Hewitt asked.

"Maybe it's lodged in the cabin roof."

Hewitt scanned the roof. It was a pitched, shingled roof with a protruding metal woodstove flue. "I went over Riley's radio traffic with dispatch," he said. "Except for the brawl at the Carrizozo bar and a fifteen-minute coffee break with Craig Bolt, Riley made no contact with anyone else after he left the crash scene."

"We can't be completely sure of that," Clayton said.

"I know," Hewitt replied. "But if Riley did encounter someone unofficially without notifying dispatch, it happened toward the end of his shift."

Clayton nodded and said nothing. It wasn't unusual for the sheriff to cruise the county at odd hours without notifying dispatch that he was on duty. It was a good way to stay on top of what the troops were doing in the field. He wondered if Hewitt had shadowed Riley during the early part of his shift.

"I'll ask Chief Bolt to find you a ladder," Hewitt said.

"I'm also going to need something other than my truck to drive," Clayton said.

Hewitt glanced at the Ford Explorer that had been assigned to Tim Riley less than sixteen hours ago. "It's got a rebuilt engine, good tires, and a new clutch."

Clayton nodded. It was either the Explorer or the only other available sheriff's vehicle, a six-year-old Crown Victoria that needed new shocks, burned over a quart of oil a day, and was about to throw a rod.

"Ten-four," he said, not completely happy with the idea of driving the murdered deputy's unit.

"I'll get you that ladder," Hewitt said as he went to find Bolt. "Be careful when you climb up there."

Clayton stared at Tim Riley's unit. It was an Apache tradition to believe newly deceased people wanted to have some of the living journey with them to the other side. The most dangerous time for this to happen was the four days after death, when the dead person was still present, although invisible. During this period, they revisited the critical events in their lives and remained close to the important people they were about to leave behind.

Clayton figured getting murdered had to be an event of great consequence for Tim Riley, one he would definitely have to revisit. That meant Riley's invisible presence would be hanging around over the next few days, and Clayton would have to stay alert and balanced to avoid any witchery that might come his way.

A village fire engine pulled to a stop on the street. A firefighter climbed out of the cab, waved at Clayton, and asked where to put the ladder. Clayton pointed to the spot and helped the man carry the ladder to the side of the cabin. He spent an hour on the roof inspecting every fiberglass shingle, examining the plumbing vent protrusions, and studying the woodstove flue. He checked the eaves, the gutters, and the downspouts. He went over every inch of the side of the cabin, high and low, where the slug could have impacted. He looked for any evidence that it could have ricocheted. Finally he gave up, climbed down, and helped the firefighter put the ladder back on the truck.

"There's nothing up there," Clayton said before Hewitt had a chance to ask.

Hewitt handed Clayton a piece of paper. "This is a list of the people we know Riley had contact with since he moved down here. There may be more."

There were over thirty names on the list. Some worked at local businesses, several were real estate agents, and a few were people Clayton had introduced to Riley earlier in the week.

"Use whomever you want to help you work that list," Hewitt added.

"Thanks," Clayton said. "Any word on Riley's missing wife?"

"Not yet. Maybe something will break on that end."

"Yeah," Clayton said without enthusiasm, wondering if his father, Kevin Kerney, was involved in the Santa Fe investigation.

"Where is Cañoncito?" he asked Hewitt.

"I have no idea," Hewitt replied.


In Cañoncito, the news that Deputy Riley had been shot dead turned a missing person case into a full-scale homicide investigation. Chief Deputy Leonard Jessup of the Santa Fe S.O. called out his major felony investigators, his crime scene team, and asked Kerney to provide additional detectives to assist. Aside from Detective Matt Chacon, who was already on his way, Kerney had Sergeant Ramona Pino and two more detectives roll to the scene.

Helen Muiz rejected Kerney's suggestion to go home and await further developments. Although the double-wide and surrounding area were now part of a homicide investigation and thus closed to civilians, Kerney didn't force the issue. Helen's long and distinguished record of service with the department, the strong support she'd given him during his tenure as chief, and their friendship that extended back to Kerney's rookie year as a cop entitled her to all due consideration.

To make way for the investigators and the techs, Kerney took Helen and Ruben to his police vehicle, where they sat with the dome light on, the motor running, and the heater cranking out warm air.

Kerney asked Helen to tell him about her baby sister, and he learned that Denise had lived with five or six men during her wanderlust years, none of whom the family had ever met. According to both Helen and Ruben, Denise had volunteered very little information about her past relationships and would brush off any serious attempt to discuss her time away from Santa Fe. It was as if she had erased from scrutiny a dozen years of her life.

Kerney did learn that Denise had left Santa Fe two days after her high school graduation party, taking with her all of the money she'd saved for college, cash she'd received as presents from relatives, plus two hundred dollars she'd stolen from her mother's purse. There had been gossip at the time that Denise had taken the money and left town to get an abortion, but those rumors soon died away.

Kerney asked for clarity about Denise's rapid departure. Helen said Denise left because of conflict with her father that centered around his refusal to let her go away to college. Because of her rebellious nature, he wanted her to live at home and go to the community college for her first two years.

"Was going away to college a financial issue?" Kerney asked.

Helen, who sat on the front passenger seat next to Kerney, shook her head. "Not at all. Daddy just wanted to keep an eye on her. He'd just sold his plumbing and heating business and had settled my grandfather's estate. Each of us children received money from the sale of Grandfather's foothills property, although Denise had to wait until she was twenty-one to receive her share."

"Why would Denise leave home because of a spat over where she could go to college?" Kerney asked.

"It went deeper than that," Ruben said from the backseat of Kerney's cruiser.

Kerney turned to Ruben. "Do you think she was pregnant when she left home?"

"She may have been, but it's one of those topics that's never discussed in the family," Ruben replied.

Helen shook her head. "Because it wasn't true."

"Then why is the topic always such a sore spot with you and Denise?" Ruben countered.

"Go on," Kerney said to Ruben before Helen could reply.

"Denise was super smart, totally bored with Santa Fe, and very unchallenged in high school. You could call the crowd she hung out with a fringe, arty group. They were into theater, film, acting, music, art, and smoking a little pot. Denise had aspirations; she wanted to strike out on her own, see the world, and she didn't want to be held back. She had big dreams to make it as a singer or actress."

"You seem to know a great deal about your sister-in-law's teenage years," Kerney said.

Ruben smiled. "I was the head of the guidance and counseling department at the high school during the time Denise was enrolled. As Helen's husband, I couldn't counsel her directly, but I did stay informed of her progress. She dropped out of the gifted program her sophomore year, although she continued to take advance placement classes in subjects that interested her."

Kerney was about to direct the conversation to Denise's relationship with her husband when Detective Matt Chacon stepped onto the deck of the double-wide and motioned to him. Kerney excused himself and went to see what Chacon had discovered.

"Did you find anything interesting on the computers?" he asked. Through the open door Kerney could see deputies and detectives carefully examining the furnishings, carpet, walls, and curtains, looking for trace evidence.

"It's what I didn't find that's interesting, Chief," Matt replied. "Both computers have had the hard drives completely erased and reformatted using what I think was a bootleg recovery system that can't be traced back to a manufacturer. Everything on the computers was wiped clean. Whoever did this didn't want whatever was on the computers to be retrieved."

"Can't you restore the hard drive data?"

"It's not a question of retrieval," Matt replied. "The drives have been scoured and sterilized of all information. It doesn't take a computer geek to do it. An hour or two of Internet research can give anyone the information they need to permanently purge files, folders, and data. However, I can tell you that this was done twenty-four hours ago."

"What about any removable storage devices?"

"Both computers have CD and flash drive capacity, but I haven't found any compact disks or portable storage devices in the house. I'm assuming whoever erased the hard drives took them. I dusted both machines for fingerprints. They'd been wiped clean."

"This is not good news," Kerney said.

"I know it isn't, Chief," Matt replied. "But most people pay their monthly IP bills automatically through online checking or a charge to a credit card. Sergeant Pino is looking for banking and credit card statements. If we can determine the IP provider, we can get a court order and access e-mail account information."

"Do the same with the cell phone and landline accounts."

"It's on the list," Matt said. "I'm going to take both computers back to the office and go through everything again. Sometimes a recovery program will miss, skip, or write over an old file or folder. Maybe I'll get lucky."

"Okay." Kerney gave Matt a pat on the back. Soon after becoming chief, he'd promoted Chacon to detective, and although the young officer didn't know it, he was about to receive his sergeant stripes and be put in charge of the Property Crimes Unit. "Keep at it," Kerney said.

"Will do, Chief."

When Kerney returned to his police unit, Helen quizzed him about his conversation with Chacon. He short-circuited the facts and told her that Matt hadn't yet found anything of interest on the computers, but would conduct a more comprehensive examination at police headquarters.

By daybreak, Ruben had talked his exhausted wife into going home. Inside the double-wide, Sergeant Ramona Pino, two SFPD detectives, and three sheriff's investigators were continuing the house search. Kerney joined Chief Deputy Leonard Jessup in the

RV that served as the sheriff's office mobile command center, and asked him to talk about Tim Riley.

Jessup eased his bulk into a chair behind a small bolted-down table and motioned for Kerney to join him. Jessup's pale blue eyes were weary. The deep creases below his chubby cheeks pulled down the corners of his mouth and gave him a perpetual hangdog expression. In contrast to his dour appearance, Jessup had a high-pitched voice. A true tenor, he was the mainstay of a barbershop quartet that performed locally and at regional competitions.

"Tim was a solid, dependable officer," Jessup said, "and we were sorry to lose him."

"No personality conflicts with other officers or problems with the brass?"

"None."

"Then why did he leave?" Kerney asked.

Jessup shrugged his shoulders. "He didn't give a reason other than to say he'd accepted a job with the Lincoln County S.O." He handed Kerney a file folder. "That's Riley's personnel file. Look it over for yourself. He received solid performance evaluations, had no disciplinary actions, and received several commendations from his supervisors and one from the board of county commissioners."

Kerney paged through the paperwork. "What about his personal and family life?"

"That I don't know anything about," Jessup replied. "He wasn't one to socialize much with other officers. I met his wife maybe twice, once at a retirement party and once at some community fund-raising event. I didn't even know she was Helen Muiz's kid sister."

Outside the RV window, detectives and investigators were loading boxes of evidence into the back of the S.O. crime lab van.

On the driveway that led from the double-wide to the county road, S.O. patrol vehicles, state police units, and SFPD vehicles were arriving, along with members of a search and rescue team.

Jessup stood up and nodded toward an unmarked sedan that came to a stop near a staging area for searchers that had been set up in front of the stables. "The sheriff has arrived. He wants us to scour this area until we either find Denise Riley's body or we know that she isn't here to be found."

Kerney followed Jessup out of the RV and looked at the mesa that rose above the narrow valley, much of it still in deep shadows. There was a lot of rugged country to cover and places where a body could be hidden so that no matter how exhaustive the search, it might never be found.

At the staging area, Kerney joined Leonard Jessup, Sheriff Luciano Salgado, the state police captain who commanded the district office, and an emergency room doctor who also served as the search and rescue director. Together, they went over the sheriff's search plan, which consisted of a concentrated sweep of the valley and surrounding area before moving into the higher country. When the searchers had assembled, Salgado divided the personnel into teams and gave out grid assignments. A sober and silent group of three dozen men and women fanned out in all four directions, the quiet broken only by the rough, querulous sound of Mexican jays in the tall pines and the low whine of a commercial jet thirty thousand feet overhead.

Kerney spent a few minutes alone with Luciano Salgado, who had retired as a SFPD patrol sergeant six years ago to accept an appointment as chief deputy for the S.O, and was now serving his first term as the duly elected sheriff. Luciano asked if he could continue to use Kerney's detectives throughout the day. He wanted Ramona Pino to work with his major crimes unit supervisor on an evidence search of the stable and the P.D. detectives to assist in a follow-up neighborhood canvass of all residents.

Kerney readily agreed and passed on the assignments to Sergeant Pino. Back at his unit he called Sara on his cell phone.

"I didn't wake you up, did I?" he asked.

"Patrick did that a half hour ago," Sara replied, sounding perfectly normal. "We've had our breakfast and now he's petitioning me to go horseback riding."

"Are you feeling up to it?"

"I am. Have you found Helen's missing sister?"

"Not yet. But we have learned that the woman's husband, a police officer, was murdered last night in Lincoln County."

"Does that mean you won't be home anytime soon?"

"No," Kerney replied. "This case is not under my jurisdiction. I've given the sheriff's department all the help they've asked for and done as much for Helen Muiz as I can at this point. I don't need to stay here watching other people work."

"Too many chiefs?" Sara asked.

"Something like that. I'll be home soon."

Kerney disconnected and went to find Ramona Pino to tell her he'd be leaving. He found her in the tack room at the stables with Don Mielke, the major crimes unit supervisor for the sheriff's department.

"Don't come in, Chief," Ramona said when Kerney appeared in the doorway.

Kerney looked around. An upended saddle was on the hard-packed dirt floor, some of the halters and bridles lay in a heap under the wall hooks, and there were scuff marks in the dirt that looked as if something had been dragged out into the corral, where the two horses whinnied and snorted for their morning oats.

"Any hard evidence of a struggle?" Kerney asked.

"Not yet," Mielke replied.

Beyond the corral, next to a horse trailer, a medium-size black-and-white mutt with a long coat joined the chorus. "Do you know if the Rileys had a dog?" Kerney asked.

"There was a picture in the house of Riley's wife kneeling next to a dog," Ramona said.

Kerney pointed at the mutt who had taken up a position at the back of the trailer. "That dog?"

"Maybe," Ramona said.

"Has it been here all night?"

"I didn't see or hear it earlier," Ramona replied.

"Has anyone checked that horse trailer?" Kerney asked.

"Not that I know of," Mielke replied.

"Let's do it," Kerney said, stepping off in the direction of the trailer.

The barking dog fell silent and backed off when Kerney approached, but it stayed nearby, watchful, and seemed unwilling to scamper away. The trailer, built to haul two horses, was padlocked. Kerney turned to Mielke and asked him to find some bolt cutters. Ramona Pino dropped down on one knee and looked back at the stables and corral. Although it was impossible to tell for sure, what seemed to be drag marks in the dirt ran from the tack room to the horse trailer. She pointed them out to Kerney.

"Ten-to-one odds says we can call off the search as soon as Mielke brings those bolt cutters," Kerney said.

Ramona shook her head. "I learned a long time ago never to bet against you, Chief."

Mielke returned, snapped the locks with the bolt cutters, and swung open the doors. Inside one of the trailer stalls was the rigid body of a woman facedown on a bed of blood-soaked straw.

"Okay," Kerney said as he exhaled and turned to Mielke. "You'd better get your bosses over here pronto."

"Yeah," Mielke replied.

# Chapter Three

The discovery of the body set off a chain of procedural events common to all murder investigations. Kerney backed off so Ramona Pino and Don Mielke could work without his interference, and informed Sheriff Salgado about the unidentified female victim.

By radio, Salgado got the word out to the searchers and asked them to suspend operations and maintain their positions until a positive ID could be made. Kerney took Salgado and his chief deputy, Leonard Jessup, to the horse trailer, which had already been cordoned off, and from behind the police line the three men watched as Mielke and Pino established a wider crime scene perimeter.

After roping off a larger area that extended from the tack room to the horse trailer, they began documenting and processing the scene. Mielke photographed the body as it lay, leaving it untouched and unmoved. Although it was highly likely the dead woman was Denise Riley, protocol required the body remain as it had been found until the medical investigator arrived.

Mielke moved on to photograph the horse trailer, the drag marks in the dirt, and the interior of the tack room, while Ramona Pino inspected the victim and made a list of the woman's clothing, which included notations of the condition of the garments and any visible damage and stains. The woman's jeans barely covered her buttocks, and flecks of straw adhered to exposed skin at the small of her back.

Ramona wondered if the woman's jeans had been rearranged by the perpetrator. If so, it signaled that the killer probably knew the victim. She made a closer visual inspection of the victim's exposed right forearm and left hand and saw what appeared to be bruising—quite possibly defensive wounds. Had the crime started out as a sexual assault and escalated to murder?

She wrote down her observations and speculations, drew a rough sketch of the body in relation to the corral and tack room, measured off all distances, and then began a search for trace evidence on the surfaces of the horse trailer.

When the MI arrived and declared the victim dead, the body was turned faceup and two facts became readily apparent. First, comparison with the driver's license photo Ramona had found in the purse inside the double-wide showed that the dead woman was indeed Denise Riley. Second, her throat had been cut.

Salgado promptly called off the search and released all off-duty and nonessential personnel who had volunteered their time. As the searchers returned to the staging area and quietly began to disperse, Kerney, Salgado, and Jessup thanked each of them personally for coming out. The three men silently watched as the searchers loaded gear and equipment into their police units and emergency vehicles and left the area in a line of cars that stretched the length of the long dirt driveway.

As the last vehicle turned onto the county road, Sheriff Luciano Salgado turned to Kerney. "Are you going to tell Helen Muiz?" he asked.

"I'll go over to her house right now," Kerney replied.

"Let her know that I'll be in touch with her real soon," Salgado said.

"Maybe you'll have some answers for her by then."

"God, I hope so," Salgado replied with a sigh. "How long can I use Sergeant Pino and your detectives?"

"As long as you need them," Kerney replied, thinking it was unlikely that the two separate homicides of Riley and his wife would be cleared anytime soon.

"Thanks," Salgado said.

Kerney nodded in reply and headed to his unit. Before driving off, he tried reaching Sara at home by phone. There was no answer, so he called her cell phone and got a voice message that told him that Sara and Patrick were off on an early morning horseback ride.

The message pleased Kerney. Being with Patrick was the best medicine for what ailed Sara. That sweet, happy, smart-as-a-whip little boy buoyed her spirits and got her thinking about all the good things life had to offer.

He put the unit in gear and headed for town, his thoughts turning as dark as the gunmetal gray March sky that masked the morning sun. Far too often over the course of his career, he'd brought the news of a loved one's death to family members. Most times, they had been complete strangers or only slightly known to him through the course of an investigation. But it was never an easy thing to do.

This time it would be worse. He would have to tell a woman he'd known, liked, and respected for over twenty years that the death of her brother-in-law was not the worst of it. The kid sister she'd adored was dead, murdered just as her husband had been hours ago in Lincoln County.

Ruben and Helen Muiz lived in a historic double adobe home that had been in her family since the early twentieth century. Ancient cottonwoods and pines screened the house from the dirt lane that ran around the back side of the hill to a new fourteen-thousand-square foot adobe mansion built by a

Chicago real estate developer who came to Santa Fe every summer for the opera season.

The cars that lined the driveway to the Muiz residence told Kerney that the family had gathered in the wake of the bad news of Tim Riley's murder and Denise's disappearance. He parked on the lane and walked toward the house, thinking that over the years his friendship with Helen had been basically work-related and he knew very little about Helen's siblings or her extended family. The circumstances of the last eight hours were about to change all that.

He rang the doorbell and was soon greeted by Ruben Muiz, who stared at him with bleary eyes ringed with dark circles. Beyond the entry hall in a nearby room, he could hear the low sounds of hushed conversation.

"What have you learned?" Ruben asked.

"Is Helen sleeping?" Kerney countered.

"Nobody's sleeping," Ruben said tersely. "Everybody's here. Tell me what you found out about Denise."

Kerney touched Ruben on the shoulder. "Take it easy," he said gently as people began crowding into the entry hall.

"Sorry," Ruben said, lowering his voice.

"Why don't you get everyone together and let me talk to them as a group."

"Yes, of course," Ruben said, ushering Kerney into a large living room filled with twenty-some somber people who stopped talking and stared at him with great intensity.

Helen sat on a couch with several women and a man clustered nearby who looked to be her sisters and brother. Other men hovering close by Kerney took to be the sisters' husbands.

He crossed the room, trying to keep his expression passive, reached Helen, took her by the hand, and shook his head once. She gasped and began sobbing. He stepped away as the sisters closed in around Helen, the women choking back tears, crying, reaching to embrace one another and clasp hands. He backed off to a far corner of the room and waited patiently for the grieving to subside and the questioning to begin. The family's anguish was about to become a hell of a lot more distressing once they learned how Denise had died.

The report that Tim Riley's wife had also been murdered reached Clayton by way of a phone call from Sergeant Ramona Pino. Clayton had worked with Pino once before, on a case involving a revenge killer intent on wiping out Kevin Kerney and his entire bloodline, including Clayton and his family. The perp had almost succeeded, but Clayton had gunned him down in Santa Fe before he could kill Kerney, Sara, and their brand-new baby boy, Patrick.

After winding up the search for evidence at Tim Riley's rented cabin, Clayton convened a meeting of his team at the Capitan town hall and brought them up to speed on what he knew about Denise Riley's murder in Santa Fe County.

"I doubt that these murders are coincidental," Clayton told the group, "but until we have either a motive or a suspect, I want some people backtracking on Tim Riley's time here in Lincoln County. I want an accounting for every minute of every day in the week Riley was here."

Clayton paused and looked around the room, which contained every available deputy plus Paul Hewitt, Craig Bolt, and the two Capitan village officers. "I'll get to the assignments in a minute, but remember this: I don't want reports coming in with any gaps," he warned. "I want his entire week reconstructed. Names, dates, times, places—you all know the drill. You'll be looking for any unusual event, altercation, heated exchange, or misunderstanding that may have happened which could have led—no matter how remotely—to his murder."

"What if Riley's murder has nothing to do with anybody in Lincoln County?" Chief Craig Bolt asked.

"It's very possible," Clayton answered. "When a husband and wife get murdered in separate locations within hours of each other, it makes you wonder if maybe all was not sweetness and light on the home front. But with no motive and no suspect, we have to focus on the victims for now. So as soon as this meeting is over, some of you are going to start an all-out, deep background check on both Tim Riley and his wife. I'm sure the Santa Fe County S.O. will be doing the same."

Clayton walked to the whiteboard, drew a line down the middle, and wrote Tim Riley's name on one side and Denise Riley's name on the other.

"Here are some things to think about," he said. "At the cabin crime scene, the killer probably spent a minimum amount of time in the area and quickly killed his victim after he arrived home. Very little physical evidence was left behind. In fact, all we have so far is a partial footprint on the cabin porch that is probably from a man's boot, size eight, which correlates with my theory that the killer may be small in stature—not more than five seven or eight. Murder weapon, a shotgun, fired at point-blank range of no more than four feet." Clayton wrote the information under Tim's name.

"In Santa Fe," Clayton continued, "Denise Riley's throat was cut with a knife after she'd been attacked in a tack room in a barn at the couple's double-wide in Cañoncito. She was dragged to a nearby horse trailer, killed there, and then locked in the trailer. It's possible that she was sexually assaulted either prior to or after her death. A detective at the scene thinks the killer made an attempt to partially cover the lower half of the victim's body, which suggests the perp knew the decedent. Time of death was approximately sixteen to twenty hours before Tim Riley's murder."

Clayton wrote down the information under Denise's name. "Don't let the differences in the methods between the two homicides make you think we are dealing with two distinct perpetrators."

He turned to the whiteboard once again and underlined Tim Riley's name. "At first glance, our homicide looks professional. However, that doesn't necessarily mean it was a contract killing carried out by a specialist."

"But it could mean exactly that," Paul Hewitt said from the back of the cramped room. "Basically, the killer waited in ambush, fired one shot from close range at a sure kill area of the body, the head, and left behind little physical evidence."

"I'm not discounting those facts, Sheriff," Clayton replied. "But from my analysis of the crime scene I think the shooter could have killed Deputy Riley when his back was turned, but chose instead to let his victim see it coming. Additionally, by literally taking Riley's face off with a shotgun slug, the killer depersonalized his victim. It's as if he tried to erase the most easily recognizable part of the man. To me, that makes the murder decidedly personal, just as the killing of Denise Riley appears to be."

"Personal in what way?" Hewitt asked.

"If I knew that, I'd have motive," Clayton replied. "The one thing I'm fairly sure of, as I mentioned before, is that the shooter is male, possibly slight in build, and shorter than Riley by two to three inches."

Clayton wrote the physical information of the shooter on the chalkboard. "I'm guessing that we're dealing with a single perpetrator, and I agree with Chief Bolt that chances are slim to none that our killer is local. With that in mind, we need to be surveying motels, gas stations, eateries, and be talking to people about any strangers who might have recently been asking about Riley or the Lincoln County Sheriff's Office."

Clayton put the chalk on the tray. "Finally, we need to retrace everywhere Riley went while on patrol last night."

"I'll do that," Paul Hewitt said.

"I've got you down to handle the news media, Sheriff."

"The media can wait," Hewitt growled. "Besides, we've got nothing to tell them." He looked around the room. "So I expect all of you to keep your lips zipped about this case until further notice. It's 'No comment' to any questions. Got that?"

Heads nodded.

"Okay," Clayton said as he looked at the sixteen officers in the room. Excluding himself, Hewitt, and Bolt, only two of the field officers had any solid investigative experience. "Here are your assignments."

He read off names and tasks, putting the heaviest burden on himself and the two experienced officers, knowing that it meant double shifts until they broke the case or it became too cold to work full-time any longer.

Clayton closed his notebook, looked at the sober faces of the officers sitting in front of him, and nodded at the door. "Let's go out and catch this killer," he said.

Sara's favorite gelding, a baldfaced dark sorrel named Gipsy, and Patrick's pony, Pablito, were missing from the corral when Kerney arrived home. He saddled Hondo and rode up the hill, past the ancient piñon tree where Soldier, the wild mustang he'd bought, gentled, and trained years ago during his bachelor days, was buried. He paused for a minute and then turned in a westerly direction toward the live spring at the edge of the ranch property that was always a favorite horseback riding destination for the family.

A fresh pile of horse apples near the water tank and windmill told Kerney he was on the right trail. He clamped his cowboy hat down hard, lowered his head against a stiff, cold southwesterly wind, rode Hondo at a slow trot, and tried to clear his mind of the events of the last ten or so hours. The Cañoncito crime scene had been grim enough, but the impact on the family of the devastating news of Denise Riley's murder had been heart-wrenching to witness.

The wind eased. Kerney raised his eyes and blinked away some dust as he reached the top of the small hill that overlooked the pond and live stream. Several hundred years ago, during the days of the Spanish conquistadors, the pond had been a stop along a wagon road that ran from the village of Galisteo to El Rancho De Las Golondrinas, a way station on the El Camino Real south of Santa Fe. The ruts of the road were still visible under the overarching bare branches of several old cottonwood trees that once shaded a hacienda, which was now nothing more than a rock rubble foundation covered by cactus and shrubs.

Under the trees, Gipsy and Pablito stood quietly. Down by the stream, Kerney spotted Sara and Patrick watching a small flock of Canadian geese that had stopped during their northerly spring migration to feed on the tall grass that surrounded the pond.

Hondo's whinny startled the geese, and the flock rose skyward, honking deeply in unison, the sound of their wings creating a back-beat rhythm as they circled and flew north in a loose formation.

Kerney rode down to his wife and son, and Patrick gave him a stern look when he arrived.

"You scared the birds away, Daddy," he said.

"That was Hondo, not me." Kerney patted Hondo's withers, bent low in the saddle, and extended his hand. Patrick grabbed on and Kerney swung him up onto his lap. "You're getting heavy."

"I'll be four this year," Patrick announced proudly.

"That's a fact," Kerney said, smiling down at Sara. The cold March wind had put some color in her face, highlighting the line of freckles that ran across her cheeks and nose. "Are you ready to head home?" he asked.

Sara smiled. "Now that you've scared the geese away, we might as well."

Kerney groaned.

"Did you find Helen's sister?" Sara asked.

Kerney nodded. "We did," he said flatly.

"Not good?"

"It doesn't get any worse."

Sara stepped to Hondo and put her hand on Kerney's leg. "What are you going to do about it?"

"I don't know if I can do anything more." Kerney jiggled the reins and Hondo broke into a walk. "In three weeks I'm going to be just another retired cop, a civilian, and it may take a lot more time than that to put this case to rest."

"But it happened to a family member of one of your people, on your watch," Sara said, her head suddenly filled with the images of the firefight in Iraq, the wounded soldiers on the ground. The acid smell of gunpowder filled her nostrils.

"I know," Kerney replied. He reined up next to Pablito and put Patrick on his saddle.

"Can we come back to see the birds tomorrow?" Patrick asked.

Sara swung into the saddle, and Gipsy pranced sideways next to Pablito. "Yes, we can."

"Does anybody besides me want blueberry pancakes when we get home?" Kerney asked. It was one of Patrick's favorite meals.

"I already had breakfast," Patrick said glumly as the threesome wheeled their horses toward home. "Cereal."

"Is there a rule that you can only eat breakfast once a day?" Kerney asked his son.

Patrick shrugged and gave his mother a questioning look.

"I think there are special times when breakfast is a meal you can have twice a day," Sara said with a laugh.

"The boss says yes to blueberry pancakes," Kerney said.

Patrick grinned and spurred Pablito into a trot. "Okay," he yelled, taking the lead on the trail.

Clayton Istee always looked forward to evening meals with his family. As a police officer, he'd missed far too many of them over the years, and now that the children were getting older—Wendell had turned eight and Hannah was approaching six—he knew it was more important than ever to be home for dinner as much as possible. He didn't want to become one of those cops who sacrificed their personal lives or lost their families through divorce all for the sake of the job.

He'd called Grace late in the day to tell her he'd be home for dinner no matter what, and when he finally broke away from the investigation he was fairly certain that there would be no new developments that would interfere with his plans. In fact, in terms of developing leads, identifying suspects, and collecting any useful evidence, the day had been a complete and utter bust.

Clayton rolled the unit to a stop next to his pickup truck, which Sheriff Hewitt had arranged to have brought back to his house, and beeped the horn twice to announce his arrival. As he dismounted the vehicle, his son, Wendell, threw open the front door, bounded across the porch, and ran to the unit to greet him.

"I saw you on TV," Wendell said, looking up at his father. "The evening news."

Clayton nodded and said nothing. Earlier in the day, a camera crew from an Albuquerque television station had filmed him and the state police crime scene techs carrying evidence from the cabin.

Politely, Wendell waited a moment to see if his father was taking his time to consider a response. Clayton said nothing.

"The man who died," Wendell said. "The deputy . . ."

Clayton pressed his forefinger against his son's mouth before he could say more. "It is best for us not to speak about that. What has your mother fixed for dinner?"

"Spaghetti," Wendell said. "With meatballs."

Clayton rubbed Wendell's head. "Good. I'm hungry."

"Me too," Wendell said.

In the kitchen, Grace was ladling spaghetti sauce onto plates of pasta while Hannah set the table. Without being asked, Wendell pitched in and helped his sister.

Clayton got quick kisses from his wife and daughter, along with instructions to go wash up for dinner. He locked his sidearm away in the gun cabinet where he kept his hunting rifles, gave his hands and face a good scrub, and returned to find his family seated at the table awaiting his arrival.

He eased into his chair and glanced from Wendell to Hannah. "Whose turn is it to tell us everything they did at school today?"

"It's my turn," Hannah said as she twisted her fork around some pasta.

"Okay," Clayton said, smiling at his beautiful daughter, who had her mother's eyes, small bones, and finely chiseled features. "Let's hear all about it."

Hannah took a bite of spaghetti and then began recounting her day at school.

After the table had been cleared, the dishes done, and the children put to bed, Clayton and Grace snuggled together on the living room couch.

"Your mother wants you to call her," Grace said.

Clayton raised an eyebrow. Isabel Istee, a former member of the tribal council, continued to exert considerable influence over government affairs and was always pushing Clayton to get involved in politics. "Did she say what was on her mind?" he asked.

"No," Grace replied, "but I can hazard a guess. Rumor has

it that the tribal police chief position is about to open up, and after your close encounter with Bambi's father yesterday, Isabel wants you off the streets and safely ensconced behind a desk. Today's murder of the deputy only makes it a more urgent issue for her."

"But not for you?" Clayton queried.

"I know you love your job."

"You're avoiding my question."

Grace shifted her weight and sighed. "I want you to be safe. Last night and today have been scary for me."

Clayton pulled back his head and scanned Grace's face. "In spite of my mother's agenda, I have never wanted to be the tribal police chief."

Grace placed her hand gently on Clayton's chest. "I know. Let's not get into a fight over this. Just call your mother."

"Maybe later. Just so you know, over the next week I'll be gone most of the time. I'm driving to Albuquerque in the morning for the autopsy, and from there I'm going up to Santa Fe."

"Will you see your father?" Grace asked.

Clayton shook his head in mock disbelief. Until several years ago, he'd never known who his father was, but a chance meeting with Kerney on the Mescalero Reservation had forced his mother to admit to the truth. "You just love referring to Kerney as my father, don't you?" he said.

"Well, he is your father," Grace replied sweetly, "and I do my best to encourage you to think of him that way."

"I'm working on it," Clayton said with a smile. "Yes, I will see him, and also pay my respects to Sara and say hello to Patrick if time allows."

Grace poked him in the ribs with a stiff finger. "You make sure that time allows, Sergeant Istee."

Clayton laughed. "The hardest part of being a Mescalero is dealing with the matriarchy."

Early in the morning over coffee in an eatery on Cerrillos Road near police headquarters, Detective Sergeant Ramona Pino asked Detective Matt Chacon to give her an update on his attempt to recover data from hard drives taken from the computers at the Riley residence.

"Nada, zip, zilch," Matt replied, chewing on a toothpick, which was his habit, "but all may not be lost, to turn a phrase."

"That's cute, Matt," Ramona said. "Give me details."

"Details, I don't have, but I do have an idea about what it took to scour those hard drives, which can tell us something about the person who did it."

"Explain," Ramona said.

"Most of your typical computer users will either purchase or download a free hard-drive eraser utility that does a fairly adequate job of destroying data. However, a good computer forensic specialist can often find information that hasn't been overwritten in clusters because of something called file slack."

Ramona rolled her eyes skyward. "This is all so very riveting."

Matt laughed. "Be patient, Sarge, I'm getting there. In this particular case, both hard drives were cleaned and sanitized to the max."

"How is that done?"

"Simply put, by repeatedly overwriting and replacing hard-drive surface information with random numbers or characters. On hard drives that have been cleansed by your typical software end user, I'll normally find file slack that has been dumped from the computer's memory, which makes it possible to identify passwords, log-on information, and prior computer usage we call legacy data. But not this time. Everything was as clean as a whistle. I'm betting whoever did this is no average user when it comes to

computers. In fact, it could well be the individual is an IT specialist. But if not, he or she is a gifted amateur techie."

"And you can tell this by how the hard drives were erased."

"Yep. Whoever did this used the techniques and standards
set by the Department of Defense to cleanse computer hard
drives."

"What else have you got?"

Matt looked surprised. "Nothing right now. I was waiting on
you to tell me what Internet service provider the victims used so
I could get a subpoena to access their records."

Ramona drained her coffee and gave Chacon an apologetic
look. With the discovery of Denise Riley's body in the horse
trailer and the ensuing work that it entailed, she'd totally forgotten to follow up as promised.

"Never mind," Matt said with a smile. "I'll do it. Do you
know if the evidence search at the residence turned up any
floppy disks, zip drives, or compact disks? I didn't see any when
I was there."

"I'll take a look at the evidence sheets when I meet with the
sheriff's investigators and let you know."

"Thanks." Matt slid out of the booth. "Also, ask about any
software. If they secured anything like that during the search,
have them give me a call. I'll pick it up for analysis."

"Coffee's on me," Ramona said.

"Thanks," Matt said, knowing full well that it served as a
partial apology on Ramona's part.

Outside the restaurant, Ramona took a call on her cell phone
from Don Mielke of the sheriff's department asking her to show
up for an investigative team meeting at the sheriff's office in fifteen minutes. She told him that she was on her way, passed the
word of the meeting by radio to the two other detectives Chief
Kerney had assigned to the case, and drove out of the parking

lot, still feeling a bit miffed with herself for failing to get Matt Chacon the information he needed.

Several years ago, the county had built a new law enforcement complex on Highway 14, a state road that ran from Santa Fe through the old mining towns of Cerrillos, Madrid, and Golden, into the Ortiz Mountains, and down the back side of the Sandia Mountains that rose up east of the city of Albuquerque.

Designated a scenic route and named the Turquoise Trail, most of Highway 14 was indeed picturesque, with views of high, heavily forested peaks and several old mining towns along the way that were definitely worth a stop.

One such town was Cerrillos, named for the nearby hills, where according to fact or legend—Ramona wasn't sure which—Thomas Edison, the inventor of the lightbulb, had experimented with a precious metal extraction method he'd devised. When the effort failed, Edison shut down his operation and returned to his laboratory in New Jersey to invent other wonderful gadgets.

However, miles before travelers reached Cerrillos or the other old mining towns, they had to pass a cluster of institutional buildings outside the city limits that paid homage to a decision that had been made by the city fathers years before statehood. When the legislature had given Santa Fe first choice of either being home to the territorial prison or the college, the city officials had picked the pokey. At the time it had supposedly been a no-brainer; the prison would bring many more jobs to the community than a college ever could. Which meant that Santa Fe missed out on being the home of the largest university in the state, which Ramona saw as a slow-growth blessing in disguise.

Travelers on the Turquoise Trail thus encountered the stark and foreboding old prison a short distance from Santa Fe. The scene of a bloody, ghastly riot in 1980, it was now closed and rented out to filmmakers as a movie set. Visible nearby were the modern, high-security penitentiary that had been built to replace it, enclosed by towering fences topped with concertina wire; the neat and tidy Corrections Department headquarters and training academy, where the bureaucrats looked after the welfare, safety, and rehabilitation of their incarcerated clients and trained their guards to manage and control the inmate population to keep them from rioting again; and finally, across the road, the Santa Fe County Adult Detention Center and the separate law enforcement complex that housed the S.O.

Inside the county law enforcement building, a group of deputies, sheriff's investigators, and several state police agents were milling around in a large conference room waiting for the meeting to begin. At the front of the room behind a large table, the sheriff; his chief deputy, Leonard Jessup; and Don Mielke, who ran the major crimes unit for the S.O. and carried the rank of major, were engaged in quiet conversation. On the table was a stack of folders.

Ramona took a seat at the back of the room, where she was soon joined by her two detectives. After a few late stragglers wandered in, Sheriff Salgado convened the meeting while Mielke and Jessup distributed the folders, which contained copies of the briefing report.

Ramona flipped though the document as Sheriff Salgado highlighted preliminary findings from the crime scene and subsequent follow-up activities. All in all, the S.O. had done a creditable job, and Ramona didn't see any missteps or gaps in the work that had been carried out on the case so far.

Salgado ended his presentation by announcing that the autopsy on Denise Riley would be conducted in Albuquerque later in the afternoon. He turned the meeting over to Major Mielke, who passed out copies of an initial criminal investigation report of the murder of Deputy Tim Riley, prepared by Sergeant Clayton Istee of the Lincoln County Sheriff's Office.

Ramona read through the report, wondering how many people in the room other than herself knew that Clayton was Chief Kerney's son. While it wasn't a secret, it wasn't common knowledge either.

She stopped speculating about it and returned her attention to the case. Mielke was warning the group not to let the investigation stall because there was no motive and no suspect.

"Don't pin your hopes on forensic evidence solving this case," he said as he leaned against the table, "and in spite of the different modus operandi, we agree with the Lincoln County S.O. that there is a strong likelihood that the murders are linked."

One of the state police agents raised a hand. "What about this theory by the Lincoln County S.O. investigator that the killer is probably a male, approximately five-seven to five-eight in height, who wears a size eight shoe and knew his victim?" he asked in a smug, mildly skeptical tone. "Can we put any stock in it?"

The state cop's attitude rankled Ramona. "I've worked with Sergeant Istee in the past," she said before Mielke could reply, "and I wouldn't bet against him. His analysis that these homicides are personal is right on, and I'm convinced that Denise Riley's killer either redressed her or rearranged her clothing after she was dead. That makes both murders personal."

The state cop threw up his hands in mock surrender. "Hey, I was just asking," he said, but his eyes weren't smiling.

"Sergeant Istee has given us a start on a profile for our perp," Mielke said. "We need to use it when we're out there asking questions."

"The perp may also have more than a passing knowledge of computer technology," Ramona added. "According to Detective Matt Chacon, whoever scoured the hard drives on the two computers removed from the Riley residence is not your typical personal computer user. Also, both the desktop and laptop had been wiped clean of prints."

"Let's add that to what we know and move on to assignments," Mielke said. "Sheriff Salgado and Sheriff Hewitt out of Lincoln County have decided to consolidate the two murder cases into one shared investigation. Myself and Sergeant Istee will serve as case supervisors, and we will both, I repeat *both,* have equal authority."

Mielke looked directly at every officer in the room. "Are there any questions about that? Good. Our starting point is an in-depth look at our victims. The question I want answered is why these persons were murdered. We'll use the FBI crime classification protocols for violent crimes."

Mielke went over the protocols item by item, handed out assignments, and fielded some questions.

"Before we mount up, there's one more thing," he said. "In a few days, we'll be burying Deputy Tim Riley and his wife, Denise. Most of us in this room knew Tim, worked with him, liked him, and liked his wife. They were family to us."

He paused and scanned every face in the room. "I don't expect a miracle between now and the funeral, but I want to see steady progress on this investigation every single day. We are going to grind it out until we catch this killer."

After most of the officers had filed out of the conference room, Ramona approached Mielke and asked to take a look at the evidence inventory. He took her to his office, which was adjacent to the suite that housed the sheriff and his chief deputy, and had her sit while he thumbed through the stacks of paper on his desk.

Mielke was middle-aged but looked older than his years. Tall with slightly stooped shoulders, he had a slim build, a narrow chest, and a gaunt face that gave him an emaciated look. Although his eyes were clear and his hands steady, Mielke was known to be a binge drinker, who'd been on some legendary benders at the Fraternal Order of Police bar on Airport Road.

Ramona hoped the major would stay sober until the case was closed, but if he blew it, at least she knew she could count on Clayton Istee to hang tough.

He fished out a file and handed it across the desk to Ramona. "What are you looking for?" he asked.

"Zip drives, floppy disks, compact disks, and any software programs found at the Riley residence," Ramona replied as she flipped through the inventory forms.

"We didn't find any of that stuff," Mielke said.

"I'd like to go out and take another look," Ramona said.

"Suit yourself, but if you find anything bring it here and log it in with our evidence custodian. In fact, have Matt Chacon drop off those computers to us so we can keep the chain of evidence intact."

"Ten-four," Ramona replied.

Mielke looked at his watch. "I need to get down to Albuquerque for the autopsies. The chief medical investigator and his senior pathologist are personally doing both Riley and his wife."

Outside Mielke's office, Ramona found her two detectives waiting in the break room. At the meeting, Mielke had assigned Ramona and her people the task of learning what Tim and Denise Riley's Cañoncito neighbors knew about the couple. It was just one piece of what cops did to develop a victimology, a cop shop word for an exhaustive, comprehensive, up-to-the-minute history of a crime victim's life. When completed, everything that could be known about an individual would be, in the hopes that it would lead to the killer.

During the process of collecting information, officers would delve into every aspect of the victim's life, review in minute detail the elements of the crime, analyze the crime scene, pore over the forensic findings, locate and interview witnesses, family members, past and present associates, and friends, serve search warrants, and scrutinize autopsy results.

Sometimes the technique worked and sometimes it didn't. Ramona and the detectives divided up the list of neighbors and drove out to Cañoncito in their separate vehicles to start the interviews. From experience, Ramona knew that the process might not put a killer in their sights, but it rarely failed to reveal a victim's secrets.

# ChapterFour

At daybreak Clayton Istee entered the sheriff's office in the Lincoln County Courthouse to find Paul Hewitt at his desk reviewing the previous day's logs, field narratives, lead sheets, witness statements, and supplemental reports that had been turned in by the investigative team. Successful homicide investigations often hinged on not letting minor questions go unanswered. And in order to know what questions needed to be asked, it was necessary to stay on top of the volume of information that continued to accumulate.

Clayton was grateful to have the sheriff lend another pair of eyes and his superior cop instincts to the pile of paperwork. At home, over his first and only cup of coffee for the day, he had prepared an updated officer assignment sheet. He handed it to Hewitt.

The sheriff gestured at an empty chair as he looked over the assignment sheet. Clayton hadn't designated a second in command to run the show while he attended the autopsy in Albuquerque and then went to Santa Fe to meet with the team investigating Denise Riley's murder.

He drained his coffee, put the empty mug on the desk, swiveled in his desk chair, grabbed the coffeepot from the sideboard, and refilled his mug. Day and night, Hewitt kept a pot of coffee going in his office and he drank prodigious amounts of it. "Who's covering for you while you're gone?" he asked.

"I was hoping you'd volunteer, Sheriff," Clayton said from his seat across from the big oak desk that inmates incarcerated years ago at the old Santa Fe Prison had made as part of their rehabilitation program.

Hewitt nodded. "Good choice, Sergeant."

Clayton smiled. Paul Hewitt wasn't known for a sense of humor, but when it did surface it was usually as dry as a New Mexico spring wind.

"Everybody should have completed their assignments before I get back from Santa Fe," he said. "If nothing new or promising develops, have them back up and start all over again."

Hewitt leaned back. The springs of his old wooden desk chair squeaked in protest. "I can't see keeping this investigation going full bore unless we get a break or a credible lead sometime soon. When do we get the forensics back?"

"The state crime lab said they would give it priority, but they didn't make any promises."

Mug in hand, Hewitt took another jolt of java. "Want some?" he asked.

Clayton shook his head. What Hewitt called coffee was nothing more than high-octane sludge.

Hewitt put the mug down, put his elbows on the desk, and intertwined his fingers. "You do appreciate that solving this case may rest largely with the Santa Fe County sheriff."

"Is that a good or bad thing?"

"Luciano Salgado is a retired traffic cop who never made it past the rank of sergeant when he was with the Santa Fe P.D. He's a good-hearted, likable guy but something of a dim bulb in the gray matter department."

"That's not encouraging. What about his ranking officers?"

Hewitt wrapped his hand around the coffee mug. "Leonard Jessup, his chief deputy, wants to be the next sheriff. I've heard that he pretty much runs the S.O. for Salgado, who doesn't like to spend a lot of time at the office. Jessup worked for fifteen years as an agent with the Department of Public Safety SID before Salgado tapped him to be his chief deputy."

Clayton grunted. SID—Special Investigations Division—enforced alcohol, tobacco, and gaming laws within the state, and although it was important work, Jessup's years of experience busting clerks who sold liquor and cigarettes to underage minors was no substitute for investigating violent crimes and major felony cases.

"What's the scoop on this Major Mielke I'm supposed to work with?" he asked.

"Like Salgado he's a hometown Santa Fe boy," Hewitt replied. "The difference is that Mielke's been with the S.O. since the day he pinned on his shield. He worked his way up through the ranks and has survived in his exempt position through two administrations. He's got the credentials: FBI Academy courses, plus he's a graduate of their executive development program for local law enforcement administrators. He's the guy with the hands-on, major case investigating experience in the department."

"Let's hope his hands don't get tied by the powers that be," Clayton said. "What's he like?"

Hewitt reflected momentarily. "Personable and quiet spoken. Other than that, I really don't know him well. Physically, he's tall, thin, middle-age. I'd put him in his forties but he looks a bit more worse for wear. Rumor has it that he's something of a ladies' man and drinks too much."

"That's great," Clayton said.

"He doesn't outrank you on this investigation. Work around him if you have to."

Clayton stayed quiet. By culture and personality, he didn't

find silence or gaps in conversation uncomfortable. As a consequence, Hewitt had learned to wait him out.

"This could get sticky," Clayton finally said.

"What are you thinking?" Hewitt asked.

"Why is Salgado retaining control of the Denise Riley homicide investigation when every indication points to a connection between her murder and that of her husband's? He should have turned the case over to the state police."

"He can't just walk away from this," Hewitt replied. "I know I sure as hell can't either."

"I'm not saying either of you need to. But without any viable suspects there is no way the Santa Fe Sheriff's Office can avoid investigating itself. At the very least, it will require taking a very careful look at the personal and professional relationships Riley and his wife had with members of the department."

Hewitt slugged down more coffee. "That's where you come in, Sergeant. Sheriff Salgado and I have talked it over. Rather than call in the state police, who often take great pleasure at being heavy-handed in such matters, you're going to take charge of an investigation that probes Tim and Denise Riley's past and present relationship with members of the Santa Fe S.O. and their families. Three Santa Fe Police Department officers will be assigned to assist you, Sergeant Ramona Pino and two detectives. Sheriff Salgado assures me that you and your team will be allowed to follow any and all legitimate lines of questioning. If you run into any obstacles, you are to immediately let me and Salgado know, and we'll deal with it."

Clayton nodded and said nothing more on the subject, although he knew it wouldn't be that easy. Getting cops to cooperate in an investigation that could point a finger at one of their own as a murder suspect wasn't going to be straightened out and made smooth as silk by written or verbal orders issued by Paul Hewitt and Luciano Salgado. Besides that, cops were crafty; they could obviate and obfuscate with the best of the con artists and criminals they dealt with on a daily basis.

"We still need to locate a next of kin for Tim Riley," Hewitt said, taking Clayton's silence as deference to his rank, which it was.

"He has an ex-wife and an eighteen-year-old son who lives on his own," Clayton replied. "I don't know where, and I'm not sure if Riley's parents are living or dead."

"Find out," Hewitt said, "and get me the whereabouts of the son as soon as you are able."

"Ten-four," Clayton said. "How long do I stay up in Santa Fe?"

"For as long as it takes to do the job," Hewitt replied. "Chief Kerney has offered to put you up at his ranch for the duration of your stay and he has advised me that you are not allowed to turn down his invitation."

Thrown off guard, Clayton blinked once and clamped his jaw shut. Finally he said, "How did this invitation come about?"

"I called him," Hewitt replied. "When we're at meetings together, he always asks about you, and I know for a fact that he's eager to do anything he can for you and your family."

Paul Hewitt would never meddle in his personal family life without encouragement, and the only person Clayton could think of who would put him up to such a trick was his wife, Grace.

After a long silence, he looked at his watch and said, "I'd better go home and pack if I expect to get up to Albuquerque in time for the autopsy."

"Good idea," Hewitt replied. He opened the center desk drawer and handed Clayton a check. "That should cover your per diem expenses in Santa Fe for the first week. Let me know when you need more."

Clayton folded the check, put it in his shirt pocket, and gave Paul Hewitt a long, measured look.

"Is there anything else, Sergeant?" Hewitt asked, a smile playing on his lips.

Slowly Clayton got to his feet, turned, and left Paul Hewitt's office without saying another word.

To accommodate working parents, the tribal child development center opened at five-thirty on weekday mornings, and it was Grace's week to pull the early shift. Intent on having some words with his wife, Clayton bypassed going home to pack and drove directly to the center.

Built with profits from gaming, it was a new facility in the village of Mescalero, within easy walking distance of the tribal administration building. The front of the building consisted of a long sloping roof that overhung a series of windows bracketed by two arched entrances at the corners, which were supported by concrete columns made to look like cut stone blocks.

Grace's car was in the parking lot, and Clayton barged through the entrance with every intention of confronting Grace immediately with his suspicions. He slowed down when he spotted her sitting on the rug in the middle of the play area, holding a crying child in her arms. Three other children, all sleepy-eyed toddlers, were at a small table waiting for Grace to give them a breakfast snack, which sometimes comprised their entire morning meal.

Grace looked up and saw Clayton, waved him off with a shake of her head, and nodded in the direction of her office. Clayton headed toward the rear of the building knowing that he'd find Wendell and Hannah in Grace's office. When she pulled the early shift during the school year, the children came with her and then took the bus from the center to school.

Through the open office door, Clayton saw his son sitting at his mother's desk reading a book while his little sister stood close by, sounding out some of the words Wendell was reading.

"Stop bothering me," Wendell snapped, pushing Hannah away hard with his hand.

"I don't ever want to see you push your sister like that again," Clayton said as he stepped into the office.

Red-faced, Wendell lowered his head and gazed at the desktop.

"Apologize," Clayton demanded.

"Sorry," Wendell mumbled.

"Say it like you mean it," Clayton ordered.

Wendell straightened up and looked at his sister. "I'm sorry, Hannah."

"That's okay," replied Hannah, who had taken her brother's physical rebuff in stride. "What are you doing here, Daddy?"

"I came to tell both of you and your mother that I have to work up in Santa Fe for a while. I'll be staying there."

"Will you be gone for a long time?" Wendell asked.

"I don't think so. But I'll be back in time for us to go turkey hunting together."

Wendell smiled. For the past two years in the early spring, his father had taken him turkey hunting. They had yet to bag a bird, but from a distance they had seen some big toms through the breaks in the thick underbrush.

"*If* you promise to look after your sister and treat her with respect," Clayton added.

"I promise," Wendell said solemnly.

"Good." Through the glass wall that looked out on the common area where the children congregated, Clayton saw Grace approaching her office. "Now both of you give me a minute alone with your mother."

He got a hug from both children as they left the office.

Grace smiled at Hannah and Wendell as they scooted around her. "I thought you were on your way to Albuquerque and Santa Fe," she said.

"Don't act like you don't know," Clayton replied.

Grace's smile vanished. "Know what?"

"I think you put a bee in Paul Hewitt's bonnet about me staying with Kerney while I'm in Santa Fe."

Grace shook her head, walked behind her desk, and sat. "I did no such thing."

"Then why would Hewitt tell me that he knows Kerney would do anything to help me and my family?"

"Kerney could have told him so," Grace said. "If not, Sheriff Hewitt probably figured it out for himself when Kerney gave him a check for fifty thousand dollars to help us get back on our feet after our house was destroyed."

"Hewitt told me that money came from a wealthy citizen who wanted to remain anonymous."

Grace laughed harshly. "And you believed him?"

"Of course."

"Then you've been deluding yourself," Grace replied. "Kerney was that wealthy citizen."

Clayton gave Grace a speculative look. His wife was not a woman who told lies. "You know this for a fact?" he asked.

"I do."

"And the sheriff told you?"

Grace smiled sweetly. "He did, after I explained to him that as Apaches we would be sorely embarrassed and lose face if we could not acknowledge another person's generosity."

Clayton almost choked in disbelief. What Grace had told Paul Hewitt was an absolute fabrication. In fact, the reverse was usually the case. Among the Mescalero, when giving or receiving a kindness it was polite to avoid making a big to-do about it, which served only to cause embarrassment. Gifts offered had to be accepted without question or fanfare. At best, one might say one was grateful for another's generosity, but only on the rarest of occasions.

"Why would you tell him such a thing?" he asked.

"Since we rarely share our customs with outsiders, how would he know otherwise?" Grace asked. "Besides, surely you suspected that Kerney gave that fifty thousand dollars to us. I think in your heart you've known all along where the money came from and just didn't want to admit it to yourself."

Although he knew his wife was right, Clayton shook his head vigorously. "Why didn't you tell me the truth?"

"Because I had no desire to deal with your false pride." Grace rose, approached Clayton, and looked up at him with serious eyes. "So tell me, in this matter, who has been the better Apache? Kerney, who in spite of your pride, found a way to help us *as part of his family*? Or you, who has rejected most of his attempted kindnesses as though he were the enemy?"

Grace's words struck home. As a child, Clayton's uncles had taught him the four laws of the Mescalero Apaches: honesty, generosity, pride, and bravery. But a man could not be proud, brave, or honest unless he was first and foremost generous.

From the time he'd turned down Kerney's offer to help him rebuild his home, Clayton had felt ill at ease with his decision. Whether Kerney knew it or not, in the ways of the Apache people, Clayton had insulted him. To repeat such an offense would show Clayton to be a man who'd lost his dignity.

"I will stay with Kerney and his family while I'm in Santa Fe," he said with great seriousness.

Grace giggled. "Don't make it sound like you've been sentenced to a week in the county jail."

Clayton laughed in spite of himself and gave Grace a hug. The sound of the school bus horn outside the building ended the conversation. Grace and Clayton walked their children to the entrance, watched them board the bus, and waved when it drove away.

"I'll call you tonight," Clayton said.

"See that you do."

Grace raised her face for a kiss and Clayton brushed her lips with his.

"You can do better than that," she said as she grabbed his arm and pressed closely against him.

He gave her the full treatment—lips, corners of her eyes, tip of her nose, nape of her neck, a nibble on her earlobe—and left her smiling at the door.

There was no doubt in Clayton's mind that the nervous man sitting outside the New Mexico chief medical investigator's office, thumbing through an open file folder was Major Don Mielke of the Santa Fe County Sheriff's Office. He was thin and haggard-looking with long legs, a narrow frame, slightly rounded shoulders, and the rosy complexion of a man who drank too much.

Clayton stepped up to Mielke and introduced himself. Mielke nodded, gestured to an empty chair, and shook Clayton's hand after he sat down.

"My chief deputy said you'd be here for the autopsies," Mielke said.

Clayton caught the faint scent of a cough drop on Mielke's breath. "When do we get started?" he asked.

Mielke looked at his watch. "The chief MI and his senior pathologist will be here in ten minutes. They'll do the autopsies simultaneously, so I'm glad you showed up on time. I'll cover Denise Riley, you take Tim Riley."

Clayton nodded. "Did you know them well?"

Mielke shot Clayton a sharp look. "Yeah, you could say that, but let's save your interrogation into my relationships with the deceased until after we finish up here."

Clayton smiled apologetically. Mielke's annoyance at his inno-cent-sounding question signaled that the fun and games had begun.

"I only asked because I thought you might have an idea, a theory, or maybe even a half-baked guess about why they were killed."

Mielke shook his head. "If I had one single, off-the-wall, scatterbrained notion about who did this or why, I wouldn't be sitting here with you, Istee."

Clayton kept smiling. The major's answer was a neat feint that gave absolutely nothing away. "That's good to know."

A lab assistant opened the swinging door and invited Clayton and Mielke to enter. Inside the autopsy room, a stark, brightly lit, spotlessly clean space, Tim and Denise Riley had been reunited for what might be the very last time, unless they were to be buried together. Their stiff bodies were stretched out on adjoining tables still clothed in the garments they'd worn dying.

All that had been human about them was gone. Under the harsh light Tim Riley's mangled face looked even more gruesome, and although Clayton could see that Denise Riley had once been lovely to look at, her slashed throat spoiled the image.

He stepped up to the table for a closer inspection of the fatal wound. It was a straight, clean cut that severed the jugular and showed no evidence of hesitation. The incised cut had edges that were sharp and even, which made Clayton suspect that the killer had struck from behind his victim with one swift swipe of his knife. He wondered why there had been no mention of such a clean kill in the reports he'd received from the Santa Fe S.O.

The two pathologists who entered the room were suited up and ready to go to work. After introductions were made, Clayton stepped back and watched the procedure. Talking quietly into the overhead microphones above the tables, the doctors dictated their findings as they first noted the state of the victims' clothing, the physical characteristics of the bodies, and the visible evidence of injuries and wounds.

Although he would never admit it, Clayton had a hard time

staying for any length of time in the presence of death. He forced himself to remain still. It wasn't the autopsy that got to him as much as it was the Apache belief that before the dead went to where the ancestors dwelled they could infect you with a ghost sickness that could kill.

To ward it off, it was an Apache custom to wear black, and Clayton had come to the autopsies fully protected. He wore a black leather jacket, black jeans, black cowboy boots, and a sturdy black belt with a silver buckle that held up his holstered sidearm. Even the white cowboy shirt he wore had black stitching around the cuffs, collar, and pockets, and his shield, clipped to his belt, had a diagonal black stripe to signify the death of a fellow officer.

The doctor assigned to Tim Riley had worked his way through the last phase of his external examination. The lab assistant, who'd been photographing both bodies, swabbing cavities, combing for pubic hairs, and taking fingernail clippings, began to bag and tag Riley's clothing.

When he got to the shield that had been pinned above the left pocket of Riley's uniform shirt, Clayton stepped forward and held out his hand. "Let me have that," he said.

The tech gave the pathologist a questioning look.

"I don't think keeping the badge in evidence will help catch the officer's killer," the doctor said. "Give it to the sergeant. Just note where it went on your evidence log."

The tech did as he was told.

Clayton pocketed the shield, which he would return to Paul Hewitt, who would in turn eventually give it to Riley's son. He stepped back out of the way just as the pathologist made the first long incision down Riley's naked torso.

The doctor working on Denise Riley's body had already cut her open and was busy inspecting the internal organs. Slowly, he raised his head, looked at Don Mielke, and said, "This woman was pregnant. She was almost at the end of her first trimester when she died."

Clayton considered whether or not Riley had known that his wife was pregnant. Tim hadn't mentioned it, but that didn't necessarily mean anything more than it was none of Clayton's business. However, surely a wife thrilled to be having a baby would give her husband the joyful news and tell family and friends of the upcoming blessed event.

Clayton watched Mielke speed-dial his cell phone, turn his head away, and whisper so as not to be overheard. Obviously, Mielke thought the pregnancy was important news that might have a direct bearing on the case.

Without additional information from Mielke, Clayton didn't know what to think. Maybe Denise hadn't known that she was pregnant. The possibility couldn't be discounted without further probing.

Mielke closed his cell phone, looked at Clayton, glanced in the direction of the double doors, and stepped outside the autopsy suite. Clayton followed.

"I just advised my people about the pregnancy," Mielke said.

"I figured as much," Clayton said. "Was this the first you'd heard of it?"

Mielke nodded.

"What made you jump on it so fast?"

"Tim told me that after his first wife gave birth to their son, she demanded that he get a vasectomy, which he did. As far as I know he never tried to have the procedure reversed."

"So Denise was carrying somebody else's child."

"I'd say it's very likely." Mielke paused. "But what's interesting is that Denise always made the point of telling the other officers' wives how much she enjoyed not being a mother, and she made no bones about being pleased that Tim couldn't get her pregnant."

"And that was okay with Tim?" Clayton asked.

"Yeah. He said at his age he had no desire to start a new family."

Mielke rubbed his chin as though he was trying to wipe away a bewildered look that crossed his face.

"You seem surprised by all of this," Clayton said.

"They acted like the perfectly happy couple, but you never know."

"You never do," Clayton echoed. "So maybe now we have a motive."

"We've got something," Mielke said, sounding decidedly upbeat.

"We'll need DNA testing done on Denise and the fetus," Clayton said, somewhat surprised by Mielke's positive reaction.

"As soon as possible," Mielke added. "I'm sure you'll want every male officer of my department to voluntarily provide a mouth swab sample for DNA analysis."

"I'll want a sample from every male *employee*, sworn or civilian," Clayton said, "and it will have to be taken in my presence or by someone I designate from outside your department."

"Agreed." Mielke walked to the swinging doors, paused, turned, and gave Clayton a tight smile. "In a way, I'm glad she was pregnant."

"Why is that?"

"Because I honestly don't believe Denise would have had an affair with anybody at the S.O."

Clayton gave Mielke a questioning look.

"Except for Tim, I don't think she liked cops," he explained. "At least not the officers in my department."

"Including you?" Clayton asked.

Mielke scoffed as he pushed his way back into the autopsy suite. "Let me be the first in line to give you a DNA sample, Sergeant Istee," he said in a low voice.

"That would be great," Clayton whispered in reply, thinking that once again Mielke had handily jumped over a seemingly innocuous question.

The pathologists had made good progress during Clayton and Mielke's absence from the suite. Internal organs had been removed, analyzed, and weighed, and fluid specimens from the gastrointestinal tracts had been collected for toxicology testing. The doctor working on Denise Riley reported no vaginal or anal bruising or tearing, but didn't rule out sexual contact prior to death.

Mielke asked to have DNA testing done on Denise and her fetus as soon as possible.

"I've already dictated a priority request to have it done ASAP," the doctor replied.

Clayton stepped up to the table where the other doctor was busy placing some of Tim Riley's detached internal organs into his chest cavity. "Will you look and see if he had a vasectomy?"

"He sure did," the doctor replied, glancing up at Clayton, "and it was a done by a darn good surgeon, too."

"Is there any evidence that the procedure was reversed?'

"Nope, the part of the vas deferens that was removed hasn't been toyed with, at least not surgically."

Clayton shook his head in dismay at the bad joke. "Thanks."

The doctor looked over at Denise's body on the adjoining table. "These two were husband and wife, right?"

"Correct."

"Well then, Detective, I'd be looking for the guy who got the wife pregnant."

"That's a great idea," Clayton replied.

When Clayton arrived at the Santa Fe County Sheriff's Office the March sun was low in the west, pallid in a windblown, dusty sky.

He'd followed Mielke up from Albuquerque and used the time to speculate about the major. Mielke had shared a good deal of personal information about Tim and Denise Riley, which made Clayton wonder about the exact nature of his friendship with the couple. Was it Tim who'd been Mielke's buddy, or had Denise been the primary object of the major's attention?

It was a question that needed an answer, and Mielke's willingness to be first in line to give a DNA sample didn't necessarily put the issue to rest.

Clayton parked next to Mielke's unit in the rear lot and followed him through the restricted access employee entrance, down a brightly lit corridor, and into a large briefing room that had been set up as a command center for the investigation. Mielke introduced him to several uniformed deputies who were filling out paperwork at a worktable, and it earned Clayton measured looks and freeze-dried smiles. News of the nature of his mission had obviously preceded him.

After Mielke excused himself to go find the sheriff, Clayton used his time waiting to study the investigation task and duty assignments that had been posted on a large chalkboard mounted on the rear wall of the room.

Mielke came back before Clayton could digest all the information, to tell him that Sheriff Salgado was in the workout room and would meet with him there. He followed Mielke down another hallway, marveling at the space, the relative newness of the building, the number of individual offices that lined the corridors, the existence of an actual walk-in evidence storeroom, and a secure armory for weapons and ammunition. By comparison, it made the cramped space of the Lincoln County Sheriff's Office in the county courthouse in Carrizozo seem like a shabby suite of low-rent offices.

The workout room for the deputies was nothing less than a fully equipped gym, with lockers, showers, and bathrooms and every piece of exercise equipment needed for weight training and cardiovascular fitness. It was as nice as the private gym in Ruidoso that Clayton paid money to every month and never got to use half as much as he should have.

Dressed in sweats and putting in some time on a motorized treadmill, Sheriff Salgado was the only person in the gym. He jogged at a pace no faster than a slow walk, sweating heavily, red in the face and panting hard.

Salgado's thick waist and inner tube–size love handles bulged against his sweatshirt, and his double chin jiggled up and down as he moved. Clayton half expected the man to stroke out or collapse from a heart attack at any moment.

As Clayton and Mielke approached, Salgado turned off the machine, wiped the sweat from his face with a gym towel, stepped off the treadmill, and gave Clayton a hearty handshake.

"Glad you could come up and give us a hand," Salgado said, flashing a politician's sunny smile.

"It's good to be here," Clayton said. "I think this case is going to take our combined efforts to get it solved."

"That's right, that's right," Salgado said. "I want you to use the training and planning lieutenant's office in the administrative wing so you can have quick access to me if you need it."

Clayton didn't like the idea at all. It would immediately create ill will for him. "I'd rather not inconvenience the lieutenant. Isn't there someplace else you can put me?""

"It's a done deal," Salgado said. "The lieutenant will double up with one of the patrol commanders while you're here. Don't worry about it. Everybody's on board to catch this killer. That's the important thing. You need something, you tell me and I'll get it for you. Where do you want to start?"

"With you," Clayton replied. "I'd like to interview you as soon as possible."

Salgado looked at his watch. "First things first. Major Mielke will get you settled in, and Sergeant Pino and her P.D. detectives are coming in from the field to meet with you. I'll see you in my office in the morning. Just let my secretary know what time you want to meet."

"Thank you, Sheriff," Clayton said, not sure if Salgado was a dim bulb as Paul Hewitt had said, a wily old street cop, or a bit of both.

Salgado slapped him on the back and headed for the showers. Outside the gym, Clayton and Mielke fell in behind two officers who were sauntering down the corridor engrossed in conversation.

"Maldonado was in the briefing room when that sheriff's sergeant from Lincoln County showed up," the first officer said.

"So what did he think?" his buddy replied.

"He said he almost cracked up when he first saw the guy. Said he was dressed like some Apache Johnny Cash wannabe all in black."

"He's Apache?"

The first deputy nodded. "I bet his first name is probably Geronimo or something like that. Maldonado says wait until you see him. He's got long black hair pulled back in a ponytail."

His buddy laughed. "Maybe he's a New Age Indian who chews peyote buttons and has spirit visions. And this guy is the hotshot investigator who's going to find a killer among us? I almost wish the sheriff had asked the state police to do the internal investigation."

"You got that right, bro."

From the corner of his eye, Clayton could see Mielke watching him, waiting for a reaction. Clayton cleared his throat loudly, and the deputies turned their heads at the sound and didn't recover their composure quickly enough to mask their surprise.

"Have a pleasant evening, gentlemen," Clayton said as he passed them by.

Mielke didn't say a word, but he wasn't smiling either. He led Clayton to the L-shaped administrative wing and showed him his assigned office. It was next door to where the major hung his hat and in clear view of Sheriff Salgado's corner suite, the chief deputy's adjoining office, and a reception area where the sheriff's executive secretary resided. It offered zero privacy for people coming and going, and with a large glass window, with no venetian blind, that looked out on the reception area, it put Clayton and whoever was with him under constant observation.

Mielke introduced Clayton to the sheriff's secretary so he could make an appointment to interview Salgado in the morning. The secretary, a middle-aged Hispanic woman named Joanne Castillo, consulted her daily planner and gave Clayton an early morning appointment with the sheriff. She handed Clayton a key to his new office and made him sign for it.

Accompanied by Mielke, Clayton unlocked the door and looked around. One wall of bookshelves held bound reports, training manuals, and some law enforcement textbooks. On the wall behind the desk was an assortment of framed certificates that its usual occupant had received for completing training and recertification courses.

The lieutenant had cleared out his desk and provided an empty metal filing cabinet for Clayton to use. On top of the desk was a three-ring binder casebook which Mielke told him was up-to-date except for the field reports that were still being prepared.

"Have you arranged for lodging?" Mielke asked. "There are several decent motels that offer reasonable rates for law enforcement officers."

"It's all taken care of," Clayton replied, unwilling to be more specific about where he was staying and why.

"We'll need to know how to reach you."

Clayton found a ruled writing tablet in the top drawer of the desk, wrote down a number, and handed it to Mielke. "Call my cell phone."

"That'll work." Mielke pocketed the note and glanced at his

wristwatch. "Sergeant Pino and her detectives should be here in a few. If you need me, call dispatch. Until these murders are solved I'm available twenty-four/seven."

Mielke left and Clayton settled behind the desk. He opened the casebook and started reading, but he couldn't shake the thought that Salgado and Mielke's cooperation was a pretense.

*To hide what?* Clayton asked himself just as Ramona Pino stepped through the door and gave him the first authentic smile he'd seen since arriving in Santa Fe.

"It's good to see you, Clayton," she said as she stepped to the desk and shook his hand.

"You too. Where are your detectives?"

"We just got in." Ramona took a seat in the chair next to the desk. "They're doing their reports."

"You heard that Denise was three months pregnant?"

Ramona nodded. "And that the daddy couldn't be Tim Riley."

"Did you know him?" Clayton asked.

"In passing. He seemed competent. A quiet guy, not the macho type."

"Any scuttlebutt about why he left the Santa Fe S.O.?"

"None that I heard."

"What has Mielke had you doing?"

"Interviewing and re-interviewing the Rileys' neighbors. We've talked to most of them twice, but several are out of town and unavailable. One guy is a long-haul trucker who isn't answering his cell phone, and there's a retired couple who are vacationing somewhere in Mexico in their motor home."

"Has anything come up?" Clayton asked hopefully.

"Nope." Ramona looked over her shoulder and through the window that gave a view of Salgado's secretary at her desk. "So they've put you in this fishbowl to keep an eye on you."

"Yeah, but I don't intend to stay here all day every day.

In fact, initially I want to keep our interviews with the commissioned personnel informal and low-key. Let's meet with the deputies in the field, in their squad cars, over coffee, in the break room, or at their homes whenever we can. Have you encountered any male deputies or employees who seem a little skittish to you?"

"No, but based on how this killer went about his business, I wouldn't expect him to be anything but cool and collected. Do we even have anything more than a hunch that suggests the murderer could be a cop?"

Clayton shook his head. "It's all theory at this point."

"Great. Okay, how do you want to do this?"

Clayton said he wanted the first round of interviews to start in the morning. He'd take the brass, the administrative staff, and the civilian office workers. Ramona and her two detectives would divvy up the three shifts, including all officers and the regional dispatchers housed at the facility. The four of them would convene every morning to set their schedule, and debrief every evening.

"Let's meet here in this office at 8 A.M.," he said as he stood up and tucked the casebook under his arm.

"You got it," Ramona said as she got to her feet. "Are you going to see Chief Kerney while you're here?"

"Yeah, in about thirty minutes. I'm staying at his place."

Ramona followed Clayton out of the office. "I'm going to miss him when he retires at the end of the month."

Clayton locked the door. "Raising cutting horses and running a ranch sounds like a pretty good way to retire to me."

Ramona laughed. She knew the story of how Kerney had inherited his wealth from a famous Southwestern spinster artist who'd been his mother's best childhood friend and college roommate. "Think I could get to do something like that on a retired sergeant's salary?"

"Maybe if you supplemented your retirement income as a security guard, you could swing buying yourself a broken-down pony."

Ramona chuckled. "That's an ugly thing to say about somebody's future prospects, Sergeant."

"I know it," Clayton replied with a smile.

The sheriff's office door was closed, Mielke was away from his desk, and the secretary was nowhere to be seen. In the briefing room, Ramona introduced Clayton to her two detectives, Jesse Calabaza and Steve Johnson. He spent a few minutes talking to the detectives about his plans for the next day, before excusing himself.

Outside, the night sky was a low blanket of clouds pushed along by a cold wind that carried the sting of light sleet and the promise of heavy snow. He was northbound on Interstate 25, traveling in the foothills of the Sangre de Cristo Mountains, when the storm hit. He slowed the unit way down, put it into four-wheel drive, and made his way carefully through the whiteout to the exit that would take him to the Galisteo Basin and then on to Kerney's ranch.

When Clayton arrived, the dashboard clock told him that the snowstorm had more than doubled the time he had figured to reach the ranch. Through the swirling blizzard, the lights from inside the ranch house looked warm and inviting.

He knew that he would be warmly welcomed, and although he didn't think he deserved such treatment, he would put his pride aside as Grace had suggested and act like a dignified Apache.

He killed the engine and grabbed his luggage from the passenger seat. The outside lights winked on and the front door opened. With his head up and his face chilled by the wind-driven snow, Clayton walked up the path and said hello to his father.

# ChapterFive

Kerney's house wasn't ostentatious, but it was clearly the home of a well-heeled man and his family. The rooms were large, the ceilings high, and the art on the walls original and highly collectible.

Over the years Kerney had frequently invited Clayton and his family to visit, but they had accepted only once. At Grace's urging, they'd phoned and been persuaded to come for dinner on the last evening of a long weekend visit to the state capital and several of the nearby pueblos. Although Kerney had repeatedly invited them to stay at the ranch, Clayton, not wanting to impose, had booked the family into a budget motel on Cerrillos Road.

Patrick had just turned a year old at the time, so it had been a good two and a half years or more since Clayton had stepped over the threshold into Kerney's house. He put his luggage on the floor and shook Kerney's outstretched hand.

"Welcome," Kerney said with a warm smile.

Clayton nodded. "Some weather out there."

"It's a humdinger of a storm, and desperately needed."

Clayton removed his leather jacket and draped it over his luggage. "I hope it heads south to Mescalero."

Before the two men could say more, Patrick scooted between them, stopped in his tracks and gazed up at his half brother.

"You're Clayton," he said emphatically.

"That's right," Clayton replied.

Patrick stuck his hand out. "Let's shake hands."

"Okay." Clayton bent down and shook Patrick's hand. When he rose up, Sara was standing next to Kerney. She stepped forward, gave him a quick hug, and released him.

"It's so good to see you," she said.

"And you," Clayton said. "I am happy to see that you are home and recovering from your wounds. Kerney e-mailed me to say you'd been decorated and promoted. Congratulations."

"Thank you," Sara said politely. "I'm so glad you're staying with us. Since you were last here, we've built a guest wing. It's totally self-contained with its own private entrance, but I do hope you'll take your meals with us when you can."

Sara had spoken hurriedly, as though she was trying hard to put him at ease. Or was it that she wished to avoid any conversation about her wartime experiences in Iraq? Clayton decided it was probably a bit of both.

He smiled. "Since I'm not much of a cook, and meals of cold pizza and fast-food burgers get old real fast, I'll be glad to eat with you when my schedule allows."

"Good," Sara said. "We're big on stews and soups in this household, so there will always be something for you in the refrigerator."

Before Clayton could protest that he didn't need any special treatment, Patrick tugged at his hand.

"I'll show you where you're going to stay," he said with the authority of one who knew exactly where he was going. "It's got a kitchen, a TV, and *two* bedrooms. My uncle, aunt, and cousins stay there when they visit. So do my grandma and grandpa."

"Okay," Clayton said as he grabbed his luggage and jacket. "Lead on."

Patrick didn't move. "Are you really my brother? My dad says you are."

Clayton dropped down on one knee and looked Patrick squarely in the eye while he continued to hold his hand. "I am your older brother, a Mescalero Apache, and a policeman."

Patrick nodded in confused agreement. "That's what my dad told me. He said you were all those things and a father too."

"That's true. Wendell and Hannah are my children. They're a little bit older than you. You've only met them a couple of times and you were probably too young to remember. What do you think about that?"

Patrick paused and thought it over. "It's okay," he said. "I'm too young to be a dad, but someday *I'd* like to be an older brother."

Clayton laughed and looked up at Kerney and Sara. "Maybe someday you will be. You'll have to talk to your parents about that."

Kerney smiled and slipped his arm around Sara's waist. "He already has."

"We're currently in negotiations," Sara added. "Dinner's in fifteen minutes."

"I'll be ready," Clayton replied as Patrick led him away.


Conversation at the dinner table stayed away from weighty subjects such as the homicide investigations and Sara's combat experiences in Iraq. Instead, the three adults and Patrick talked about family matters. Clayton spoke of Grace's job as director of the tribal child development center, and Wendell's and Hannah's progress in school. Sara talked about the visit her parents had made to the ranch after her release from the army hospital, and Patrick went on at some length about his older cousins in Montana whom he'd visited with Kerney last fall.

"Are Wendell and Hannah my cousins?" he asked Clayton.

"No, they are your nephew and niece," Clayton answered.

"You're their uncle," Kerney added.

Patrick cast an unbelieving look at his father and turned his attention to Sara for an explanation. "Is Dad teasing me?"

"No," Sara said. "You are Wendell and Hannah's uncle."

Disbelieving, Patrick shook his head. "I can't be. Uncles are grown-ups, not kids."

His pronouncement was met with laughter, and it took some patient explaining before Patrick got comfortable with the idea that he was an uncle. By the end of the discussion, he seemed quite pleased with his newfound status in Clayton's family.

"But uncles still have to put on their pajamas, brush their teeth, and get ready for bed," Sara said as she plucked Patrick from his chair and carried him toward his bedroom.

"I'll pull KP," Kerney said, pushing back from the table.

Clayton joined in to help clear the table and load the dishwasher. Never having served in the military, he'd wanted to learn more about Sara's combat experiences, but had been reluctant to ask. As he towel-dried a pot too big for the dishwasher, he asked Kerney if she was doing all right.

"It's a tough transition to make, especially after getting wounded," he replied. "But she's coming along. We'll be moving to London soon after I retire. She's being posted there as a military attaché to the U.S. Embassy."

"For how long?"

Kerney took the dried pot from Clayton and stowed it in the appropriate kitchen cabinet. "Three years. Then she'll have her full twenty years in for retirement and we'll come back to New Mexico permanently."

"That's a long time to be gone," Clayton said.

Kerney closed the dishwasher and turned it on. "We'll return every year during her annual leave, and I'll come back with Patrick occasionally on shorter trips."

"Are you looking forward to living in London?"

Kerney folded the dish towel and hung it on the rack. "You know in a way I am, as long as I can get back every now and then for some New Mexico sunshine and a green chili fix."

Kerney gestured toward the door to the living room, and after Clayton had settled into one of two oversize easy chairs separated by a hand-carved nineteenth-century Spanish colonial chest that served as a coffee table, Kerney offered him a cordial.

"No, thanks. It would only make me sleepy." Clayton leaned forward in the chair and waited until Kerney sat down across from him. "How involved are you in the investigation?"

"I want it solved, preferably before I retire. Denise Riley's sister, Helen Muiz, who is also retiring, has been with the department for over thirty-five years. More important, she's a friend. I don't want this case hanging over our heads when we both walk out the door for the last time."

"Has Sergeant Pino been keeping you briefed?"

"She has," Kerney answered, "right down to her concern that Sheriff Salgado may be sabotaging the investigation while spouting platitudes about giving you his full cooperation. What do you need?"

"I need some fresh eyes to look at everything and everybody again. I need somebody to analyze what's been done up until now and tell me what we're missing. I need more people digging deep into Denise and Tim Riley's lives and their recent activities."

"I thought your assignment was to investigate the relationship between the Rileys and sheriff's office personnel to determine if there are any possible suspects."

"It is."

"Wouldn't doing what you suggest mean you'd be stepping on Don Mielke's toes?"

"It means stomping on them big-time," Clayton replied, "but with good cause."

Kerney sat quietly for a moment. Without saying it directly, Clayton was asking him to muscle in on the investigation. He had no quarrel with Clayton's assessment of the situation. He read it the same way. Salgado was at best a lightweight police administrator; his chief deputy, Leonard Jessup, was no better, and Don Mielke was competent but unreliable.

Ineffective, muddled leadership coupled with a complex, difficult case could only spell disaster. The investigation would most probably bog down and wind up in a cold case file to be trumpeted every few years in the print media as one of Santa Fe's major unsolved crimes.

Concerned almost to the point of distraction about the well-being of Sara, Kerney had done nothing on the case other than assign staff to work with the S.O. and ask to be kept informed of the progress, or the lack of it.

Had he been shirking his responsibility to Helen Muiz, her family, and the men and women under his command? He didn't like the way that notion made him feel. Clayton's face—including his eyes—was composed and watchful. Clearly, he wanted Kerney to step up to the plate.

Kerney leaned forward. "Bring me up to speed on your end of the investigation down in Lincoln County and then we'll figure out a way to get around Salgado and his underlings."

Clayton's expression lightened and he started talking. By the time Sara brought Patrick out to say good night, the two men were deep in conversation. Much later, when Sara came out of the library to say that she was retiring for the night, they were still at it.

They decided their best strategy was to have Paul Hewitt

ask for additional assistance from Kerney's department. Because Hewitt had jurisdiction over the Lincoln County homicide, there was no way Salgado could challenge the appropriateness of the request.

Kerney, in turn, would allocate all available resources of his department to the investigation and assume direct oversight of the joint operation.

"We're probably going to need to have Paul come up here for a face-to-face with Salgado," Kerney said. "I'll put the idea to him when I call him in the morning."

Clayton nodded, yawned, and stood. "Good deal. Are you and Sara serious about adding to your family?"

Kerney got to his feet. "Absolutely, but it may not happen as quickly as Patrick would like. Right now Sara's questioning the wisdom of bringing another child into the world."

"That's understandable seeing what she has been through," Clayton said.

"Exactly," Kerney said. "Do you think, when the time comes, Patrick will enjoy his role as an older brother?"

The carefully worded, pointed question went right to the heart of Clayton's uneasiness about his relationship with Kerney. He could either respond to it truthfully or sidestep the issue and give a trite answer.

Clayton decided to be candid. "We both know that Patrick is much more ready to be an older brother than I was to be a father's son. I'm sorry it took me so long to warm to the idea."

Kerney smiled. "Knowing you as I do, I'm proud to be your father."

Kerney's direct expression of his feelings toward him took Clayton by surprise, and for a moment he didn't reply. Finally he said, "Thank you."

It came out sounding stiff and lame. Embarrassed, he noted the lateness of the hour, said good night, and retired to the guest suite.

———

Sunup found Kerney in the horse barn mucking out stalls, laying down fresh hay, and putting out oats for his horse, Hondo; Patrick's pony, Pablito; Sara's mare, Ginger; Gipsy, one other gelding; and Comeuppance, Kerney's stallion at stud. Housed in a separate wing of the barn with his own paddock, Comeuppance sired foals that Kerney and his partner, Riley Burke, raised and trained as cutting horses. It was Riley who did most of the work, but he was away for a few days with his wife and his parents, attending a meeting of the New Mexico Cattle Growers Association in Tucumcari, so the morning chores fell to Kerney.

Last night's blizzard had fizzled out, leaving behind less than two inches of snow on the ground that would quickly melt under a clear sky and bright sun. Still, any moisture was welcome, and it gave Kerney hope that more might be on the way, although the absence of clouds argued against it.

He was breaking the ice in the water troughs when the sound of a car engine caught his attention. Across the meadow he watched Clayton drive away in his Lincoln County S.O. unit.

Back at the house all was quiet. Sara, who was ranch born and raised, had always fallen asleep easily and was by nature an early riser. But since her discharge from the hospital, her sleeping patterns had been erratic. She would stay awake late into the night and sleep through most of the morning. Or she would fall into a fitful sleep for several hours, tossing and turning, before getting out of bed and dozing on the couch, where Kerney would often find her when he awoke.

Her doctor saw it as a symptom of depression and gave her a prescription that she'd refused to get filled. Sara had firm opinions about not taking drugs unless it was absolutely necessary. But this time Kerney, who understood and appreciated her point of view, truly believed she was wrong not to take the medication.

He went into the library, closed the door, found Paul Hewitt's cell phone number in his address book, and dialed it. Breathing heavily, Hewitt answered abruptly.

"This is Kevin Kerney. Have I called at a bad time?"

"No, you haven't," Hewitt said, pausing for a breath. "I'm riding an exercise bike at my gym and I'm about out of steam. What can I do for you?"

"We've got a situation up here I think you need to know about." He filled Hewitt in on the state of affairs with the Santa Fe S.O., laid out the plan he'd hatched with Clayton, and asked Paul if he would be willing to come up to Santa Fe and flex some muscle at Salgado.

"Sounds like you're in good enough shape to do it," he added with a chuckle.

"Oh yeah," Hewitt grunted. "I'm looking forward to the day I kiss my health club membership good-bye, sit in my rocking chair, and grow a nice potbelly."

"I'll believe that when I see it," Kerney replied.

"What time do you want me up there?"

"If you'd get off the phone, we could stop talking and you could start driving," Kerney said. "While you're traveling, I'm going over to Salgado's house and tell him exactly what we want him to do this morning."

"What is it we want him to do?" Hewitt asked.

Kerney ran it down.

"Sounds like a plan," Hewitt replied before he abruptly disconnected.

From the living room Kerney heard Sara and Patrick talking in the kitchen. He found them at the table reading a picture book together. Although *Pablito the Pony* remained one of Patrick's favorite stories, he'd recently expanded his literary horizons to a newly discovered book about Herman and Poppy, two horses who formed a unique and lasting friendship. Patrick hadn't quite learned all the words yet, so Sara was reading those parts he'd yet to master.

Kerney poured himself a second cup of coffee, pulled a chair next to Sara, and joined his wife and son at the table.

When they had finished reading the story, Patrick closed the book. "The end," he said. "I bet Pablito, Herman, and Poppy would all be friends if they knew each other."

"You're absolutely right," Sara said.

"Do you think so, Daddy?"

"They would be best friends," Kerney replied, turning his attention to Sara, who looked a little more rested and less withdrawn. "Did you sleep well?"

"Maybe Herman and Poppy could live on our ranch with my pony, Pablito," Patrick said hopefully.

"Herman and Poppy are storybook animals," Sara said.

"But Pablito was just a storybook pony until Daddy and I went and got him," Patrick replied with great certainty about his scheme to bring the three horses together.

"The day will come when you'll be able to ride every horse on the ranch whenever you want," Kerney said in hopes of putting to rest Patrick's idea of adding Herman and Poppy to the herd.

Patrick thought hard. "*Every* horse includes Comeuppance, right?"

"Yes, it does," Kerney answered slowly as Sara cocked an eye at him. "Your mother and I will decide when that day has arrived."

"How about this morning?"

"No, not this morning. And not tomorrow morning, either. You've got a lot more to learn about horses and riding first, and you've got to get bigger, too."

"How much bigger, Dad? This big?" Patrick held his hand a few inches above his head.

Kerney raised Patrick's hand a few more inches. "More like this, Patrick. Don't worry. You're growing fast."

Patrick smiled at the happy thought, and Sara chuckled. "You got yourself out of a tight spot there, Kerney."

Delighted by Sara's cheerfulness, Kerney asked, "How did you sleep?"

"Well enough," she replied. "I see that Clayton has already left. How did the two of you get along last night?"

"Much better than I anticipated. I think there's actually a chance we can be friends."

"That's good news."

Patrick got down from his chair and went to the glass patio doors that looked out on the meadow and the horse barn. "It snowed last night," he announced excitedly. "We have to make a snowman."

Kerney walked to Patrick, picked him up, and carried him back to the kitchen table. "I can't help you, sport. I have to go to work today."

"That's okay," Patrick said, wiggling to be set free. "I can make it myself. Put me down."

Kerney lowered Patrick and he ran to get dressed.

"Will you be working all day?" Sara asked.

"Yes." Kerney sat next to her. "Today and every day, if necessary, until we either catch Denise Riley's killer or I get put out to pasture at the end of the month. Whichever comes first."

"That's a relief," Sara said.

"Meaning exactly what?"

Sara smiled, and for the first time since her return home there was a sparkle in her eyes. "Meaning that I've been wanting to tell you for days to just leave me the hell alone until I feel better. Just knowing you're not going to be around every minute worrying about me has already lifted my spirits considerably."

"Have I been that much of a nuisance?"

Sara shrugged. "In a good way."

"But you want me gone," Kerney added.

"Not permanently."

"How reassuring." He leaned close and kissed her. "Perhaps retiring is a bad idea. I would be constantly underfoot."

"There's no backing out of that now, Kerney." Sara poked him lightly on the bicep. "We're all going to London together. That's the deal."

"Yes, it is." Kerney stood. "So I'd better get cracking."

By the time Kerney left, Sara and Patrick were busy building a snowman in the meadow, unconcerned that it would be a melted puddle by noon. He drove the ranch road to the highway with his spirits lifted for the first time in weeks, hopeful that Sara had turned the corner and was on her way to a full recovery.

Clayton arrived at the law enforcement center to discover that none of the S.O. honchos were around. When he asked Salgado's secretary if the sheriff was ready to meet with him, he was told without further explanation that Salgado had been delayed and she didn't know when he would arrive. Frustrated by the sheriff's cavalier attitude, Clayton went to his borrowed office, where he found the desk piled high with reports, and started the arduous task of reading through every document. Two hours later he looked up to see a clear-eyed Don Mielke standing in the doorway.

"Come with me," Mielke said, and without waiting for a response he started down the hallway.

In the briefing room he introduced Clayton to a state police crime lab tech named Stan Steiner, who had been sent over to take saliva samples from all male personnel.

Steiner, a young man with a serious hair-loss problem, a high forehead, and wide-set brown eyes, had the look of a person who'd found his calling among test tubes and microscopes and was completely ill at ease in the alien environment of the sheriff's department. After a limp handshake and a mumbled greeting, he quickly returned to the task of setting up for the onslaught of male deputies and civilian employees who would soon be lining up to have their mouths swabbed.

"Just so there is no question about evidence contamination, Sheriff Salgado thought it best to have the state police crime lab gather the saliva samples," Mielke explained as they left the room.

"That's smart thinking," Clayton said.

"Also," Mielke continued, "he decided to order all male correctional officers at the county detention center and all male police dispatchers to give samples. He wants to make absolutely sure every male employee under his command is screened."

"That's good," Clayton said, wondering what Kerney and Paul Hewitt had already done to cause such a quantum leap in Salgado's procedural IQ. He briefly considered the possibility that Salgado had wised up on his own. He couldn't dismiss it out of hand, but it seemed highly unlikely.

Mielke stopped in front of Clayton's office. "The sheriff is hiring a private laboratory to do the DNA testing," he said, "so that we can get a fast turnaround on the results. The medical investigator will send DNA material from the fetus to the private laboratory for comparison."

"Excellent," Clayton said.

"By the way," Mielke said, "at the sheriff's request, the state police will cover our patrol calls while you and your team take statements from on-duty personnel. That should give you and your team adequate time without feeling rushed."

"Tell the sheriff this helps a lot," Clayton said.

"Then you're all set," Mielke turned on his heel and walked away.

Clayton checked the time. Ramona and her two detectives were due to arrive in thirty minutes. He needed to create an interview outline along with questions to be asked before they began talking to all the male deputies, correctional officers, and dispatchers.

While welcome, the sudden and unexpected high level of cooperation from Salgado made the task before him only more daunting. With an inner laugh, he reminded himself that Kerney was apparently doing what he had asked. He looked forward to learning exactly what tactics had been employed.

Late last night, the trucker Ramona Pino had been unable to make direct contact with had called the Santa Fe P.D. and left word that he would be home no later than 7 A.M.

In the morning, Ramona sent her two detectives off to link up with Clayton at the S.O. and drove out to Cañoncito to interview the trucker. On the way, she mentally reviewed the substance of the statement that the man, Roy Mirabal, had given to a deputy. An independent livestock trucker, Mirabal had supposedly been gone from his residence during the time the murder occurred, hauling a load of cattle from Las Vegas to a Roswell feed lot, although no attempt had been made to verify the information. Additionally, Mirabal, who lived alone, said he'd been home the night that Denise Riley had been reported missing, and had been awakened by a man who'd asked him if he'd seen Denise or knew where she might be. According to Mirabal, the man pounding on his front door had identified himself as Denise Riley's brother-in-law.

Last night, Ramona had called Ruben Muiz and asked him about his late-night conversation with Roy Mirabal. Ruben had confirmed the story, but added a comment that ratcheted

Ramona's interest in Mirabal up a few notches. Ruben said that after learning that Denise was missing, Mirabal had asked if she'd run off. Ramona was eager to find out why Mirabal asked such a intriguing question.

She pulled to a stop next to an older-model tractor trailer and knocked on the door of a rather run-down double-wide mounted on concrete blocks. Mirabal opened up and inspected Ramona's police credentials before stepping aside to let her enter.

In his late fifties, he had a round face, a heavy two-day beard, and a trucker's potbelly that spilled over a large fake rodeo belt buckle. He wore a badly wrinkled Western shirt, blue jeans, and scuffed steel-toe work boots.

The inside of the double-wide looked no better than the outside. Cheap floor-to-ceiling wood laminate paneling darkened the front room, and a long sectional couch with tattered armrests positioned in front of a large-screen television dominated the space. Stretched out on an overstuffed easy chair covered in a dull gray throw was the largest domestic cat Ramona had seen in a very long time. It raised its head, cast a lazy look in Ramona's direction, and promptly lost interest. From somewhere inside the trailer came the smell of a litter box that desperately needed emptying.

Ramona thanked Mirabal for meeting with her. "Have you been driving all night?" she asked in an attempt to put him at ease.

"No," Mirabal replied. "I took a rest break in Lubbock. Your message said you had some questions for me about the Rileys."

"I'll get to that in a minute," Ramona replied with a smile. "But first could you show me your trip paperwork for the load you hauled during the time Denise Riley was murdered?"

Mirabal licked his upper teeth with his tongue and looked slightly confused. "I don't know exactly when she was murdered. The deputy who came here just asked if I'd been home two or three days ago—I don't remember the exact date—and I told him no, I'd been on a run to a Roswell feedlot, and from there I picked up a load of cows in West Texas for delivery to a rancher down in Fort Sumner. I was gone at least thirty-six hours."

Ramona nodded understandingly. "I'm sure there isn't a problem, Mr. Mirabal. If I can just take a look at your paperwork, we can clear this up right away."

Mirabal reached for a briefcase on the couch, snapped it open, pulled out a clipboard, and gave it to Ramona. "Look all you want," he said.

A quick scan of the documents confirmed Mirabal's story, but Ramona's cop instincts weren't completely satisfied. Paperwork could easily be forged. Mirabal could have deliberately cast an aspersion on Denise to deflect suspicion from himself. Ramona decided to contact the feedlot operator and the rancher to make sure his story checked out 100 percent. She jotted down names and phone numbers before returning the clipboard to Mirabal.

"You gonna check up on me?" Mirabal asked.

"Yes, and that should take care of it, if you're telling the truth," she said. "Except I do have one more question."

"What that?"

"When Mr. Muiz came to your door looking for Denise, you asked him if she'd run off."

"Yeah, I remember saying that."

"I'm wondering why you weren't surprised to learn that Denise had gone missing."

Mirabal shrugged. "I can't say I know anything for sure. It was just some things I saw and heard."

Ramona gestured at the couch. "Why don't we sit down and you can tell me about it."

"There's not much to tell." Mirabal hoisted the cat off the easy chair, dumped it on the carpet, and plopped down. The cat arched its back, stretched, looked insulted, and padded away to the kitchen.

Ramona took a cautious seat on the edge of a couch cushion. "What exactly did you see and hear?" she asked.

"Well, I don't work regular hours; no long-haul trucker does. So I'm home at different times, day and night. With Riley a deputy sheriff and all, his schedule would change from days to swing to nights. Sometimes I'd be here when he was working graveyard or swing shift and I'd see Denise walking down her driveway at night. I'd hear a car engine on the country road, see headlights. When the wind was right, I'd hear voices. Then the car would drive away and an hour or two later come back. Before you know it, there would be Denise walking back up the driveway to her house."

"You could tell it was Denise?" Ramona asked.

"On moonlit nights I could. Other times I just figured it had to be her. When I could hear voices, it was her voice for sure. The other voice was a man's."

"Did you hear what was said?" Ramona asked.

Mirabal shook his head. "Not really. Sometimes they would laugh, or I'd catch a word to two on the wind."

"Did you ever see the man, see the vehicle?"

"Nope."

"How often did Denise walk down the lane to the county road at night?"

"I can't say for sure, because I'd be gone a good deal of the time. But I do know she was meeting somebody who she didn't want visiting her at home and didn't want to be seen with, so I'm thinking she's probably screwing around with a guy her husband knew. Least ways, that's the way I saw it."

"That makes sense. When was the last time you saw Denise walking down the lane?"

"Three nights before her brother-in-law came pounding on my door. I saw the beam of her flashlight from my kitchen window as she walked down her driveway. Five minutes later, I saw her coming back toward her double-wide."

"Can you be sure it was Denise?"

"No, but who else would it be? Anyway, she was gone and back in a hurry, which was real unusual."

"As far as you know, whenever she met somebody at the end of her driveway it was always at night," Ramona said. "Is that correct?"

"Yeah, if you put it that way. I know she worked during the day. But I can't tell you where she went when she drove away in her car by herself."

"Did you ever visit socially with the Rileys?"

"Never did. Every now and then, I'd see them at the supermarket or the gas station and we'd say howdy and spend a few minutes passing the time of day. When they were together they seemed happy enough. I never saw them arguing or fighting."

"Did you ever talk to Riley about his wife's nocturnal behavior?"

"I don't butt into other people's business. Like I said, I had my suspicions, but that's all. Besides, they weren't real friendly neighbors. Can't say that I'm very friendly either."

"Was there any hostility between you and the Rileys?"

Mirabal shook his head. "Nope."

Ramona went over Mirabal's story with him again to jog his memory in case he'd forgotten something. The only new bit of information he recalled was that he'd started noticing Denise's late-night rendezvous behavior about two years ago.

She thanked Mirabal for his time, gave him her business card, and left Cañoncito. By the time she reached the sheriff's office, she'd talked by cell phone to the rancher and the feedlot operator. Not surprisingly, Mirabal's alibi had held up.

Inside the S.O., Ramona swung by the regional dispatch center and asked for the whereabouts of Deputy John Quintana, the officer who'd initially interviewed Roy Mirabal. The supervisor, Joanne Bustos, a tiny, middle-aged woman who bordered on

being anorexic, told her that Quintana was in the building meeting with the lieutenant in charge of training and planning.

"How long has Quintana been with the S.O.?" Ramona
asked.

"Less that six months." Joanne opened the door to the hallway and stepped outside. Ramona followed.

"He's a cadet," Joanne continued, "so he hasn't been to the
law enforcement academy yet. I think he's scheduled to start with
the next class."

Ramona had known Joanne Bustos from the day she'd been
hired as a night dispatcher back when the P.D. had its own separate communication center. She'd always been a good source of
back-channel information and gossip.

"What else do you know about him?" she asked.

Although the hallway was empty, Joanne lowered her voice.
"He's struggling on the job. He gets lost a lot when he's sent out
on calls, still has trouble remembering his ten-codes, and from
what I hear his paperwork and reports are totally subpar."

"So why is he still wearing a shield and carrying a weapon?"

"He's Sheriff Salgado's nephew. I understand his patrol supervisor is hoping and praying that he'll flunk out of the academy."

"Ah," Ramona said. "Enough said. Thanks."

"Anytime."

Not at all surprised by Joanne's revelation about Deputy
Quintana, and encouraged by what Roy Mirabal had told her
about Denise Riley, Ramona left Bustos and went in search of
Clayton Istee.


After several hours spent interviewing deputies about their relationships with Tim and Denise Riley, Clayton was beginning to
think that there was no logical, earthly reason the couple had been
murdered. Although the Rileys pretty much kept to themselves,

they were well liked, and Tim was considered by his peers to be one of the best—if not the best—patrol officer on the force.

None of the men seemed resistant to questions or defensive, and all seemed equally upset about the murders. Although it was too soon to tell for sure, Clayton wondered if the one man in the department who knew the most about Tim and Denise Riley's personal life might be Don Mielke.

The high point of his morning came when Ramona Pino arrived and briefed him on the substance of her interview with Roy Mirabal. The downside was not having knowledge of Denise's nighttime assignations sooner. Now everyone along the stretch of county road to the Rileys' double-wide would have to be interviewed again, this time to see if they could help ID the mystery driver or provide a description of the vehicle.

It was a possible major lead in the investigation that had remained uncovered due to the incompetence of a cadet deputy and the stupidity of a supervisor who'd had allowed an untrained rookie to conduct a major felony case interview.

Clayton shared his frustration with Mielke, who shrugged it off as an unfortunate event that had occurred in the rush to gather information as quickly as possible after Denise's body had been found.

Clayton couldn't believe Mielke's spin on the event, but given how big-time screwups were being managed at every level of government, he wondered if both Deputy Quintana and the yet-to-be-named supervisor would be commended and promoted instead of censured and sacked.

Noon came and went with no sign of Sheriff Salgado, who'd blown off his early morning appointment with Clayton and still had not yet made an appearance at the office. Furthermore, Clayton hadn't seen or heard from Kerney or Sheriff Hewitt. He wondered if his assumption that they had already put the squeeze on Salgado was correct.

He was reviewing interview summaries with Ramona Pino when Detective Matt Chacon from the SFPD showed up carting a box containing the computers secured from the Riley residence along with the software and zip drives uncovered in a subsequent search of the double-wide.

Chacon put the box on the table and gave the two sergeants a wan smile. "Here's everything Major Mielke wanted returned to evidence," he said. "The bad news is that after an exhaustive examination I've found nothing useful at all. But it confirmed my suspicion that whoever erased the hard drives was no amateur."

"Is that it?" Ramona asked, noting that Matt's smile telegraphed he had more to tell. She nodded at a straight-back office chair.

Chacon sat, took the toothpick out of the corner of his mouth, and said, "I uncovered some interesting, perplexing information. After I located Denise and Tim Riley's e-mail, cell phone, and landline telephone accounts, I served a court order to access them. The cell phone and e-mail accounts had been almost completely emptied. In fact, the only calls on file consisted of the unsuccessful half a dozen or so attempts Tim Riley made to reach his wife on the night he was murdered."

Clayton, who'd been half-listening while working on an updated investigators assignment schedule, gave Matt Chacon his full attention. "What do you mean, the accounts had been emptied?" he asked.

"Except for Tim Riley's few failed attempts to call home, the records had been purged," Matt reiterated, "and it was done a few hours after Denise was murdered."

"Purged by who?" Ramona asked.

Matt shrugged. "The service providers claim it was a security breach and they assure me that the information didn't get dumped accidentally or on purpose by their personnel. But I have no way to verify if they're telling the truth. If they are leveling with me, that leaves two possibilities. Either a world-class hacker broke into their systems, which I seriously doubt, or we're dealing with something that's far beyond our reach."

"Why not a hacker?" Ramona asked. "Didn't you initially think that a computer geek or a techie could have wiped the Rileys' computers clean?"

"And what exactly is it that is far beyond our reach?" Clayton demanded.

Matt turned to Ramona. "I did say it could be a hacker, but the security specialists for the Internet provider and the cell phone companies tell me that whoever penetrated their firewalls and erased the e-mail and call records also found and scoured redundancy files that backed up the data. Furthermore, it was a surgical strike that targeted only the Rileys' records. Not only that, all the accounts were accessed and cleansed simultaneously."

He glanced at Clayton. "Which gets to your question. I'm not the world's greatest expert, but it doesn't seem likely that one individual, even a brilliant one, could do all that so quickly after the Rileys' deaths. If it was a lone hacker, it had to have been planned well in advance."

Clayton leaned back and studied Chacon. "So take a guess and tell me what you think we are dealing with here."

Matt twisted his toothpick between his thumb and forefinger before responding. "An organization with ultrahigh-tech computer savvy and megabucks would be my guess. That could mean any number of multinational corporations or government agencies, foreign or domestic. I know that doesn't help much."

"Can we track the computer break-ins back to the source?" Ramona asked.

"Maybe," Matt replied, "but not without outside help and even then it could take months. The FBI is investigating."

"It could be years before they tell us anything," Clayton said, shaking his head in dismay. As a former tribal police officer, he'd experienced firsthand uppity federal agents who loved keeping local cops in the dark.

"This raises some big questions about our victims," Ramona said. "What did Tim and Denise Riley know—or do—that got them killed?"

"And who wants to keep it secret?" Clayton added.

"Exactly," Ramona said.

Clayton pawed through the papers on the desk. "Before I left Carrizozo, I assigned a deputy to do a deep background check on Tim Riley. Has Mielke started one on Denise?"

Ramona flipped through the assignment sheet on her clipboard. "No."

"What do we know about her?"

Before Ramona could answer, Mielke stepped into the office. He gave Matt Chacon a brief nod and looked directly at Clayton and Ramona.

"Chief Kerney and Sheriff Hewitt are with Sheriff Salgado in his conference room, and they'd like the three of us to join them," he said.

"Not a problem," Clayton replied, stifling a smile as he pushed back his chair. "Has anyone interviewed Denise Riley's employer?"

"The insurance agent was questioned," Mielke replied, "and was eliminated as a suspect. He's gay and lives with his longtime partner. His parents have been visiting from Buffalo for the past week. He has an airtight alibi. You should have the report."

Clayton said, "I mean did anyone interview the insurance agent in depth about Denise?"

"Not yet," Mielke said.

"Matt," Ramona said, "after you log in the evidence with the S.O., go have a chat with the man about Denise."

Chacon nodded, picked up the box of computer evidence, stepped around Mielke, and left.

"Did Chacon find anything useful on the computers?" Mielke asked.

"Not on the computers," Ramona said.

Mielke turned his attention to Clayton. "What does that mean?"

Clayton gave the major a broad, reassuring smile. "Detective Chacon has made some helpful discoveries. I'll brief you after our meeting with the brass. What's that all about?"

"We'll soon find out," Mielke replied as he stepped into the hallway behind Ramona. "Did you know that Sheriff Hewitt was coming up here?"

"I haven't talked to my boss since I left Lincoln County," Clayton said as he followed along.

"Uh-huh," Mielke grunted, shooting Clayton a sour look.


The meeting was short and sweet. Wearing his game face, Salgado announced that effective immediately Chief Kerney was officially in charge of all aspects of the homicide investigation. Santa Fe S.O. and P.D. supervisory personnel assigned to the case would report directly to him. Sheriff Hewitt would continue to head up the Lincoln County investigation and work cooperatively with Kerney and Salgado. Clayton would stay on in Santa Fe as a lead investigator, and additional officers and resources would be made available from the Santa Fe P.D.

"This task force is the best way to get the job done," Salgado said in his closing remarks. "I want everybody behind it one hundred percent."

Mielke looked like he was seething inside, and Salgado's chief deputy, Leonard Jessup, had a constipated expression. The two other senior sheriff's deputies in attendance, both captains, seemed completely nonplussed. The meeting ended with Kerney calling for a supervisory briefing at 1600 hours.

"We'll want to know everything you've got," he said, glancing from Mielke to Clayton to Ramona. "Get ready for tough questions if we don't like what we hear, and get ready for some reshuffling if we don't like the way things have been run."

Paul Hewitt nodded in agreement to emphasize the threat.

Outside the conference room Mielke scurried to his office with his two captains and quickly closed the door.

"I'd like to be a fly on the wall for that conversation," Ramona said as she and Clayton passed by. "Did we just witness a palace coup?"

"I think it was more like an abdication," Clayton replied. He smiled at Salgado's secretary, who shot him a decidedly unfriendly look in return.

Ramona caught the exchange. "But certainly not a voluntary one based on the spiteful once-over you just got from Salgado's secretary," she whispered. "Did you have anything to do with this?"

Clayton gave Ramona a sideways glance but kept a straight face. "Me? Like you, I'm just a lowly sergeant." Politely he stood aside to allow Ramona to enter his temporary office.

"Ah, I see," Ramona said as she walked through the doorway. "First you give Mielke a non-answer about whether or not you knew Hewitt was in Santa Fe and now I get one about Salgado's abdication. Is that any way to trust your partner?"

"Are we partners?" Clayton asked with a smile, quickly warming to the idea.

"For the duration," Ramona said.

"Then close the door and I'll tell you what's up."

# Chapter Six

Denise Riley's former employer owned an independent insurance agency in a huge open-air mall on Cerrillos Road. A few Santa Fe–style touches—earthtoned stucco exteriors, flat roofs, "rough-hewn" wooden posts, and fake buttresses—could not disguise the fact that it was a glorified strip mall with a big-box discount department store and a mega-supermarket mixed in with an assortment of franchise restaurants and national chain stores that sold books, electronics, home accessories, and clothing.

Sandwiched between a brand-name shoe outlet and a cellular phone store, the insurance agency had a front window with a lovely view of the parking lot that served the big discount department store. Inside, Matt Chacon encountered a middle-aged man probably in his early forties, who had the muscular build of a welterweight on a trim five-eight frame. He had short brown hair, brown eyes below thick brows, a strong chin, and a pronounced British accent.

"What happened to Denise is bloody awful," John Culley said after Chacon introduced himself. "I don't know what I will do without her."

Major Mielke hadn't said anything about John Culley being British. Matt wondered what else Mielke might have forgotten or failed to mention. "I understand your parents are visiting from Buffalo," he said.

"My partner's parents, not mine," Culley replied with a wave of his hand. "My dear widowed mother, who is safely ensconced in her Tunbridge Wells cottage, thankfully has no desire to venture forth to visit me in the new world. Have you ever been to Buffalo? No? Regardless what the time of year might be, I cannot recommend it in any season."

Matt loved the way Brits talked. It wasn't just the accent he enjoyed hearing; he liked the way they used the language and seemed so comfortable making conversation.

Culley was just one of a number of Brits living in Santa Fe, including prominent artists, successful business owners, scientists who worked at the national laboratory in nearby Los Alamos, and some who were simply filthy rich and hobnobbed with the area's other wealthy residents at charity events, the opera, and art openings. Members of British nobility—Matt couldn't remember their names or titles—owned a large, secluded estate outside the city and were occasionally mentioned in the local newspaper.

The Brits composed one part of a rather extensive community of western European expatriates who lived in Santa Fe. Some of the Brits were full-time residents and others part-timers who either regularly returned to Europe or wintered in Florida.

Aside from illegal Mexican workers who'd been coming to Santa Fe forever, the ranks of foreign migrants living in the city had recently swelled, as more and more Middle Eastern businessmen had moved in and opened retail stores that catered to the tourist trade.

"I take it Tunbridge Wells is in England," Matt said.

"Indeed, it is," Culley replied. "In Kent, actually. Lovely castles and gardens. Have you been?"

Matt shook his head. "I don't get a chance to travel that much."

"Pity," Culley said. "There is so much to see in the world."

"What can you tell me about Denise's personal life?" Matt asked.

"Shall we sit?" Culley asked as he stepped to his desk and settled into a chair.

Matt pulled up a side chair and joined Culley at his desk, which was modern, European-looking, and shaped somewhat like an unshelled peanut. On it was a laptop, a cordless phone, a leather desk pad, and a matching leather letter and pen holder. The other desk in the office was of the same design but smaller. Denise Riley's nameplate was prominently displayed on an otherwise empty desktop. There were framed Southwestern landscape prints on the walls, and a large, freestanding clear plastic rack of randomly arranged boxes that was abstract in design and positioned near the entrance. It served as a display case for various insurance company brochures. A bank of two-drawer black file cabinets lined the wall behind Denise's desk, and behind Culley's desk stood a credenza that held several membership certificates from local civic organizations and the photograph of a good-looking man Matt took to be Culley's partner.

"How long did Denise work for you?" Matt asked.

"I hired her soon after I started the business. I was renting a small one-room office on St. Francis Drive at the time and had placed an advertisement in the paper for a receptionist. Denise was the first to respond and I hired her immediately."

Matt took a notebook out of his coat pocket and flipped to a blank page. "When was that?"

"I started the business seven years ago this spring."

"So you knew Denise before she married Tim Riley?"

Culley smiled. "Yes, indeed. I witnessed the entire courtship. It was quite a whirlwind romance. They made a splendid couple."

"Did the romance last?" Matt asked.

"Well, I suppose the honeymoon phase ended as it always does, but they were very loving to each other as far as I could tell.

Telephone calls back and forth, occasional luncheon dates when Tim had days off during the workweek—that sort of thing."

"Would you say Denise was a faithful wife?"

Culley raised his eyebrows. "What an astonishing question. Denise was an extremely attractive woman, and a number of my male clients were very flirtatious with her both on the telephone and when they came into the office. She always handled it with aplomb and never acted inappropriately. But to answer you more directly, I never had an occasion to think of her as the unfaithful type."

Matt wrote down an abbreviated version of Culley's remarks in his notebook. "Did you know that she was almost three months pregnant at the time of her death?"

Culley shook his head. "Now you have me totally flummoxed. According to Denise, her husband was unable to give her a child. I suppose that's why you asked if I thought she might be unfaithful. Could it be that she might have sought out a sperm donor?"

"It's possible," Matt said. "Did she talk to you about a desire to have children?"

"We didn't have that kind of a relationship," Culley replied. "We got along well as employer and employee, but we were not close personal friends."

"Are you saying that she didn't share much of her personal life with you?"

Culley smiled. "Exactly so. Nor did I share much of mine with her. I think both of us liked it that way."

"Professional relationships at work are always best." Matt glanced at Denise's nearby vacant desk. "Still, you worked together in close proximity. I'm sure you took telephone messages for her, greeted friends and family who occasionally dropped by to see her when she was out of the office, overheard snatches of her phone conversations."

"Yes, of course," Culley said before Matt could continue,

"and I've been trying to think of a person, a man perhaps, she might have particularly favored. But no one comes to mind, other than Tim, her sisters, and her brother. They were the ones most likely to call or stop by."

"If you think of someone, let me know." Matt closed the notebook and handed Culley a business card. "I'd like to review Denise's employee file."

Culley looked slighted embarrassed. "I'm afraid there is no employee file other than salary and income tax information that my accountant maintains." He wrote down the accountant's name and phone number on a telephone message slip and handed it to Chacon.

"You didn't get a résumé, verify her past employment, and check her references before you hired her?" Matt asked.

"I saw no need to, and my intuition about Denise was spot-on. She worked out perfectly."

Matt glanced at the empty desk again. "Did Denise do her work on a computer?"

"Yes, a desktop model. I tried to use it yesterday and it froze and crashed. Fortunately, I have all my records and files backed up and I can access them from my laptop."

"Where is the desktop computer now?"

Culley waved his hand. "For all I care, it's in transit to a computer graveyard in India to be salvaged. The technician who services my computers came out and told me it wasn't worth the trouble or expense to fix it. I had him take it away. He's building a new one for me, and I've ordered a larger monitor and a faster printer to go with it."

Matt asked for and got the name of the company Culley used to service his computers. He tore a fresh piece of paper from his notepad and put it in front of the Englishman. "I need your written permission allowing me to take custody of your old computer. Please sign and date the authorization."

Culley picked up a pen. "Yes, of course, but whatever for?"

"I can't talk about what we do in ongoing investigations."

"Of course you can't." Culley scribbled his consent and handed it to Matt, signed and dated.

"Have you had any recent break-ins or burglaries?"

"No, not a one."

"Who else besides you, Denise Riley, and your clients have access to the office?"

"The leasing agent has a key, as does the cleaning lady I employ to tidy up my house and the office."

"I may need to speak with both of those people," Matt said.

Culley wrote down names and phone numbers, and handed the slip of paper to Matt. "This is becoming rather worrisome, Detective."

Matt smiled reassuringly. "Rest easy, Mr. Culley. Sometimes the solution to a crime is in the details, so it's important not to overlook any information that might be helpful."

Culley's worried expression cleared. "I absolutely understand."

"Are you a U.S. citizen, Mr. Culley?"

"No, I am not, and as long as the current incumbent resides in the White House, I'm inclined to remain a British citizen. However, I do have permanent resident status."

"What brought you to New Mexico?" Matt asked.

"D. H. Lawrence and the promise of blue skies," Culley replied.

Although intelligent and knowledgeable in his chosen field, Matt was the product of the local school system and one year of study at the area community college. He flipped open his notepad. "Is this Mr. Lawrence a friend of yours?"

Culley repressed a smile and carefully chose his words. "You could say that, Detective Chacon. He was a very famous and controversial writer born in the Midlands of England who lived in northern New Mexico for a time early in the twentieth century. It was through his writing that I first became fascinated with New Mexico."

Matt appreciated the fact that Culley had shown no condescension about his scant knowledge of modern literature. He closed the notebook and stood. "That should do it for now, but I may need to speak with you again."

"I am at your disposal, Detective." Culley rose and came around his desk. "It would be my pleasure to do whatever I can to help advance your inquiries. Whoever did these terrible, murderous acts must be brought to justice."

The word *indeed* was on the tip of Matt's tongue. Instead he asked, "Do you have proof of your permanent resident status with you?"

"Yes," Culley replied. "Would you like to see it?"

"Indeed I would," Matt said, unable to resist the impulse.


The computer repair and service company John Culley used was housed in a small adobe building at the back of an industrial lot tucked near the railroad tracks on Baca Street. A small sign on the outside of the building read "Roadrunner Computer Repair and Service." Matt entered to find a man sitting at a large workbench in the middle of a room filled with monitors, keyboards, printers, laptops, and CPUs. He looked up, saw Matt, and got to his feet.

"Are you Steve Griego?" Matt showed the man his police credentials.

The man, who looked to be in his late thirties, nodded. "I am. Pardon the mess, but it's always like this around here."

"You have a desktop computer belonging to John Culley." Matt held out Culley's signed consent. "I've come to pick it up."

Griego read the note and pointed to a desktop computer and assorted paraphernalia in a box on the floor near the door.

"There it is. Please take it away and don't bring it back. I've got no use for it."

"Is it intact?"

"I haven't cannibalized it if that's what you mean."

"That's what I mean. Culley told me the unit was completely worthless. When you powered it up, what did you find?"

"Nothing. When it crashed, it took all the files and folders with it. I tried system restore and nothing happened. Tried it again, and the same thing—nada. The operating system and software is so outdated on the unit I told Culley he'd be smart to trash it and get something with greater capacity and speed."

"Did you run any diagnostics?"

"Culley said not to bother, just to build him a new CPU. The old one is an off-the-shelf discounted model that was out-of-date the day he bought it. What do police want with Culley's old computer?"

"It's a secret, so I can't tell you," Matt replied. "How would you rate Culley's skills as a computer user?"

Griego laughed. "At the bottom of the barrel along with ninety percent of all the people who own personal computers. He's the kind of customer who would have his receptionist schedule a service call because the unit was running slow. I'd go out, run the disk cleanup and defragmenter utilities, and that would be it. It didn't matter how many times I showed them how to do it themselves, they'd forget or just didn't want to be bothered."

"So neither Culley nor Denise Riley was computer savvy."

"Not so far as I saw."

"Do you have any employees who may have serviced the Culley account?"

"You're kidding me, right?" Griego said with a hearty laugh.

Griego's likable personality made Matt smile. "I guess I must have been." He picked up the box with Culley's old computer and stood in the doorway. "Thanks for your time."

"No sweat. Remember to dispose of that CPU properly when you're done with it. You can't just throw it in the trash."

"I'll keep that in mind," Matt replied.


The 4 P.M. meeting with lead investigators and supervisors called by Chief Kerney and Sheriff Hewitt started on time with all present and accounted for and no dillydallying. Kerney and Hewitt impressed Clayton with the way they asked questions, took suggestions, revised task force operations, established targeted goals, gave constructive criticism, and made sure Sheriff Salgado got full credit for putting the new plan in place. Just by watching the two top cops in action, Clayton learned a hell of a lot about the right way to organize a well-functioning major felony interagency task force. The effect on the men and women in the room was palpable. Everybody seemed re-energized, ready to dig in and start over again.

At the tail end of the meeting, Sheriff Hewitt brought the team up to speed on the Lincoln County murder investigation. With significantly less resources and far fewer personnel than the Santa Fe S.O., Lincoln County deputies had pieced together a complete accounting of Riley's week on and off the job, identified all the persons Riley had come into contact with during his time in Lincoln County, and made substantial headway on Riley's background check. Information from the air force, including several former commanding officers, Riley's ex-wife, some old high school mates, and one surviving uncle who resided in an assisted living facility in Dayton, Ohio, seemed to prove that Tim Riley had been exactly whom he professed to be.

After Hewitt finished, Salgado passed out a synopsis of Riley's known personal history that included updated information. He had entered the air force at the age of eighteen, after graduating from high school. He rose to the rank of master sergeant E-8 and served twenty years and two months before retiring. His service record showed overseas postings to England, Japan, Germany, and Kuwait, where he was stationed during Gulf War One. His last duty assignment was at Holloman Air Force Base adjacent to White Sands Missile Range near the city of Alamogordo, less than an hour's drive from Lincoln County.

Riley was the father of one child, an eighteen-year-old son named Brian, whereabouts currently unknown, who had stayed with Tim and Denise for a time last summer. While in Santa Fe, Brian worked for a month as a busboy in a downtown restaurant before being fired for tardiness. A National Crime Information Center criminal records check showed no wants and warrants and no arrest record for the boy.

Tim Riley had moved to Santa Fe soon after his retirement and applied for a deputy sheriff vacancy with the Santa Fe Sheriff's Office. Because of his extensive experience as a noncommissioned military police officer and criminal investigator, he was hired and sent to the New Mexico Law Enforcement Academy to complete an accelerated police officer certification course. Upon his return to the S.O., he was assigned to the patrol division, where he remained until he resigned to accept the Lincoln County job.

A year after arriving in Santa Fe, Riley married Denise Louise Roybal in a civil ceremony performed by a county magistrate. Financial records showed that the couple had lived within their means and neither were deeply in debt nor had unusually large unexplained monetary assets. Riley's vasectomy had been verified by autopsy, and there was no evidence of surgery to reverse the procedure.

Riley had divorced Eunice, his first wife, ten years ago. Eunice, currently living in North Carolina, had been interviewed by the local police. According to their report, she was employed as a veterinarian's assistant at a small animal clinic and had a live-in boyfriend named Ernest Arnett who worked as an independent electrical contractor. Interviews with the woman's employer, neighbors, and friends verified that she'd been in North Carolina during the time of the two homicides.

When told of Tim Riley's murder, Eunice was unable to think of any person who had reason to kill him. However, since she'd had little contact with him for over eight years, she had no idea who Riley's current friends or enemies might be.

When asked about her son, she stated she had no knowledge of Brian's whereabouts, noting that the boy had left home soon after turning eighteen because of a personality conflict with her boyfriend. She expressed surprise on being told of Brian's visit to Santa Fe, saying she had not known about it and stating he and Tim had not been close since the divorce. According to the interviewing officer, she showed little sorrow about her ex-husband's death.

Kerney and Hewitt ended the meeting with four priority goals established: find Brian Riley as quickly as possible and determine if he was to be treated as a suspect; identify the unknown person Denise Riley had been secretly seeing; delve deeply into Denise's past, particularly those years when she was living away from Santa Fe; and complete the gathering of saliva samples for DNA comparison testing.

Outside the conference room, Clayton gave Paul Mielke the scoop on Matt Chacon's conversation with Denise's employer and the tale of the office desktop computer that had crashed the day after her murder.

"Detective Chacon secured the computer," Clayton noted, "and will let us know if he finds anything."

"Do we know if Riley's son is a computer whiz?"

"That's a good question," Clayton replied. "We should ask the North Carolina authorities to check it out."

"I'll give them a call," Mielke said as he walked away.

A few minutes later Paul Hewitt caught up with Clayton in

his borrowed office. "We've got to find Brian Riley," he said from the doorway.

"I heard you and Chief Kerney loud and clear on that, Sheriff. I'm on it."

"How are you on it, Sergeant?"

"Ramona Pino is en route to the restaurant where the boy worked to see if she can scout up some information. Two SFPD detectives are making the rounds of juvie hangouts in the city to locate anyone who knows him or where he is. I've got a deputy calling the North Carolina high school authorities and Tim Riley's ex-wife to get a list of classmates he might have stayed in touch with. We're also putting the word out to snitches on the street."

"Very good," Hewitt said. "I'm heading home to Lincoln County. I want daily updates from you, Sergeant."

"I'll route them through Chief Kerney and Sheriff Salgado," Clayton replied.

Hewitt nodded. "You're going to make a first-rate police chief someday."

"Thanks for the compliment, Sheriff, but that's a long way off, if ever."

"You never know," Hewitt said as he waved good-bye.


The downtown restaurant where Brian Riley had briefly worked as a busboy catered to patrons who could easily afford a two-hundred-dollar bottle of wine to complement their perfectly plated, expensive gourmet meals. Except for Chief Kerney, who'd inherited some megabucks from an old family friend, Ramona Pino thought it highly unlikely that any member of the Santa Fe Police Department had ever eaten at the establishment.

The swanky restaurant, according to several old-timers on the force, stood on the site of the long-gone downtown bus depot, which had housed a small diner renowned for serving the best green-chili cheeseburgers in town. Back in those days, uniformed officers assigned to Plaza foot patrol almost always chowed down at the diner, which had a varied menu, good food, and reasonable prices.

But that was then, and the new Santa Fe was now a vastly different place. Since the transformation of the bus depot into a world-class restaurant, just about everything else in the downtown part of the city had also changed. Plaza businesses that catered to locals had vanished, replaced by stores and eateries that served the tourist trade. The price of a nice dinner in a fancy Santa Fe restaurant to celebrate a special occasion was now way beyond the means of the average citizen, which definitely included the men and women sworn to protect and serve.

Many officers, including those who had working spouses, were holding down part-time second jobs. A growing number couldn't afford to live in Santa Fe and were now commuting from the boomtown city of Rio Rancho that sprawled along the Rio Grande west of Albuquerque. The joke going around the department was that when a major disaster hit the city, FEMA would probably lumber into Santa Fe faster than the officers who lived out of town could arrive.

Inside the restaurant, the hostess area at the top of the stairs was unoccupied. Servers were setting up a long row of tables for what appeared to be a large dinner party. At the bar in the back of the room, a bartender was polishing glassware and talking to a man who wore a chef's coat with the sleeves rolled up to his elbows.

Ramona approached, identified herself, and asked to speak to the manager, owner, or whoever was in charge. The man in the chef's coat told her the manager, Pearce Byers, was in the back. He went through the kitchen double doors to get him.

While Ramona waited, the bartender, a strapping six-footer

with a leering smile on his pretty-boy face, gave Ramona the once-over. The guy looked to be the bad-boy type who preyed on women and lived off them when he could.

Ramona stared him down.

Pearce Byers came out of the kitchen and advanced quickly on Ramona. Dressed in a linen shirt and wool slacks, he had a scowl on his face that pinched his eyebrows together. "What can I do for you, Officer?" he asked.

"I'm Detective Sergeant Pino," Ramona said as she handed him her business card, "and I need a few minutes of your time."

Byers glanced at the card and stuck it in his shirt pocket. "Certainly. A few minutes. Sorry to be so rushed, but I have a party of twenty arriving any time now and a number of early pre-concert bookings for the piano recital at the Lensic Performing Arts Center."

Ramona surveyed the dining room. All was ready for the alleged onslaught and there wasn't a customer in sight. "I need to talk to anyone on your staff who might be able to put me in touch with Brian Riley. He worked as a busboy here last summer."

Byers looked thoughtful. "The name doesn't ring a bell."

"He was here for a very short period of time," Ramona said. "No more than a month. I was told he was fired for tardiness."

"Oh, yes," Byers said, touching his finger to his lips. "I tend to forget the problem children we hire who slip through our screening process. As I recall, we took a chance on him because his father was a police officer. But he wasn't fired for tardiness; he was canned for coming to work stoned."

"On drugs or alcohol?"

"Does it really matter?" Byers answered. "But to answer your question, not only did he show up stoned, but he was caught smoking pot on breaks behind the building with an apprentice cook. We fired them both."

"Who was the cook?" Ramona asked.

"Randy Velarde. He was enrolled in the culinary arts program at the community college."

"I need to see Velarde's employment application. Riley's also."

Byers looked past Ramona toward a large group of people who'd arrived at the hostess area. "Can't this wait until later?"

"No, it can't," Ramona answered.

Byers sighed in frustration, called one of the servers over, asked him to seat the waiting party, and told Ramona he'd be right back with the employment applications.

The pretty-boy bartender, who'd been listening with great interest, leaned over the bar. "If you can't find Randy at home, he may be in class at the community college."

"Do you know that for a fact?" Ramona asked.

Pretty Boy nodded. "When I ran into him a month or so ago, he said he was working days as a grocery store stocker and taking classes at night and one morning on his days off."

"Did he say what store he was working at?"

"No."

"Thanks," Ramona said.

Pretty Boy didn't answer right away. He was distracted by a very attractive woman with long brown hair who hurried up the stairs and joined the just-seated party. He gave the woman a thorough once-over before returning his attention to Ramona.

"Yeah, no problem."

"Do you know where I can find Brian Riley?"

"Nope, that I don't know," Pretty Boy said as he went to the end of the bar to take drink orders from a couple with Palm Springs tans.

Byers returned with the employment applications, slapped the papers on the bar in front of Ramona, and hurried away to greet arriving customers at the hostess area. Ramona copied down the information she needed and made her way to the kitchen, where she asked the executive chef and several of her assistants about

Randy Velarde's work in the kitchen. They characterized him as moody, inconsistent, and a pothead. The one cook who vaguely remembered Brian Riley put him in the same category.

Byers came bursting through the double doors just as Ramona was writing down names and phone numbers.

"You can't be in here," he sputtered angrily. "This is unacceptable."

"I'm done," Ramona said with a smile.

"Next time, come back after we're closed."

Ramona closed her notebook. "I'll keep that in mind."

Tranquilo Casitas, Space 39 was the address Randy Velarde had listed on his job application. It was a run-down trailer park on Agua Fria Street just inside the city limits, located between a sand-and-gravel operation and a small subdivision of "starter homes" on tiny lots. Hardly a tranquil place to live, it was a well-known trouble spot. Patrol officers were frequently called to the location to quell domestic disputes, break up gang fights, and investigate break-ins and burglaries that were usually drug-related.

On the way to the trailer park, Ramona ran a check on Randy Velarde. He had a clean sheet, but given the fact that he'd been fired for smoking marijuana on the job, Ramona doubted that Velarde was an upstanding citizen.

She pulled into Tranquilo Casitas and bumped her way down a paved asphalt lane that had so many potholes it resembled a bombed-out Baghdad roadway. All of the mobile homes in the park were older single-wides, and many were in disrepair. Some had plastic sheeting on the roof held in place by automobile tires. Others had broken windows covered with scrap plywood. A few were missing the skirting used to hide the concrete blocks that elevated the trailers off the ground.

The single-wide at space 39 was no better or worse than all

the rest. On one side of the trailer jutted a half-finished covered porch made of plywood. Scrap lumber and construction trash littered the area. The hulk of an old Japanese subcompact pickup truck sat in the mud ruts of the parking space. Ramona climbed three rickety wooden steps that rose to the plywood front porch, and with her badge case open to display her shield and police ID, she knocked on the door. A young teenage girl, no more than five-one and a hundred pounds, opened up. She had an infant riding on her hip. The distinctive smell of grass wafted out the door.

"I'd like to speak to Randy Velarde," said Ramona, who wasn't at all interested in making a misdemeanor arrest on a pot possession charge.

"My brother's not here right now. Why do you need to see him?"

Ramona studied the girl's face. She looked clear-eyed and seemed alert to her surroundings. "I'm trying to locate someone Randy worked with last summer, Brian Riley."

The girl pushed the baby's tiny hand away from the front of her blouse. No more than four or five months old, the infant had a dirty face and a urine-stained diaper. "What did Brian do?"

"Nothing," Ramona replied. "Do you know him?"

"Yeah, sort of. He stayed here for a couple nights last summer before he left town."

"Where did he go?"

The baby started to cry. The girl pulled a pacifier from her pants pocket and stuck it in the baby's mouth. "I don't know. I didn't talk to him much."

"Why was he staying here?"

"I think he had a fight with his father or his stepmother. Something like that."

"Would Randy know where Brian went?"

The baby spit out the pacifier. The girl picked it up, put it in her pocket, and shifted the baby to her other hip. "Maybe. Look, I've got to feed him."

Ramona heard a toilet flush. "Where is Randy?"

The girl put her hand on the door. "In class at the community college. He doesn't get home until after nine."

"Is the baby's mother working?"

"I'm his mother," the girl said, jiggling the baby on her hip. "He's my little *hijo*."

"Where's *your* mother?"

"Working."

"What does she do?"

"She's a housekeeper at the hospital."

"Is there anyone here with you?"

"Javier, my *hijo*'s father."

"What's your name?" Ramona asked.

"Vanessa Velarde."

"How old are you?"

"Fifteen."

"Are you in school?"

Vanessa shook her head. "There's no one to look after my *hijo* during the day but me."

Ramona smiled understandingly. "A baby is a lot of responsibility to take on. Let me see what I can do to get you some help."

Vanessa smirked and gave Ramona a sour look. "I don't need any help. School sucks, so I dropped out. Next year I'll get my GED and then I'll get a job." She closed the trailer door in Ramona's face.

Ramona walked to her unit and drove away. In her years on the force she'd yet to meet any fifteen-year-olds who were mature enough to know what was best for them. On Agua Fria Street, she pulled to the side of the road, called the lieutenant in charge of the juvenile division, and gave her the heads-up on Vanessa

Velarde. The lieutenant promised to contact social services and request that a caseworker make a home visit.

Ramona knew it could be days or weeks before a caseworker showed up at the trailer to determine if Vanessa and her baby needed protective services. She glumly wondered if any good would come from bringing social services into the picture. Even with help, being a low-income, fifteen-year-old dropout with a new baby was a hell of a deep hole to climb out of.

The Santa Fe Community College, a relatively new institution of higher education established some twenty-odd years ago in cramped, temporary quarters in a Cerrillos Road business park, was now located outside town on a modern campus near a rapidly growing residential area that fronted I-25.

At the administration office Ramona was directed to Ms. Carpenter's classroom, where some twenty culinary arts students, all dressed in loose-fitting cook's jackets, stood at a food prep area watching their instructor demonstrate how to properly bone an uncooked chicken. Ramona, a notoriously bad cook with little interest in the subject, found Ms. Carpenter's skill with a knife impressive. Carpenter made short order of the task without slicing any of her fingers. After she'd finished the demonstration, Ramona pulled her aside and asked her to ID Randy Velarde.

"He's not in trouble," Ramona added. "I'm trying to locate a friend of his."

Carpenter, a skinny woman in her fifties, with a wide mouth and big teeth, smiled in relief and called over a plump young man with a fleshy face and the start of a second chin. He looked fretful when Ramona identified herself as a detective and asked him to step into the hallway with her. Outside the classroom she asked Velarde if he knew where Brian Riley was living.

"I'm not sure," Velarde replied. "Maybe down in Albuquerque. That's where he said he was living the last time I saw him."

"And when was that?"

"Three months or so ago at a club in town. He was with some college girl. They'd driven up to Santa Fe to party."

"Have you heard from him since then?"

"Nope, but we weren't that tight to begin with."

"You were tight enough to smoke pot with him on the job and get fired for it," Ramona rebutted. "Tight enough to let him crash with you last summer for a couple of days."

"That doesn't mean we're bros," Velarde replied. "Yeah, I smoked pot with him once or twice, and yeah, I let him sleep on my bedroom floor. So what? Why are you looking for him anyway?"

"His father and stepmother have been murdered."

Velarde looked shocked. "No shit?"

"He needs to be found so he can be told," Ramona continued. "Did he say anything to you about where he might be staying in Albuquerque?"

"No, but he gave me his cell phone number in case I was in Albuquerque and wanted to hook up. I never called him 'cause I've been too busy with school and work." Velarde unclipped his cell phone from his belt, browsed through the menu, and read off a number.

Ramona scribbled it on the back of her notebook. "Thanks. That's a big help. Your sister said Brian stayed with you last summer because of an argument he had with his father or stepmother. Was that what went down?"

Velarde shook his head. "Not even. His stepmother gave him money to move out of her house. I mean a wad of money. Don't ask me why. He stayed with me for two days until the guy he was selling his car to came through with the cash. Then I took him to a motorcycle dealership on Cerrillos Road where he bought a used Harley. That was the last time I saw him until three months ago."

"Did you actually see him buy the Harley?" Ramona asked.

Velarde nodded. "Yeah, it cost six thousand dollars and he only got fifteen hundred cash for his car. Like I say, he had a wad of money. I don't know how much."

"You're sure Brian told you his stepmother gave him the cash," Ramona reiterated, wondering if Riley had stolen the money.

"That's what he said."

"Did he say why she'd been so generous?"

"Nope."

"When you last saw Brian, did he mention what he was doing in Albuquerque?"

Velarde shrugged. "Nothing special that I can remember. I asked him if he was working and he just grinned and shook his head."

"Who was the girl he was with?"

"Some student at the university. She had an unusual name for a girl. I mean, like when she told me her name I thought she was joking, but she wasn't. Her name was Stanley."

"Did you get a last name?"

"Na, she never told me what it was."

"Describe her to me."

"Maybe five feet five inches, curly light blond hair, real cute-looking. She said she was from Iowa."

Ramona gave him a business card. "If you think of anything else or if Brian gets in touch with you, call me."

Randy nodded, put the card in his pocket, and went back into the classroom.

On her way down the empty hallway to the campus parking lot, Ramona called Clayton and filled him in on her discoveries.

"That's real good work," Clayton said. "We need to find out

what exactly went on between the boy and his stepmother. Did she really give him money, or is he a thief and a possible murder suspect to boot?"

"I can start looking for him in Albuquerque tomorrow morning," Ramona suggested.

"I'll take it from here," Clayton replied. "Chief Kerney has assigned all his available detectives to the case. I need a supervisor to ride roughshod over them. That's you."

"Okay."

"Detective Chacon tells me that the desktop computer Denise Riley used at work that crashed wasn't tampered with at all. It had an outdated disk operating system that somehow disabled the system restore feature. The files on the hard drive weren't wiped. He's working on recovering the data, but what he's found so far is just insurance business–related stuff."

"My enthusiasm for new information today has just bottomed out," Ramona said as she passed through the automatic doors and walked toward her unmarked unit. "I'm going home."

"I wish I could say the same. Do you have someone there waiting for you?"

"No," Ramona replied as she slid behind the steering wheel. "I'm going to practice boning an uncooked chicken."

New information uncovered by Ramona Pino had caused Kerney to go straight from his office to Helen Muiz's house. Since the start of the investigation Helen had refused to deal with anyone but Kerney, and he had a few important questions to ask her that simply couldn't be put off.

Ruben answered the doorbell and took Kerney to the living room, where Helen was stretched out on the couch, covered by a comforter, a box of facial tissue within easy reach. The room was lit by one table lamp, and the window curtains were closed against the darkness of the night.

Helen sat, forced a smile, and made space on the couch for Kerney to join her. Ruben excused himself to answer the telephone ringing in an adjacent room.

"How are you holding up?" Kerney asked as he sat.

"I honestly don't know," Helen replied.

"It takes time for everything to settle down."

"I can't seem to stop crying." She gave Kerney a bleak, apologetic smile.

"Crying is a good thing," Kerney said.

Helen dabbed her eyes with a tissue. "You told Ruben on the phone you had some questions."

"Fairly important ones," Kerney said, "that can't wait."

"Okay," Helen replied.

"Did you know Denise was three months pregnant at the time of her death?"

Helen looked shocked. She shook her head in disbelief.

"Tim couldn't have possibly been the father of the baby, Helen," Kerney added. "I'm sure you know that."

Helen's eyes locked on Kerney's face. "Of course I know that."

"Do you have any ideas who the father might have been?"

"Maybe she was raped."

The comment stunned Kerney into silence.

"You can't discount the possibility," Helen added, sounding frenzied. "Can you?"

"Not completely," Kerney replied. "I'll grant you that some rape victims hide the sexual assault from spouses and fail to report it to law enforcement. But everything we know about your sister's attitude toward motherhood argues against such behavior. She made it very clear to family and friends alike that having children wasn't something she wanted to do. If she did become pregnant due to a rape, surely she would have had an abortion, or even more proactively taken a morning-after pill. Why are you trying so hard to protect your sister's reputation?"

Helen's shoulders sagged and her eyes moistened. "Because I can't help myself. I've always done it. Denise was the rebellious child in the family: refusing to go to Mass, staying out late, playing hooky from school, drinking, running away from home. Our father would make her stand in the living room in front of the entire family and switch her legs with his belt. It only made her more defiant. When she left Santa Fe after high school I thought she would be gone forever. Now she is."

Helen's tears returned. Kerney had learned long ago to be patient with survivors of loved ones who'd died violently and suddenly. The shock was catastrophic. It magnified grief and caused emotional ripple effects that surged uncontrollably.

After a long crying jag, Helen sniffled into a fresh tissue and forced a brave smile.

"Can you think of anybody Denise might have been sexually involved with?" Kerney asked.

"I'd be the last person to know anything about that. Denise was a very private person in some ways, especially about matters she knew the family wouldn't approve of."

"Okay," Kerney said. "Let's switch gears. What can you tell me about Tim's son, Brian?"

"I only met him once. He seemed to be a bit of a free spirit. Several times, Ruben and I invited him to come to dinner with Tim and Denise, but he never did. He didn't seem interested in Denise's family, and why should he have been? We were all strangers to him and he didn't stay in Santa Fe long enough to get to know us."

"Did Denise mention having any difficulty or problems with Brian while he stayed with them in Cañoncito?"

Helen shook her head. "She hardly talked about him at all."

"Denise may have given him a large amount of cash."

"What for?"

Kerney shrugged. "We don't know. But what we do know is that Tim and Denise didn't have a lot of money to give away. Did Tim talk to you about helping his son financially?"

"No. The only thing Tim said was that Brian's arrival in Santa Fe had come out of the blue, but they were getting along better than expected and he was hopeful that they might be friends. Why haven't you asked the boy these questions?"

"We're trying to find him so we can," Kerney replied.

Helen paused and studied Kerney's face. "Do you think he may have killed his father and my sister?"

"We have no reason to believe that."

"Don't talk to me like I'm an uninformed civilian," Helen said. "I've spent thirty-five years working with cops. You're treating him like a suspect."

"Of course we are," Kerney replied, "until we can find him and clear him or book him. Now, I have to talk to you about one more thing, and then we'll be finished and you can get some rest."

"What is it?"

"We asked the State Department to give us Denise's passport records during the years she was a traveling and working outside of the country. They have nothing on file. As far as the federal government is concerned, Denise never even applied for a U.S. passport."

"That's impossible," Helen replied. "She sent me letters from everywhere she lived."

"Did you keep them?"

"Of course." Helen pushed the comforter off her lap and stood. "Are you suggesting my sister lied about where she lived and what she did?"

"No, I'm just saying the State Department has no record of her travels. Her letters may go a long way in clearing up the confusion."

"Many of them were postmarked and stamped in other countries, and as I told you before, she often used her boyfriend's surnames."

"I'm sure they will be very helpful," Kerney said.

"Let me get them for you."

Kerney rose. "I'd prefer if you would just show me where they are."

"Are you taking them for analysis?"

"With your permission," Kerney said.

Helen nodded and moved across the living room. Kerney followed her to a small home office next to the master bedroom. It was as neat and tidy as Helen's office at police headquarters and just as well organized. Family photographs covered wall space that wasn't given over to bookcases, and a desk was positioned to give a view out a window, where Kerney could see the vague shape of a thick tree trunk in the weak light of a rising new moon.

Helen opened a desk file drawer which held hanging folders. One thick folder labeled in typed bold caps read "**DENISE'S LETTERS.**"

Kerney asked Helen for a large manila envelope, put the file inside, and sealed it. "I'll let you know what we find."

He walked with Helen back to the living room, where Ruben waited. He shook Ruben's hand, hugged Helen, said good night, let himself out, and hurried to his unit, eager to get home to check on Sara. He hadn't spoken to her all day, and even though she'd been in a good mood that morning, he still worried about her. Her bouts of depression could recur at any time.

He called in his on-duty status to dispatch as he left Helen's driveway, and received a back-channel message from Clayton that he'd gone to Albuquerque in search of Brian Riley and would stay there overnight.

Kerney decided to wait until morning to read Denise's letters before turning them over to Questioned Documents at the lab for analysis. He also decided he would ignore the speed limit on the drive home, and soon he was on U.S. 285 just about to turn off on the ranch road.

Although it had been a very long day and there were still no clear suspects in sight, Kerney felt possible breaks in the case were looming. He also knew that what looked promising at first glance often came to a screeching dead end after closer inspection. He decided not to get too optimistic.

Up ahead lights inside his ranch house winked down at him from the saddleback ridge. Kerney shut down the cop thoughts rattling around in his head and drove up the canyon, happy to be going home to his wife and son.

# Chapter Seven

Hoping to locate Brian Riley quickly, Clayton ran down the cell phone number Riley had given Randy Velarde three months earlier. But the account had lapsed and the address Riley had used when purchasing the phone was nonexistent.

After confirming that Riley had paid cash for the motorcycle, Clayton tried to nail down the source of the money Denise had allegedly given the boy. But Denise's financial accounts showed nothing more than normal credits and debits from direct deposit of her paychecks and the checks she wrote every month for routine bills and credit card payments. There was no record of her borrowing money or purchasing money orders. Additionally, none of the banks in Albuquerque or Santa Fe showed any accounts opened by Brian Riley.

If Riley had lied about Denise being the source of his money, then where did the cash come from? According to the North Carolina police, it didn't come from Riley's mother or any of his high school friends, and a check of pawnshops in Albuquerque and Santa Fe and those in Riley's hometown also drew a blank. Brian had never done business with any of them.

That meant the source of the cash Brian had flashed to his chum Velarde and used to buy the motorcycle might not have been legit. What illicit activity could have provided Riley's sudden windfall? Drug dealing immediately came to mind, but winnings from area casinos on tribal land couldn't be discounted. That theory fell flat after calls to the casinos revealed no payouts had been made to Riley.

Before leaving Santa Fe, Clayton tapped into all the usual resources for tracing runaways and people who'd gone missing. The postal service, public utilities, Internet providers, phone companies, and various municipal agencies he called had no record of providing services to Riley. A more thorough state and national criminal records check showed no arrests, wants, or warrants. Motor Vehicles reported Riley as the owner of a Harley motorcycle bought last summer in Santa Fe. But the current registration listed Brian's address as Cañoncito, which was no help at all. Because Riley owned the Harley outright, there was no lien on the cycle and thus no lender who might know where he was living.

Clayton checked for traffic violations and found none. He put out a statewide APB on Riley and the Harley, with an advisory that the boy was a person of interest in the investigation of the murders of his father and stepmother. To give his bulletin greater emphasis, Clayton personally called law enforcement agencies in the greater Albuquerque area to give them a heads-up about the search for Riley. He asked each high-ranking officer he contacted to query all sworn personnel to see if anyone had any knowledge whatsoever about the boy.

Still hoping to find an address for Riley, Clayton contacted the company that insured the motorcycle, called cable and satellite companies that provided home television and broadband services, and made inquiries at the circulation desks of local newspapers. He struck out every time and was left thinking that Riley was probably staying under the radar by living with someone—possibly a girl named Stanley.

But why? Was it a deliberate attempt to avoid being found, or simply the footloose lifestyle of a kid out on his own for the very first time? If Riley hadn't hooked up and moved in with Stanley or some other college girl, Clayton couldn't discount the possibility that the boy was either homeless or floating from one crash pad to the next in the subculture of dropouts that every college and university attracted. But he wasn't about to start querying the social service agencies and emergency shelters in Albuquerque that served the down-and-out until all other possibilities were exhausted.

He kept working the phone. Major credit card companies reported nothing useful. No area detention centers had a recent arrest of a Brian Riley that had yet to hit the system. No cell phone providers had signed up a Brian Riley for new service. None of the dozen public, private, and for-profit universities, colleges, and trade schools in Albuquerque showed a past or present enrollment for Brian Riley or a female student with the unusual given name of Stanley.

Playing a long shot, Clayton asked Detective Matt Chacon to see if he could find a young female named Stanley in any state public records database. Matt told Clayton he'd give it a try, but not to hold out too much hope.

On that upbeat note, Clayton drove to Albuquerque, rented a room at a budget motel just off Interstate 25 close to downtown, and ordered a meal at a nearby family-style franchise restaurant. It was one of those places that offered breakfast twenty-four hours a day and made up silly names for their specialty menu items.

Except for the short trip down from Santa Fe, it was the first time Clayton had been alone all day, and it gave him a chance to catch his breath, set aside thoughts of the investigation, and mull over last night's conversation with Kerney.

He'd jumped at the opportunity to take the search for Brian

Riley out of Ramona Pino's hands as a way to avoid spending a second consecutive night as Kerney's houseguest. It wasn't that Clayton was uncomfortable with Kerney and his family, or that he'd decided not to return as their guest. On the contrary, he'd felt welcomed last night and was happy that he'd finally broken the ice with Kerney.

But his oblique, partial apology for being frequently impolite, often brusque, and habitually standoffish to a man who'd never been less than gracious and generous wasn't good enough. He had to do a better job of explaining his past bad behavior, and he wanted to think about how to approach it before proceeding.

Clayton knew his shoddy behavior was a direct offshoot of a lifetime spent trying to deny his Anglo blood. Kerney had probably already sensed it, but it was Clayton's responsibility to spell it out. How to do it without coming off as a complete pigheaded, prejudiced jerk was the question, and it was still bouncing around in his head unanswered when he looked up from his plate to see a long-haired, unshaven man dressed in jeans, a leather jacket, and motorcycle boots approach his booth.

"Are you Sergeant Istee?" the man asked, flashing an APD shield.

"I am."

"Santa Fe dispatch told me where to find you." The officer sat across from Clayton. "Detective Lee Armijo, APD Narcotics."

"I never would have guessed it," Clayton said with a smile, shaking Armijo's hand.

"I haven't seen the kid you're looking for," Armijo said, "but I sure have seen his Harley."

"Where?"

"First time, up by the university. We got a tip about a drug dealer who was selling product to college students out of a house near the campus. We ran surveillance on him for two nights, sent in an undercover officer posing as a student to make a buy, and as soon as it went down we busted the dealer and shut him down."

"That's solid police work," Clayton said, "but how does it help me find Brian Riley?"

Armijo reached into a jacket pocket. "We photographed and identified everyone who went into the place during our surveillance. Ran license plate checks also."

He handed Clayton a high-quality black-and-white photograph of a slender woman throwing her leg over the seat of a motorcycle. "That's the bike plate on your ABP," Armijo added.

Clayton nodded in agreement. The motorcycle make and model squared with the one Riley had bought in Santa Fe, and the clearly readable license plate matched the MVD registration records. The woman in the photograph had her face turned away from the camera.

"Please tell me this is a photo of a young woman named Stanley something," he said.

Armijo laughed. "You ain't heard the half of it. Her full legal name is Minerva Stanley Robocker. Quite the moniker, isn't it? She's a server at a downtown bar that's popular with the college and young professional crowd. Age twenty-two, single, college dropout originally from a small farming town in Iowa. She's been here about two and a half years. Has a clean sheet. No wants and warrants. No outstanding traffic citations. According to the dealer we busted, Minerva, aka Stanley, bought small amounts of pot from him on a regular basis, probably for her own use. But just to be sure she wasn't reselling it to her customers at the nightclub, we kept a close watch on her for a while. As far as we could tell, Minerva is just one of the many young adults in our fair city who enjoy getting high on illegal substances during their free time."

"Is Brian Riley staying with her?" Clayton asked.

Armijo shook his head. "Negative. Like I said, I've only seen his motorcycle, never him. In fact, Minerva seems to have taken full possession of the bike. It's always parked at her place and she switches back and forth between driving her car or riding the Harley. I'm figuring Riley either sold it to her and she hasn't re-registered it yet, he's out of town and left it with her for safekeeping, or something else is going on that is yet to be determined."

"That about covers all the bases," Clayton said with a smile. "What else can you tell me about her?"

"She's never been married, and lives alone in a one-bedroom apartment. When Stanley, as she likes to be called, isn't serving drinks, she's either sleeping, shopping, running errands, or clubbing with friends at some of the popular watering holes. Except for smoking pot, she's not engaged in any other illegal activity we know about. But when it comes to men, Minerva isn't a prude, that's for sure. A couple of guys spent the night at her apartment during the short time we kept an eye on her. Of course, we can only assume what may have occurred."

"Of course. Do you still have her under surveillance?"

Armijo shook his head. "Not even. Minerva Stanley Robocker is your typical recreational user. She isn't going to lead us to any of the major traffickers along the I-25 drug pipeline."

"Do you mind if I question her about Riley?" Clayton asked.

"Be my guest, although I'd like to tag along."

Clayton motioned to the waitress to bring the check. "I'd appreciate the company."

"Good deal," Armijo said. "Now tell me why Riley's a person of interest in these homicides. Do you really think there's a chance he killed his father and stepmother?"

Clayton took the check from the waitress and handed her a twenty. When she walked away to make change, he said, "It's impossible to say one way or the other."

"Did he have motive, opportunity, and means?" Armijo asked.

Clayton put a healthy tip on the table. "Now you're asking me those tough legal questions that never have any easy answers."

Armijo chuckled and stood. "You don't have squat on this kid, do you?" he said as the waitress brought Clayton his change.

"That's exactly right." Clayton pocketed several bills and left the rest. "Which is why he's only a person of interest for now. Where will we find Minerva Stanley Robocker tonight?"

"Serving liquid refreshments to the sports crowd in the nightclub lounge while they watch college ESPN basketball on the fifty-inch high-definition, wall-mounted plasma television."

"Sounds like loads of fun," Clayton said. "Lead on."

"You can leave your unit at the motel," Armijo said, "and I'll drive you there."

Clayton quickly accepted Armijo's offer. He still wasn't feeling all that comfortable about driving Tim Riley's S.O. unit. The vehicle was one of the last things Riley had touched before his murder, and the thought that he might still be hanging around continued to creep Clayton out.

The downtown nightclub on Central Avenue was buzzing with a mixture of hip grad students from the university, young, single professionals, and affluent thirty-something couples. The décor was industrial chic, with exposed heating and air-conditioning ductwork suspended from the ceiling, high-tech halogen lights on long, flexible metallic elbows, steel girders painted a rust red, polished aluminum wall panels, and large mirrors strategically mounted to give patrons a view of themselves as they mingled and flirted. In the lounge area, two wide-screen wall-mounted high-definition televisions on opposite walls had attracted a noisy crowd of customers watching a basketball game. Three very attractive female servers dressed in tailored black slacks and tight-fitting scoop-neck tops dipped, scooted, and swerved their way around the patrons, delivering drinks and bar food.

Armijo pointed out Minerva Stanley Robocker, who was by far the best-looking server of the trio. She had curly blond hair, a slender body, and high cheekbones above full, rosy lips. "You'll want to talk to her outside," Armijo said. "I'll bring her to you."

Clayton nodded and watched Armijo intercept Robocker as she stepped to the bar to unload empty glasses and place a fresh drink order. She looked unhappy when Armijo flashed his shield, and then balked and shook her head when he pointed toward the exit. Armijo put his shield away, said something, and pointed at Clayton.

Robocker cast a frosty look in Clayton's direction, put her tray on the bar, said something to the bartender, and walked with Armijo toward the exit. Clayton caught up with them at the door. Outside, with Armijo behind the wheel of his unmarked police car, Clayton joined Robocker in the backseat.

"This could get me fired," Robocker said before Clayton uttered a word.

"Relax," Armijo said as he cranked the engine, turned on the car heater, and switched on the dome light. "I'll square it with your boss."

"You'd better," Minerva Stanley Robocker replied as she stared at Clayton. "So what kind of cop are you? Navajo Tribal Police? Isleta Pueblo? Something like that?"

"Why don't you let me ask the questions?" Clayton countered.

"You look like one of the Indian policemen in the television movies that have been made from those Tony Hillerman novels set on the Navajo Rez. I saw a rerun of one on public TV recently."

"My name is Sergeant Istee, Ms. Robocker. I'm with the Lincoln

County Sheriff's Office and we're investigating the murders of Brian Riley's father and stepmother. Since you've been riding his Harley lately, we thought you might know where he is."

Stanley put her hand to her throat. "His father and stepmother have been murdered?"

"Yes. We need to find Brian and tell him what's happened."

"He's probably in North Carolina. He went back there to visit some friends."

"When was that?" Clayton asked.

"Four weeks ago," Stanley replied. "Maybe a little longer."

"Have you heard from him since he left?"

Stanley shook her head. "No."

"Have any of your friends?"

Her gaze shifted away from Clayton's face. "No."

"Okay," he said, reading the lie. "Sometime last year you went up to Santa Fe with him. Tell me about that."

Stanley shrugged a shoulder. "It was just a day trip. We rode up on his Harley. I'd only been to Santa Fe once or twice before, and he offered to show me around."

"I was told he introduced you as his girlfriend."

Stanley laughed. "That was a little fib on his part. I let him get away with it to impress a friend of his. Brian's way too young for me. He's like a kid brother, nothing more."

"There's no romantic involvement between the two of you?" Clayton queried.

Stanley waved her hand to dismiss the ludicrous notion. "No way."

"Didn't you tell Brian's Santa Fe friends that you were a college student?" he asked.

"I don't know where they got that impression. I may have said something about going back to school someday. What does any of this have to do with finding Brian?"

Clayton smiled. Stanley's obvious irritation made him believe she was hiding something. He decided to see if he could annoy her some more. "I'm simply trying to get everything clear in my mind. How did Brian support himself?"

Stanley shook her head. "I don't know. He didn't talk about working or having a job, but he had money. Not a lot, but some."

"Did he tell you where his money came from?"

"No. Listen, it wasn't like I spent oodles of time with him, you know? Sometimes we would hang out together. I liked him because he wasn't always coming on to me. We could just chill."

Clayton couldn't remember the last time he'd heard anyone use the word *oodles*. "How did you meet him?"

"At a party up by the university."

"Who threw it?" Clayton asked.

"I don't know."

"Where was it held?"

"I don't remember," Stanley replied, sounding testy. "I just heard there was this party and I crashed it."

"You crashed it alone?"

"Yes, alone."

"How did you come to have possession of his Harley?"

"He left it with me while he's gone. Is there some kind of law against that?" she snapped. Clayton smiled again. Her strong reaction convinced him that she wasn't being completely truthful. He reached across her and opened the car door. "You can go back to work," he said. "Thanks for your time."

"That's it?" Stanley asked.

"For now." Clayton gave her his business card. "I may need to talk to you again, but in the meantime call me if you see Brian or if he gets in touch with you or any of your friends."

"Yeah, sure," Stanley replied.

Armijo gave Clayton a quizzical look as the young woman hurried toward the club entrance. "You know she's lying," he said when Clayton joined him in the front seat.

"Yeah. Do you want to stick around and see what she does next?"

Armijo nodded and killed the dome light. "It's going to be a while before she gets off work."

"I've got nothing better to do, have you?" Clayton asked.

"Not since my wife left me for the assistant manager at our local supermarket. And I thought she was just forgetful when it came to getting stuff we needed at the grocery store. Boy, was I stupid."

"Sorry to hear it," Clayton said.

Armijo put the car in gear. "Let's find a place were we can stake out the front entrance without being spotted, and get some people over here to cover her car and the staff entrance."

"Can you free someone up to keep an eye on her inside the club?" Clayton asked.

"Good idea." Armijo reached for the radio microphone.

While Armijo was calling for assistance, Clayton looked up and down the street. There were no crowds standing outside the nightspots waiting to get in; foot traffic was almost nonexistent along the avenue, and only a few cars were stopped at the intersection waiting for a light to change. Except for the smattering of bars and clubs on both sides of the street, most of the businesses were closed and dark.

"So where's the big-city nightlife?" he asked.

"Except for the weekends, you're looking at it," Armijo replied with a chuckle as he pulled away from the curb. "It really gets your party juices flowing, doesn't it?"

"Big-time," Clayton said.

Armijo found a spot behind a parked pickup truck that gave them good concealment, and after the officers called to assist were in place, the two men passed the time in bursts of silence and conversation.

Two hours into the stakeout, the detective inside the nightclub called Armijo and told him a customer had just walked in, slipped a small envelope to Stanley, and was on his way out the front door.

"He's six-one, about one-eighty, mid-thirties, clean-shaven, brown and brown, wearing a suede leather jacket and blue jeans," the detective said.

"I see him," Armijo said as he cranked over the engine. "You couldn't make him?"

"Negative," the detective replied. "He's not one of the usual suspects."

"Stay on Stanley," Armijo said. "We'll cover the customer."

The man outside the nightclub walked quickly to a new silver Ford Mustang and got behind the wheel.

"Are you going to stop and question?" Clayton asked as Armijo eased into traffic one car behind the Mustang, heading east on Central Avenue.

"Is that want you want to do?"

Clayton shook his head. "Let's see where he takes us."

"I like your style, Sergeant." Armijo nodded at the laptop computer that was attached by a mechanical arm to the dashboard. "Do you know how to use that thing?" he asked.

Clayton nodded. The laptop was tied into motor vehicle records and federal and state crime information systems. He had a desktop computer at work with the same capacity, but the Lincoln County Sheriff's Office had no money to put laptops in its vehicles, which put the department further behind the pack when it came to state-of-the-art technology and equipment.

Armijo swung the laptop so that Clayton could easily reach the keyboard. "Have at it," he said

By the time they had passed under the railroad tracks on Central Avenue and were climbing the hill toward the university, Clayton had the name of the registered owner and his DMV driver's license photo on the laptop screen. They were following Morton E. Birch, age thirty-two, with a home address that Armijo said was in the opposite direction.

As they passed by the university, where all the streets were named for elite private eastern colleges, Clayton accessed NCIC and state crime data banks for wants and warrants on Birch. He got no hits.

"Apparently, Mort is clean," Clayton said, glancing at the street signs, which now carried the names of dead presidents. "At least, so far."

"That only makes me believe that he's guilty of something," Armijo said as he glanced at the dashboard clock. "Our friend Minerva clocks out of work in an hour. What would you like to do about her?"

"Let's have her picked up and held for questioning. I want to know what's in that envelope."

Armijo nodded in agreement. "No problem. If she balks, we'll arrest her on the old pot charge and hold her incommunicado until we get tonight's excitement sorted out."

"You're having that much fun, are you?" Clayton asked, tongue in cheek.

"You're a bright spot in my otherwise dull, mundane existence, Sergeant," Armijo replied.

The traffic had thinned on Central Avenue, and Armijo stayed two cars behind the Mustang to avoid detection. "Looks like Birch is heading toward the Four Hills neighborhood," he said as they approached the foothills. "Wasn't there a John Birch Society that was active forty or fifty years ago? If I remember correctly from a political science class I took in college, it was an ultraconservative organization of hawks who hated communism, wanted to dismantle the United Nations, and hoped to spread capitalism and democracy throughout the world. Whatever happened to it?"

"The society members and their clones are now running the country," Clayton replied.

"Don't you want an America that's strong, safe, and secure?" Armijo asked with passionate conviction.

Clayton decided to avoid a political debate on the off chance he had misread the sarcasm in Armijo's voice. "Absolutely," he said with equal sincerity.

Armijo gave him a quizzical look and said nothing more. The Mustang turned onto Four Hills Road, and they entered a subdivision that had all the trappings of an established high-end neighborhood, with big houses on large lots, quiet streets with mature trees, and expansive front lawns.

Armijo explained that Four Hills had been the first foothills subdivision built in the city, back in the 1960s, and that it came complete with its own country club and golf course. On the empty residential streets, he killed the headlights and slowed, but kept the Mustang's taillights in view. Up ahead the car turned into a driveway. Armijo pulled to the curb and turned off the engine.

The houses on either side of the street were almost entirely obscured by evergreen trees and shrubs. Most of the houses were dark, with only a few showing some interior lights veiled behind drawn curtains and barely discernible through the branches of the trees.

"What now?" Armijo asked.

Clayton opened the passenger door. "Let me do a little sleuthing."

"Does that mean you're going to trespass on private property without reasonable suspicion or probable cause?" Armijo asked.

"I wouldn't think of it."

"I'm liking your style more all the time, Sergeant Istee," Armijo said with a laugh. "And if Birch leaves while you're out sleuthing?"

"Follow him," Clayton said, "and give me a call." He rattled off his cell phone number.

Armijo popped open the glove box and gave Clayton a night vision scope. "Here. You'll need it."

"Thanks."

"Don't get caught sleuthing."

Clayton stepped out of the vehicle. "Not a chance, Detective."

Canyon winds coursing down from the mountains had dropped the temperature considerably. Clayton quietly closed the car door, zipped up his jacket, and turned up the collar, then scooted between two houses and paused behind a tree to let his eyes adjust to the darkness. From some distance away a dog barked lethargically, paused, barked again, and fell quiet.

The houses on either side of Clayton showed no sign of life. Moving low and slow anyway to avoid rousing any light sleepers, he passed into a backyard, staying as far away from the houses as possible. Hunched over, he took careful steps to the back end of the lot, where he found concealment behind a stand of trees that graced an empty stone pond.

Clayton froze at the close yelp of a coyote. Lackluster barks from the dog resumed. In the dim moonlight he saw the coyote quickly lope across the lawn in the direction of the barking dog. The coyote vanished, and Clayton moved on to the house where Birch had parked the Mustang. From a safe distance he made a full three-sixty reconnaissance. The house, on a double lot of at least half an acre, sat at the edge of a hill that dropped off steeply. There were no houses behind it, and thick stands of trees on either side blocked views from the adjacent houses. A high privacy wall ran from the driveway of the attached garage across the front of the house and severely restricted Clayton's view. No lights showed at any of the windows.

Along with the Mustang, two other cars were parked in the driveway. From across the street, concealed behind some shrubbery, Clayton used the night scope to read the license plates. A late-model Audi coupe carried Canadian plates from British Columbia, and a domestic minivan had California tags. He called the information in to Armijo, switched his cell phone ringer off, and considered what he'd seen.

The house was a mid-sixties modern, with a vaulted roof, an expanse of glass windows that overlooked the backyard, and a soaring stone fireplace that rose above an elevated deck positioned to take in the city views below. There were no lights burning inside and no sign of activity.

He decided to take another tour of the property and crept through the trees on the north side of the house to the backyard. A closer look at the rear wall of glass through the scope revealed that some kind of material had been used to cover all the windows as well as the glass doors that opened onto the raised deck and the backyard patio. He checked all the windows on both sides of the house and found the same thing. It was impossible to see inside the house.

From the back of the lot Clayton mulled over the implications. Even though the house was almost completely secluded from prying eyes, every window had been blacked out. That meant the occupants were very serious about not wanting people to know what was going on inside. Also, the grounds at the back of the house were badly neglected, which didn't fit with the character of the neat and tidy upscale neighborhood. But at the front of the house the grounds were well cared for, which meant that the occupants were hiding whatever they were doing in plain sight.

Clayton was pondering the possibilities when a car engine kicked over. He stayed put until the sound of the departing vehicle faded in the distance and then made his way to the street, staying in the shadows of a big tree. The Mustang was gone, which meant that Armijo should be tailing Birch. A text message on his cell phone told him that was exactly what Armijo was doing.

He decided to stake out the front of the house to see what happened next, and hunkered down under some low branches with his back against the trunk. All stayed quiet until the sound of a squealing, frightened dog pierced the silence and abruptly stopped. Within minutes Clayton saw the coyote come into view as it padded down the middle of the street carrying the limp body of a small dog in its tightly clamped mouth. A negligent owner had provided the coyote with a tasty meal.

Coyote, according to the Mescalero creation story, was a jokester put on the earth to remind human beings of their weaknesses and foolish ways. Almost without thinking, Clayton silently raised his chin to acknowledge the animal. The coyote glanced in his direction and passed by without pause, trotting toward the mountains that loomed above the Four Hills neighborhood and the city below.

Among the Mescalero, if you carried out a devious trick, such as trespassing on private property without cause, which was what Clayton was doing, or if you accomplished a stellar prank, it was called "pulling a little coyote." The fact that the jokester had caught him red-handed almost made Clayton chuckle out loud.

The sound of an approaching car drew his attention back to the street. Headlights came into view and a vehicle passed by, continued up the road, and disappeared around a bend. Except for the canyon winds whistling through the trees and occasional traffic sounds that drifted over from Interstate 40, all was quiet for the next half hour. In spite of the growing cold and the deepening of the darkness, Clayton remained motionless, watching the darkened house for any sign of life, wondering what was inside.

Was it a safe house for illegal immigrants smuggled across the Mexican border? Was it a drug house run by a trafficker? Or a warehouse to store product for distribution along the infamous I-25 drug corridor? Maybe Birch and his buddies were operating a meth lab inside. Or a prostitution ring could be using it as a bordello, or to house sex slaves brought in illegally from one of the Eastern European countries. And what was with the Canadian and California license plates?

The sound of an automatic garage door opener drew Clayton's attention back to the house. No lights went on as the door rose on its tracks, but a figure emerged from the darkness, got into the minivan, drove it into the garage, and immediately closed the door.

His curiosity aroused, Clayton decided to get closer to see if he could learn more. He crossed the street, approached the garage at an angle, and pressed his ear against the door. He could hear some movement—maybe boxes being lifted—and muffled voices, but couldn't make out what was being said.

The sound of the van doors being slammed shut caused Clayton to back off quickly into the deep shadows at the side of the house and call Detective Armijo.

"Where are you?" he asked when Armijo answered.

"Still following Birch," Armijo answered. "He's made three quick stops since he left Four Hills. One at a house near the university, and two at Northeast Heights apartment complexes that cater to young singles. I've got addresses but no names yet. Right now I'm following him across the Rio Grande heading in the possible direction of Paradise Hills or Rio Rancho."

"Has our gal Minerva Stanley Robocker been questioned?" Clayton asked.

"She's being interrogated right now. The envelope Birch gave her contained an ounce of grass. She swears he's just a good friend who gave her some of his stash to tide her over until she could score. She also believes in the tooth fairy, as do I."

"Has she said anything that's useful?" Clayton asked.

"That I don't know. But she's not going anywhere until we see what shakes out with Mort Birch tonight. You'll get another crack at her if you need it."

"What about the DMV checks on the two vehicles?" Clayton asked.

"Neither vehicle has been reported stolen," Armijo replied. "Registrations show the owners, both male, to be of Vietnamese extraction. One is an immigrant to Canada with permanent resident papers, the other is a native-born U.S. citizen originally from Los Angeles now living in San Francisco. No rap sheets, wants, or warrants on either man. I've asked federal and Canadian cop shops for any intel they might have on the two subjects, but I don't expect to hear back soon. What has all your sleuthing uncovered?"

The garage door opened to the squeaky sound of metal wheels on the steel track. "Hold on," Clayton replied. "How fast can you get a unit to the Four Hills Road?"

"A couple of minutes. What's up?"

Through the scope Clayton watched the minivan back out of the garage and drive away. "The minivan with California tags just left the house headed east with two occupants, both male."

"Perhaps our Vietnamese friends," Armijo said. "I'll put a tail on them."

"Be advised they loaded something in the vehicle before leaving."

"Like what?"

"Unknown," Clayton replied. "They moved the minivan into the garage and closed the door before loading it, so I was unable to see."

"How devious," Armijo said. "What else can you tell me?"

"All the windows have been covered over, so whatever is going on inside the house the occupants don't want anyone to know about. There's more evidence to suggest that something isn't kosher, but I won't go into it right now."

"I sense cunning criminal minds at work here," Armijo said. "I'm sending detectives and my lieutenant to your location. ETA ten minutes or less."

"Roger that. No lights, no sirens, and tell them to park away from the house and come in on foot. I'll meet them at the bottom of the street."

"Affirmative. You do good sleuthing, Sergeant Istee."

The first to arrive at Clayton's location was Lee Armijo's lieutenant, Doug Bromilow, a tall man with a narrow face and a protruding lower lip that gave him a perpetually disgruntled look. Clayton filled Bromilow in on what he'd observed, walked him up the quiet street to take a look at the front of the house, and suggested where to deploy the officers for the stakeout. After everyone was in place, Clayton and Bromilow stationed themselves across from the house under the tree. An hour later Detective Armijo joined the party.

"Under watchful eyes, Mort Birch has tucked himself in for the night at his North Valley condo," he said, "and the two gentlemen in the minivan are indeed our Vietnamese friends from British Columbia and California. Apparently, they were unloading—not loading—items from the minivan in the garage. I know this to be so because while the gentlemen where having a leisurely late night meal at a restaurant, I took a peek inside the van. It was empty. Right now our suspects are at an all-night supermarket stocking up on groceries and household products. I expect they'll be arriving here in the next ten minutes or less."

Bromilow snorted. "You'd better have more to tell us than that."

"I do, LT," Armijo replied. "Facing jail time, Minerva decided to tell the truth. Mort is her new dealer. For the past month, he's been selling high-quality grass to her and her party animal friends. According to the county clerk's computer records, Mort owns this house. He inherited it by way of a special warranty deed from a bachelor uncle who died in a nursing home last year."

"Is there any connection between Riley and Birch?" Clayton asked.

Armijo nodded. "You bet there is. When his money ran out, Riley went to work for Mort, making drug deliveries on his Harley. According to Minerva, Mort advanced Riley the cash for his trip back to North Carolina, and he's way overdue returning to Albuquerque. She said Mort told her Riley had called him and said he wasn't coming back to Albuquerque until summer, and that she should just keep using the Harley until she heard from him directly."

Armijo stopped talking as the minivan approached and turned into the driveway. Two men got out and hurried inside the house carrying a number of plastic grocery bags.

"Now that the pantry is stocked, do we go in without a warrant, LT?" Armijo asked. "Or do we wake up the DA and a judge and wait for the wheels of justice to grind on ever so slowly?"

Bromilow stomped his feet against the cold that had settled into his bones. "Why don't we ask Mr. Birch nicely if we can search his house?" Without waiting for a response, he flipped open his cell phone and speed-dialed a number. "Arrest Morton Birch and bring him to my twenty, pronto. Lights and sirens if you please."

He disconnected and smiled at Armijo. "I want the people Birch visited while you had him under surveillance picked up and questioned right now. Send two detectives to each address."

"And if they won't let us in?"

"Arrest them."

"On what charges?"

Bromilow looked thoughtful. "Make something up."

Armijo smiled. "I've always admired your ability to see the bigger picture, LT."

Bromilow grunted. "Don't try to be a kiss-ass, Armijo. It doesn't suit you. Just go get it done."

As Armijo hiked down the street toward his unit, Bromilow went into action, and it was soon clear to Clayton that the lieutenant had a flair for the dramatic. First, he ordered uniformed officers who were standing by to position their units in front of the house with headlights and spotlights trained on the building and emergency lights flashing. Then, using a bullhorn, he asked the occupants inside the house to join him on the street. Other than attracting a growing number of neighborhood residents, the invitation got no response.

When Mort Birch arrived on the scene accompanied by two arresting officers, Bromilow met him in the middle of the street directly in front of the house. The flashing emergency lights were almost blinding, the house was bathed in the glare of spotlights, and the uniforms were in cover positions behind their marked police units. It was pure theater.

Bromilow gave Birch a friendly smile. "I'm Lieutenant Bromilow." He pointed at Clayton, who stood at his side. "This is Sergeant Istee. Thanks for coming."

Hands cuffed behind his back, wearing jeans, sneakers, and a lightweight shirt, Birch shivered in the cold night air. "What are you doing here at my house?" he asked.

Bromilow nodded his head at the house. "Waiting for you. This is your place and so I need your permission to enter and search it. The people inside won't even come to the door. I can only assume that they're either very reclusive or extremely rude."

"If my renters won't let you in, that's no skin off my back," Birch said.

"Legally, as the owner of the premises, you can let me inside, and that would be a huge favor to me, Mort. In fact, if you give me your permission, I promise to do everything in my power to convince the district attorney to plea-bargain your case."

"What case?" Birch snapped.

"Surely the officers told you the charges," Bromilow replied.

Birch laughed. "Yeah, a trumped-up drug bust because I stopped off at a nightclub and gave a friend of mine some grass."

"It's so much worse than that," Bromilow said gravely.

"How so?" Birch demanded.

"You're facing a major drug trafficking fall, Mort."

As far as Clayton knew, Bromilow's ploy was total poppycock. The lieutenant had sent Detective Armijo off with a half-dozen narco cops to illegally arrest citizens in the dead of night without probable cause. Narcotic cops had a reputation for playing fast and loose and covering up their maneuvers that violated the rule of law. What Bromilow had done tonight could easily be challenged in court if word of it ever got out. Clayton wondered what he'd do if he was subpoenaed to testify on Mort Birch's behalf.

"That's nonsense," Birch said.

"Try to show a more cooperative attitude," Bromilow replied in a chiding tone.

Birch replied with a shrug of his shoulders. "Like I told these officers who brought me here, I rent this place out. Whatever is going on inside, I know nothing about it."

"Then you shouldn't mind us taking a look."

Birch hesitated and shook his head. "Get a search warrant. I want a lawyer."

Bromilow sighed and shook his head sadly. "Of course, but not just yet. You'll be allowed to call a lawyer after you've been booked into jail."

Birch nodded. "Then take me to jail. I'm freezing out here."

"You don't get it, do you?" Bromilow said.

"Get what?" Birch answered.

"We've had a tail on you all night," Bromilow said. "All those people you visited after you left here. Well, they're talking."

Birch gulped hard.

"So you and I are going to stay right here until I hear what they told my people." Bromilow pointed in Clayton's direction. "By the way, where can we find Brian Riley? Sergeant Istee would like to know."

Birch glanced at Clayton. "Who?"

"Brian Riley," Clayton said. "Minerva Stanley Robocker's friend."

"The teenage kid she hung out with?"

"That's him," Clayton said.

Birch shook his head vigorously. "How the hell should I know where he is? I met him maybe twice."

Bromilow's cell phone rang. He answered quickly, listened intently, thanked the caller, and disconnected. "Okay, Mort," he said. "This is the way it's gonna go down. I've got five people in custody who say you've been dealing drugs to them. That's a major trafficking beef. Now, I've been in this cop business for a long time, so I know you're a new player in town and maybe not totally clued into what happens when you get busted, convicted, and sent to the slam. But the bottom line is, you're going to lose everything, Mort: your freedom, your Mustang, your condo, this house. Think about that, and think about what you can do to make your immediate future a little less bleak."

Mort Birch's bravado began to waver.

"I know you're probably thinking you can make bail," Bromilow continued, "and keep your freedom while the lawyers try to work some magic on your behalf. But I'm not going to let that happen, Mort. My people are going to work overtime from the moment you're booked to find, tie up, and seize every asset you have, so that no bondsman will want to take a chance on you. And believe me, I'll make sure the DA asks the judge at your preliminary hearing to set a hefty six-figure cash bond. Have you got half a million, six hundred thousand lying around?"

Mort shook his head.

"As a first-time offender who cooperated with the police, you might get a lighter sentence at a minimum security prison. Let's say five years, but out in two and a half with good behavior. Plus guys don't get raped that much in the minimum lockups."

Bromilow paused to let his words sink in. "What's going on inside the house, Mort?"

"It's a marijuana factory," Birch replied. "A pot hothouse."

"How many people are inside?"

"Two."

"Two Vietnamese men?"

"Yeah."

"Are they armed?"

"Probably."

"How do they figure in this?"

"They're part of a West Coast gang that was buying me out. A week from now they would have been back on the West Coast with the grass from this harvest and the title to the house, and I would have been completely out of the business."

Bromilow nodded sympathetically. "Sometimes it's a damn shame the way things turn out. Do I have your permission to enter the premises?"

"Yeah."

"Thanks, Mort."

Bromilow passed the word about the possibility of armed suspects to the officers and detectives on scene before hitting a button on his cell phone and requesting a SWAT team at his location pronto. He turned Birch over to a nearby officer and gave Clayton a concerned look as they walked out of the street and climbed into Bromilow's toasty-warm unmarked vehicle.

"It doesn't appear that we're going to find who you came for, Sergeant Istee." Bromilow blew into his cupped hands to warm them. "But thanks to you, we can score one for the good guys tonight."

"Let's see how it plays out," Clayton replied, thinking it had been a night filled with all kinds of jokesters and tricksters and it wasn't over yet.

# Chapter Eight

Before the SWAT team arrived, the Vietnamese men inside the house tried to make a getaway through the rear patio door. They were quickly apprehended by detectives covering the backyard, put facedown on the ground, cuffed, and searched. Each of them was packing a semiautomatic handgun and carrying over five thousand dollars in cash. Their driver's licenses didn't match the names or the Motor Vehicle Division photos of the registered owners of the vehicles parked in the driveway. When questioned, they refused to talk or reveal their true identities.

Bromilow separated them, took their photographs with a digital camera, downloaded the pictures to his laptop, sent the photos to the DEA agent on duty, and asked for help in identifying the men. Then he had the suspects placed in different squad cars under the watchful eyes of uniformed officers.

Although Mort Birch had sworn that the two Vietnamese were the only occupants in the house, Bromilow decided to play it safe and wait for SWAT before attempting entry. From an officer safety standpoint, Clayton thought it was a wise move. But then Bromilow got stupid and started showboating, making appeals over a bullhorn asking all remaining occupants to exit the house, which served only to rouse more neighbors, who began gathering behind the cordoned-off areas at either end of the street.

As Clayton watched Bromilow in the middle of the street, entreating any additional unknown occupants to peacefully exit the premises, all he could think was that the lieutenant suffered from either blatant self-destructive tendencies, a grandiose need for attention, or both.

SWAT arrived, and as soon as they were set up, Bromilow, with a look of eager anticipation, sent them in full bore. Within minutes the SWAT commander gave the all clear. Bromilow, Clayton, and a squad of APD detectives swarmed into the house to find that all the non-load-bearing interior walls had been demolished; exhaust fans had been installed in the roof to ventilate, filter, and disperse the smell of the marijuana-laden air; all the exterior windows and glass in the house had been spray-painted black; and row upon row of high-tech hydroponic growing tables contained healthy-looking, mature marijuana plants. Bromilow estimated the house held a multimillion-dollar crop.

It was a sophisticated major marijuana factory, and Clayton and the APD detectives spent a few minutes examining how it had been put together. Electrical cords and water lines ran across floors and up stairways or were tacked against the remaining load-bearing interior walls. Strands of thousand-watt grow lights hung above the tables, and a network of tubes fed a nutrient solution to the plants. Narrow walkways separated the rows to maximize the growing space. Plants five feet tall and the high humidity made the house look and feel like a single-species arboretum.

In the kitchen, which, except for one small first-floor bathroom, was the only room that had not been converted for production, there was evidence that harvesting had already begun. A stack of packaged one-pound bricks sat on a countertop. Bromilow gave it a street value of a hundred thousand dollars.

Two cots, some blankets, pillows, dirty clothes, several travel bags, and a small portable television on top of a step stool filled the breakfast nook adjacent to the kitchen. The stove cooktop and a microwave oven were cruddy with baked-on and nuked food, and the sink was filled with filthy dishes, pots, and pans. The refrigerator had been freshly stocked, as had the pantry, where Clayton spotted mouse droppings on the floor. He wondered what other kinds of varmints cohabited the premises.

SWAT pulled out, and while Bromilow and his detectives started photographing, inventorying, bagging, and tagging, Clayton went looking for anything he could find that would lead him to Brian Riley. Wearing latex gloves, he dug through every cabinet, drawer, and closet that had remained untouched in the gutted house. He examined everything in the refrigerator and freezer, poked around behind appliances, pulled out everything in the pantry, and went through all the personal items and bedding in the breakfast nook. He inspected the one bathroom the gang members had used and emptied out the contents of all the garbage cans.

In the garage, he searched through boxes, dumped out the contents of several old storage lockers, and did a thorough sweep of the area. Then he moved on to the minivan and the Audi coupe in the driveway.

He finished with nothing to show for his efforts, leaned against the front fender of the minivan, stripped off the latex gloves, and looked at the house in disgust. From what he could tell, Mort Birch, his marijuana hothouse factory, and the two Vietnamese suspects had nothing at all to do with Brian Riley. Clayton's sleuthing had scored one major bust for the good guys, but it hadn't gotten him a step closer to finding Riley.

The sound of a car coming to a stop at the end of the driveway drew Clayton's gaze. Rodney Eden, the DEA agent in charge of operations in New Mexico, got out of his vehicle and approached. In his early forties, Eden was a sandy-haired, boyish-looking man who oozed sincerity and had a winning smile to go with it.

Clayton had dealt with Eden several times on drug cases in Lincoln County and found him to be reasonable although somewhat condescending at times, which Clayton had long ago decided was a highly prized personality trait among those who worked in federal law enforcement.

"What a surprise," Eden said with his soft Tennessee drawl as he shook Clayton's hand. "What are you doing here, Sergeant Istee?"

"Looking for a kid who might have absolutely nothing to do with two homicides, and who apparently has nothing to do with drug production and trafficking either," Clayton replied dourly.

"Ah, the Riley murders," Eden said with a nod of his head. "A cop killing is bad enough, but to murder his wife." Eden paused and shook his head. "I understand you're looking for one perpetrator, is that correct?"

"That's what seems to make sense," Clayton replied.

Eden smiled in agreement. "Of course. As you asked, I put the word out to my people to keep an eye open for the kid."

"I appreciate that."

"Not at all. Now, where would I find Lieutenant Bromilow?"

Clayton nodded toward the open overhead garage door. "Inside with his troops, harvesting a multimillion-dollar cash crop of marijuana."

"Ah, the joy of it all." Eden wandered off in the direction of the detective who'd been assigned to control access to the crime scene.

The sound of another arriving vehicle caught Clayton's attention. Detective Lee Armijo pulled to a stop behind Eden's unmarked car, opened the passenger window, and called Clayton over.

"Get in, amigo," he said.

Clayton opened the door and joined Armijo. "Tell me you have something that might interest me."

"I got some factoids for you," Armijo said. "According to a DEA drug gang expert, who just called in with the news, the two Vietnamese men we busted are Tran Anh Toan, aka Rabbit, and Nguyen Hoang, aka Ricky Hoang. Both are members of a gang called the Black Wolf Crew that got its start in Canada and has been moving south over the past five years. This is the gang's first known incursion into New Mexico. You've helped us put a big dent in their expansion plans, for which APD will be eternally grateful. We may even someday give you a plaque recognizing your contribution to the department."

Clayton, who wasn't in a wisecracking mood, changed the subject. "Are there any tie-ins to my investigation?"

"Not a one, as far as we know," Armijo replied. "But our pal Morty was about to get in bed with a big-time international cartel. The Black Wolf Crew operates dozens of pot hothouses, manufactures Ecstasy powder worth tens of millions, owns private overseas investment banks, runs an international Internet-based sport betting operation, and launders their money in Vietnam by building and managing high-end hotels and upscale resorts on the central coast."

Clayton nodded and forced a smile. Armijo was enjoying recounting his factoids, and why not? It was a bust well worth feeling good about.

Armijo read the strained politeness in Clayton's expression. "Sorry, man. Here I am gloating and you've got nada."

"I still have Stanley," Clayton replied. "Where is she?"

"Since she agreed to cooperate, I saw no need to arrest her," Armijo replied. "So I've got her under wraps at her apartment in the company of a female officer."

Armijo put the car in gear. "You want to go talk to her?"

Clayton nodded.

Armijo made a U-turn. The cop manning the barricade at the end of the street let them pass. "I think once Robocker and Birch have their legal problems behind them, they ought to hook up and get married."

"Why's that?"

"Think about it; with names like Morton and Minerva, it's a marriage made in Heaven."

"Minerva is a pagan name," Clayton replied.

"Really?"

"She was the Roman goddess of wisdom and invention, along with a few other things."

"What other things?"

"Art and martial prowess, I think."

"Interesting," Armijo said. "I wonder what the name Stanley means."

"I haven't a clue," Clayton replied.

"Do you think the Romans had a goddess named Stanley?" Armijo asked. "Or maybe the Greeks?"

"Are you always like this?"

"Like what?" Armijo retorted innocently.

"So fast with the quips, the puns, the repartee."

Armijo laughed. "I just use it to hide my angst."

Clayton cracked a big smile, but didn't for a minute doubt that Armijo meant what he said. "And I suppose Bromilow showboats so he can hide his angst."

Armijo nodded. "Exactly. What do you do with yours?"

"Apaches don't do angst."

"Why not?" Armijo asked.

"We don't have a word for it."

Armijo slapped the steering wheel with his hand and laughed. "That makes total sense."


Stanley—the original meaning of her name currently unknown but under discussion by the two officers—lived in an apartment complex that catered to young singles. In the parking lot, Armijo pulled into an empty space next to Brian Riley's motorcycle, shifted in his seat, typed in something on the laptop, waited a minute, and then typed some more. Whatever came up on the screen made him smile.

"Stanley is an old English masculine surname that means 'stone clearing,'" he announced.

"The old English were also pagans," Clayton said.

"I think I saw that movie," Armijo replied, pointing the way to Stanley's apartment. It was a second-story unit located next to a staircase.

Armijo called in his location to dispatch, and the two officers climbed the stairs. Armijo rang the doorbell, and when no one answered, he stepped away from the door and called out to the officer inside. He waited a couple of beats before drawing his weapon. Clayton did the same.

Armijo knocked again, rang the bell, and called out to the officer once more. Silence. He raised a hand, counted one, two, three with his fingers and turned the doorknob. The door swung open easily.

Armijo went in low, shining the beam of his flashlight in a wide arc across the dark front room. Clayton went in high, searching for the light switch. He found it, and the harsh overhead light revealed an empty room. He cleared the nearby galley kitchen and dining area while Armijo moved toward the rear bedrooms. He returned to the front room just in time to see Armijo walk out of the bathroom, his face ashen gray. He shook his head sadly, holstered his weapon, keyed his handheld radio, and reported an officer down.

"She's dead," he added, "and I have a second body at this twenty."

Clayton stepped around Armijo and took a look. The female uniformed officer was in the bathroom sitting on the toilet seat, her hands cuffed, legs bound with duct tape, and her mouth stuffed with what looked to be a washcloth. She had one bullet hole in the center of her forehead, and the wall behind the toilet tank was reddish brown with blood splatter from the exit wound. Her sidearm, spare ammo clips, and handheld radio had been dumped in the bathtub.

In the bedroom, Minerva Stanley Robocker was stretched out facedown on the bed, hands and feet bound by duct tape, with one bullet hole at the base of her skull. Only a trickle of blood trailed down her neck and stained the bedcovers.

A breeze through the open patio door to the bedroom balcony rustled the drapes. Clayton took a look at the door and saw tool-mark scratches near the locking mechanism. The door had probably been jimmied, which meant it was most likely the killer's point of entry.

He went back and took a closer look at the side of Minerva Stanley's Robocker's face and spotted a bruise mark at the temple. He heard Armijo step into the room and glanced in his direction.

"What the fuck is going on?" Armijo asked.

"I don't know," Clayton said as he backed away from the body and followed Armijo into the front room. "But I'm guessing the killer entered through the bedroom balcony, knocked Robocker unconscious, and then dealt with the officer before returning to the bedroom to finish Robocker off."

Clayton scanned the front room carefully. Except for the two dead women and the blood that been spilled, the apartment was as neat, tidy, and undisturbed as Tim Riley's rented cabin in Capitan.

He'd spent hours in and around that cabin bagging and tagging everything he could think of that Tim Riley's killer might have come into contact with—touched, brushed against, picked up, used, or stepped on. So far, forensic analysis had not revealed one shred of helpful evidence. He had a strong hunch that the CSI search of Robocker's apartment would also yield a big fat zero in the evidence department.

He wondered who in the hell he was up against. One person? A professional? An organization of killers? The mob? The government? Spooks? And on top of all of that, where in the hell was young Brian Riley?

He stepped outside to the landing and speed-dialed Kerney's private home number. Kerney picked up on the second ring and Clayton gave him the news.

"I'll be on my way to your location five minutes after I hang up," Kerney said, his voice still filled with sleep. "You call Paul Hewitt and let him know what's happened. I'll inform Sheriff Salgado, Ramona Pino, and Major Mielke. Let APD take the lead for now until we can sort things out."

"Will do." Relieved and glad that Kerney was willing to jump into the mix, Clayton disconnected, took a deep breath, and let it out slowly. From two difference directions, he could hear the growing sounds of converging sirens.

Armijo joined Clayton on the landing, and in the light pouring through the open apartment door the two men waited silently during the last vestiges of a night neither would ever forget.

"Why don't you meet and greet the arriving troops," Clayton finally said, "while I start asking neighbors if they saw or heard anything."

After arriving in Albuquerque, Kerney ran a gauntlet of APD cops and detectives before he could get close to the crime scene and start looking for Clayton. The entire complex had been cordoned off, and in three of the buildings within Kerney's field of vision, he could see officers talking to residents outside their apartments.

He found Clayton in front of the building, where a CSI mobile lab was parked, talking with a man in a suit who had an APD captain's shield clipped to the lapel of his jacket. Another man standing next to Clayton had a unshaven face and long hair that curled over the collar of his leather jacket, and wore a detective's shield on a lanyard around his neck.

Kerney approached in time to catch an exchange between the captain and Clayton.

"I understand that you have a legitimate interest in this investigation, Sergeant Istee," the captain said, sounding put out. "But as I've already explained, this is my crime scene, my murder investigation, and it's our dead officer upstairs bound and gagged, sitting on a toilet stool with a bullet hole in her head. Until my people finish with the crime scene and do the preliminary neighborhood canvass, you *will* stay out of the way."

The captain jabbed his finger twice at Clayton to make his point, a rude gesture that no Mescalero would ever make causally or thoughtlessly.

"These murders are connected to my investigation, Captain Apodaca," Clayton replied hotly. "I need to be interviewing potential witnesses."

"You'll get your chance," Captain Apodaca replied.

"Starting right now would be good," Kerney said genially.

The APD captain gave Kerney the once-over, glanced at the chief's shield in Kerney's hand, and shook his head. "Sorry, Chief, you've got no jurisdiction in this matter."

"Don't be obtuse, Captain," Kerney replied. "Sergeant Istee and I have every right to be part of this investigation and you know it. Now, do I talk to your chief, who's giving a statement to the media down at the end of the block as we speak, or do you and I reach an understanding here and now?"

Apodaca, a short man with a shaved head and bulgy eyes, glared at Kerney and said nothing.

The man with the stubble on his chin and long hair glanced at

Clayton, then Kerney, and patted Captain Apodaca on the shoulder. "Don't be a dickhead, Jerry," he cautioned. "Do what the chief asks."

Apodaca's face turned beet red. He caught himself just as he started to sputter an angry reply, took a deep breath, and pointed at the man who'd just called him a dickhead. "Detective Armijo here will take you upstairs and sign you into the crime scene. Ask the CSI supervisor your questions, tell him what you'd like his team to look for, and coordinate with my lieutenant any canvassing you want to conduct. Detective Armijo will stay with you."

"Very well," Kerney said.

Armijo nodded, Apodaca walked away, and Kerney gave the detective a quizzical look.

"You're wondering how a detective can call a captain a dickhead and get away with it, right, Chief?" Armijo asked as the three men walked up the stairs.

"Something like that," Kerney said.

"I was little Jerry Apodaca's field training officer after he came out of the academy," Armijo said. "Without going into details, he owes me big-time."

Kerney nodded. "Enough said."

Outside Minerva Stanley Robocker's apartment, the three officers talked to the CSI supervisor and the homicide lieutenant, and after explaining that the murders might be linked to another cop killing, they were able to get both men to agree to make a concerted effort to look for anything that could be a possible tie-in to Brian Riley's disappearance and the murder of his father and stepmother. The homicide lieutenant also agreed to have his people circulate Brian Riley's photograph to all the residents in the apartment complex to see if anyone knew him or his whereabouts.

Kerney learned that the dead patrol officer, Judy Connors,

was a three-year veteran of the force who had just returned to work from a maternity leave following the birth of her first child, a son. He asked to view the crime scene, and the CSI supervisor gave him a quick tour while Clayton and Armijo waited on the landing. He returned just as the first touch of dawn spread a glimmer of light over the top of the Sandia Mountains. For a moment the sight of the young, dead policewoman and the very attractive, just-as-dead Minerva Robocker stayed with him in his mind's eye. Not even the bullet holes, their lifeless, bloodless faces, or the dried blood that stained the bedcovers and splattered the bathroom wall could erase the fact that in different ways both had been pretty women in the full bloom of their lives. It made Kerney angry and brokenhearted for the baby boy who would never know his mother, for Minerva Robocker's parents and Judy Connors's husband, a county firefighter just back from a six-month overseas deployment with the National Guard. It made him think about how close he and Patrick had come to losing Sara.

"Down at the Capitan crime scene, didn't you think it possible that Tim Riley's killer may have been a professional?" he asked Clayton after a long silence.

"That," Clayton answered, "or somebody with sufficient knowledge and skill to kill quickly, efficiently, and leave nothing behind."

"What's the difference?" Armijo asked.

"Maybe I'm splitting hairs and there is no difference." Clayton turned and looked across the parking lot and the street at an apartment complex similar to the one that had housed Robocker. It had small, semicircular enclosed patios on the ground level and undersize balconies with wrought iron railings on the second story. "But I didn't want to dismiss the possibility that the Rileys' killer is a personal acquaintance, coworker, friend, or relative who just luckily pulled off squeaky clean murders."

"And now what do you think?" Kerney asked.

"I'm open to suggestions." The sky began to brighten, and Clayton could see the buildings across the street more clearly. Most of the second-story balconies were empty and only a few apartments had lights on inside. One balcony had a small barbecue grill pushed into a corner by the sliding glass door, and several others had cheap plastic lawn chairs scattered about. He couldn't see anything of interest behind the high privacy walls of the ground floor unit.

"A cop could make a good killer," Armijo suggested.

"We've been digging deeply into that theory with the Santa Fe sheriff and his personnel," Kerney said, "and we've got nothing so far." He glanced at Clayton, who was still scanning the apartment buildings across the street. "What are you thinking?" he asked Clayton.

"I'm trying to figure out if there are any similarities in the various crime scenes," Clayton said, "but there's nothing I can reach out and touch. About all I can say is the perp is comfortable with killing, including disarming and executing a police officer, which should tell us something. Put that together with everything else we know and what have we got? Virtually no physical evidence has been left behind at any of the crime scenes. Tim Riley's body was left where he was ambushed, but Denise Riley's body was moved and left for us to find in a staged scene. Officer Connors's and Minerva Robocker's deaths were fast in-and-out killings."

"Are you talking contract killings?" Armijo interjected.

"That possibility can't be dismissed," Clayton said. There was something behind an open sliding glass door of the apartment balcony directly across the street from the Robocker unit, but Clayton couldn't quite make it out.

"What's the statistical probability of having four homicides at three different, widely separated locations, occurring within days of each other, with three of the four victims linked to one missing teenage boy, and all of the crimes carried out by different perps?"

"I was never that good at math," Armijo answered, "but I'd say it ain't hardly likely."

Clayton nodded as he studied the object in the open sliding glass balcony door. "Did that homicide lieutenant say anything about canvassing outside of the apartment complex?"

"He wasn't that specific," Kerney replied, following Clayton's gaze. "What are you looking at, Sergeant?"

"I think it's a telescope on a tripod positioned with a direct line of sight to the front door of the Robocker apartment."

Armijo turned, took a look, and then started for the stairway. "Let's go check it out."

The three men crossed the street, found the resident manager's apartment, rang the bell, and got no answer. In the parking lot, Clayton asked a woman who was leaving to take her child to day care if she knew where he could find the manager. She pointed to a man standing with a small crowd that had gathered on the sidewalk to watch the action at the crime scene.

The manager, a man with a soft belly, a sunken chest, and acne scars on his face, looked pleased when Clayton showed him his shield and led him away from the crowd to ask a few questions.

"I hear it's a murder," the man said in a squeaky, nasal voice, giving a nod of his head in the direction of the squad cars and flashing emergency lights. "Double homicide."

"Can I have your name, sir?" Clayton asked.

"Bernard Arlinger."

Clayton asked for some ID.

Arlinger showed Clayton his driver's license and said, "I didn't see anything, Officer. Wish I had, so I could help you."

"Maybe you still can, Mr. Arlinger." Clayton pointed to the apartment where he'd spotted the telescope behind the open sliding glass door. "Who lives there?"

"Nobody, right now. The tenant moved out a week ago and I'm having the unit repainted, new carpet installed, and a new kitchen sink put in. It won't be ready to rent for another five or six days."

"Has the work already started?"

Arlinger nodded. "Yeah, the old carpet has been torn out and the painting contractor is patching the drywall."

"We need to get into that apartment."

"You think it has something to do with the killings?" Arlinger's voice rose, tinny and nasal, loud enough to turn the heads of a few people Kerney and Armijo were blocking from getting close during Clayton's Q&A.

"Can you let us in?" Clayton asked.

A smile broke across Arlinger's face, and he reached for the key ring attached to his belt. "Sure thing."

At the apartment, Arlinger unlocked the door and Clayton had to clamp a hand on his arm to keep him from entering. He pulled him aside and unholstered his weapon. Both Kerney and Armijo had their sidearms out.

"I'd like you to gather all the information you have on the previous tenant and hold on to it for me. Will you do that, Mr. Arlinger? Just wait for us downstairs, okay?"

"Sure."

"Is the electric on inside the apartment?"

Arlinger shook his head. "I turned it off. The panel is in the bedroom closet."

"Okay, you can go now," Clayton said.

For several seconds Arlinger stared at the three officers with their drawn weapons before scurrying away.

"Are we set?" Kerney asked from the side of the door, glancing from Armijo to Clayton. Both had flashlights at the ready.

Armijo nodded. "I'm first in."

"Cover left," Kerney said to Clayton. "I'll take right."

"Roger that."

The trio went in fast and cleared the apartment quickly. There was no one there. Armijo found the electrical panel and turned on the lights. Except for the telescope on the tripod, some painting supplies, drop cloths, and a chalky residue from the drywall patching on the plywood subflooring, the place was empty.

"Nobody moves out of an apartment without leaving something behind," Armijo said as he opened a kitchen cabinet drawer and dumped the contents. Several grocery store coupons floated to the floor along with a box of toothpicks and a plastic bottle of over-the-counter medicine. The rest of the drawers and cabinets were empty.

"I'm calling for forensics," Armijo said.

"First," Clayton replied, "I want that telescope and tripod dusted for prints. It looks brand-new and it's not very high quality or expensive. I'll bet it was bought at either a toy store or at one of those big-box discount retailers. Ask the manager when the last trash pickup was made. We may want somebody to go dumpster diving. It would be great if we can find a sales receipt."

"I'm on it," Armijo said as he left the apartment.

Clayton studied the exposed subflooring. A wide swath of the powdery dust from the drywall repairs had been wiped with a rag. He followed the cleanup attempt from the telescope in the bedroom all the way to the front door. Any evidence of footprints in the dust had also been wiped clean around the tripod and on the balcony.

A slight chill went up Clayton's spine. Had Tim Riley's killer watched him locate and document the partial footprints left on the cabin porch in Capitan? Is that why the footprints in the apartment had been obliterated? Was the killer watching him now, or was he just being paranoid?

Clayton looked out the open balcony door to the street below. The attention of the crowd was focused on the crime scene across the way, and nobody was looking up in his direction.

"What is it?" Kerney asked as he approached.

"Nothing?"

"It's something."

"I can't be certain," Clayton replied, "but what if we're being watched by the killer?"

Kerney stepped onto the balcony and looked over the railing. "If, as you say, we're dealing with a professional, that would be totally out of character unless it serves some larger purpose. But let's have officers get names and addresses of the people on the sidewalk just in case."

Clayton punched numbers on his cell phone and asked Lee Armijo to have APD detectives follow up with the crowd. "What larger purpose?" he asked after disconnecting.

Kerney returned to the bedroom. "Assuming Brian Riley has been the target all along, the murder of Robocker and the officer could be nothing more than some tidying up."

"How so?" Clayton asked.

"Robocker may have known absolutely nothing, and was killed simply because the police had shown an interest in her."

"So the perp has been watching her apartment," Clayton said, "hoping Riley would come around, and instead the cops show up with Robocker in tow under their protection."

"Which might have been enough to convince the perp it was time to cancel Robocker just in case she had been talking."

"That can't be the larger purpose," Clayton said wearily.

Kerney patted Clayton on the arm. "I didn't say I knew what it was; just that there might be one. Let's go with the thought that we've got four homicides, five including the unborn fetus, and

Brian Riley is the key to what ties them together. Let's find him before the killer does."

"So far that's been easier said than done."

Lee Armijo returned with news that the trash had been hauled away yesterday afternoon, the tenant who'd moved out of the apartment was being interviewed by detectives, officers were tracking down the workmen who'd been in the apartment since it had become vacant, and a fresh team of detectives were about to start a new canvass at their present location.

"I put a uniform to work going through the trash bin anyway and told him to look for the packing box and assembly instructions for the telescope," Armijo said. "If he comes up empty, I told him to get a list together of any and all businesses in the city that sold that particular make and model so we could start making the rounds."

"Good deal," Clayton said.

"The forensic techs will be here in a few," Armijo added, "and they ask that you not touch anything, as you might contaminate evidence and thus prevent them from solving the crimes."

"They truly said that?" Kerney asked.

Armijo nodded. "Apparently they consider you and Sergeant Istee country cousins who have little appreciation for or knowledge of their considerable skills, or they've been watching too many crime scene investigation television shows."

"Tell them I want comparison fingerprints from the previous tenant and everyone who's been in this apartment since it was vacated," Kerney said.

"Consider it done," Armijo said as the first crime scene tech entered the apartment. He repeated Kerney's request, pointed at the bedroom door, and told the tech to start in there. "Now, if you guys have a few minutes to spare, my chief, several of his deputy chiefs, and every officer at the crime scene above the rank of sergeant are waiting for you in the mobile command center.

They very much would like to know—as my chief put it—'what the fuck is going on. '"

"Whatever," Clayton said, stifling a yawn as he headed for the door.

As the men left the apartment, Kerney noticed dark circles under Clayton's eyes. He looked totally worn out and in need of sleep. Kerney knew Clayton had been working full throttle for over twenty-four hours and was about to run out of steam.


At the mobile command center, Scott Kruger, the APD chief of police, a man Kerney knew and considered to be more of a politician than a cop, greeted him at the door, pulled him aside, and waited until Armijo and Clayton entered the vehicle before speaking.

A chunky man with a thin face, Kruger looked decidedly uptight. "Tell me this Indian cop knows what he's talking about."

"What do you mean?"

"My homicide captain tells me that this Sergeant Istee from Lincoln County says the murder of my officer and the cocktail waitress is directly related to the killings of the deputy sheriff in Capitan and his wife up in Santa Fe."

"There's good reason to believe that."

Kruger grunted. "You mean it's just a hypothesis?"

"And a very good one," Kerney noted, already tiring of Kruger's blustery style. It was a poor substitute for command presence, which the man totally lacked. "It's one that I agree with, based on Sergeant Istee's analysis."

"And this Sergeant Istee, will he walk us through how he arrived at all of his insights?" Kruger asked without trying to mask his sarcasm.

"I'm sure if you ask nicely, he will," Kerney replied.

"The dead deputy's son, this Brian Riley, he's a suspect?"

"Perhaps," Kerney replied. "We won't know until we find him."

Kruger grimaced. "So I got nothing to tell the media, right?"

"After the briefing, I'd like us to make a full-bore effort to find Brian Riley, including asking the media for their assistance. That should make for a juicy breaking-news story."

Kruger's expression brightened as he stepped toward the mobile command center's door. "Okay, Kerney, I'll stay on the same page with you for a while."

"That's great," Kerney replied, straight-faced.

The mobile command center was an oversize recreational vehicle crammed with communication equipment, computers, workstations, and now several more cops to add to the assembled crowd. Kruger pushed his way to the front of the vehicle, introduced Kerney and Clayton, and asked his homicide captain, Jerry Apodaca, to start the briefing.

Apodaca reported that the sliding glass door to the balcony of Robocker's apartment showed tool marks and had been jimmied open. He noted that shoe scuff marks had been found on the exterior stucco wall below the balcony and there were telltale abrasions on the balcony's painted wrought iron railing, suggesting that the perp had used a rope and climbed to reach Robocker's bedroom. A motion-detection pathway light behind Robocker's building had been disabled by the perp to provide concealment, and none of the residents with a view of the victim's apartment balcony reported hearing or seeing anything unusual around the time of the murders.

Although Apodaca wasn't certain about the sequence of events that occurred after the perp gained entry, the medical investigator had concluded that Officer Connors had suffered a blunt-force trauma to the head prior to being shot, which suggested the perp first disabled and disarmed the officer before proceeding with the executions. There was, Apodaca, said, no other way to describe the killings.

Apodaca reported that given the body temperature of both dead women, the MI estimated the killings took place no more than a hour before Detective Armijo and Sergeant Istee arrived at the apartment. He ended his presentation by noting the perp had to be well trained and in good physical shape to have successfully climbed into Robocker's apartment.

Next up was Armijo's lieutenant, Doug Bromilow, who ran down the sequence of events that led to the discovery of the marijuana factory in Four Hills. He deferred to Lee Armijo to provide the alleged tie-in between Morton Birch, Minerva Stanley Robocker, and Brian Riley, and then retook center stage to note that his ongoing investigation had yet to learn anything from the suspects, their known associates, witnesses, or neighbors that connected Brian Riley to any person who was part of the marijuana manufacturing and distribution scheme.

Kerney and Clayton finished up the session with a background synopsis that included the current status of the Santa Fe and Lincoln County murder investigations. Then Kruger asked for questions from the troops. The most persistent issue that surfaced, and rightfully so, was the total absence of a motive that would clearly connect the murders.

A few of the APD brass questioned the theory of a single shooter, but there was consensus that the killings were neither crimes of passion nor the work of amateurs. Kerney almost thanked the group for their stunning insight, but held back on the sarcasm and instead made a pitch to concentrate all efforts on finding the one person who might be most helpful to the investigations, Brian Riley.

The briefing ended with Kruger ordering his troops to go find Brian Riley pronto. After the exodus of officers from the stuffy, sweaty, mobile command center, Kerney watched Chief Kruger hurry down toward a small gathering of news reporters waiting behind a police barrier.

"I can't be your tour guide anymore, gentlemen," Armijo said. "My LT wants me to head back to the office and do my shift reports."

"Thanks for your help," Clayton said, shaking Armijo's hand.

"Anytime," Armijo said as he tossed off a causal hand salute in Kerney's direction.

Kerney returned the salute. "Thanks, Detective."

"Sure thing, Chief." Armijo ambled away in the direction of his unmarked unit.

Clayton turned to Kerney. "Can you drop me off at my motel so I can pick up my stuff and check out?"

"Sure," Kerney said, "but don't check out. Get some rack time. You look like you could use the sleep."

"I'm fine."

"You're running on fumes," Kerney countered, "and I don't need you searching for Brian Riley in that condition. Not when just about everyone who wears a shield in this state is looking for the kid."

"This is my investigation and I can pull my own weight," Clayton said hotly, giving Kerney an antagonistic look.

Kerney inched closer. "I'm not asking you, Sergeant. You're off duty for at least the next eight hours. Do I make myself clear?"

For a moment Clayton remained silent, staring Kerney in the eye. Then for some unknown reason he smiled and started to laugh.

"Okay, you win, what's so funny?" Kerney asked.

Still laughing, Clayton waved off Kerney's question. "Nothing. Just a thought I had."

"What thought?"

"You really want to know?"

"I do."

Clayton stopped laughing, looked at Kerney, and shook his head. "Well, it may not be funny to you, but for the first time in my entire life, my father just ordered me to go to my room and to go to bed."

Clayton walked away and started laughing again.

"That is pretty funny," Kerney said as he caught up.

"And ridiculous too," Clayton added.

The motel was a short drive from the crime scene, and by the time they arrived, Clayton was asleep and snoring heavily, his head resting against the glass of the passenger-side window. Kerney sat and watched him for a few minutes before gently shaking him awake.

Clayton rubbed his face with his hands, covered a yawn, and gave Kerney a sideways glance. "If it's all right with you, Chief, I think I'll catch a couple hours of shut-eye."

"That's a good idea," Kerney replied. "I'll see you in Santa Fe later in the day."

Clayton got out of the unit and looked in at Kerney. "See you then."

On the drive back to Santa Fe, Kerney thought about the letters Denise Riley had written home to her sister Helen Muiz during the years she'd lived away from her family. He'd only given them a quick look and hadn't formed a clear impression, but there was something hackneyed about them, especially in the later letters Denise had written. It was as though, with the passage of time, she'd depleted her storehouse of fresh things to write home about. He wanted to analyze the letters to see if he could isolate any repetitive words or phrases Denise used, identify any stock comments or observations she made, and find any threads in the letters that might point to thinly disguised, reworked fabrications.

The fact that the federal government had no record of Denise ever applying for a passport, being issued one, or traveling outside of the United States had piqued Kerney's interest. Once he finished analyzing the letters, he would deliver them to the Department of Public Safety crime lab and ask the Questioned Documents specialist to do a thorough analysis. He wanted to know what type of pens and inks were used, the manufacture of the paper and envelopes, if the stamps and cancellation marks were authentic, whether the handwriting was Denise's, and if so, was consistent throughout the letters—everything the specialist could tell him.

And of course, he wanted to have the answers right away.

# Chapter Nine

Loud pounding at the motel room door brought Clayton out of a deep, dreamless sleep. He rolled over, opened an eye, and tried to focus on the tabletop clock radio. It was exactly three hours since his head had hit the pillow. Light-headed and groggy, he got out of bed, padded barefoot to the door, and looked through the security peephole. Detective Lee Armijo was about to pound away again on the door.

"Okay, okay," Clayton yelled, hitting the light switch and opening up. "Don't you ever sleep?" he asked as Armijo stepped inside.

"I'm a narc," Lee replied. "We all take drugs to stay awake." There were dark rings under his eyes. "Get dressed while I make the coffee. I figure that's probably your drug of choice."

"I rarely self-medicate," Clayton replied.

Armijo guffawed, took the in-room coffee carafe off the machine on the dresser next to the cheap twenty-inch color TV, went to the bathroom, and filled it with water.

"What are you doing here, Detective?" Clayton asked as he stuck a leg into his jeans.

"Please, Sergeant, call me Lee. After all, we did spend last night together." Armijo returned from the bathroom, stuffed two individually wrapped packs of coffee in the machine, poured in the water, and pushed the button. The machine sighed and started to gurgle.

"But to answer your question," Armijo continued, "I started thinking that maybe Brian Riley might be involved in the drug trade as a user, given his association with Robocker, in spite of the fact that our good pal Mort Birch told us he didn't know him. So I called some of my snitches."

Clayton sat on the edge of the bed and pulled on his boots. "And?"

"One of them, Ed Duffy, a good Irish-American lad who sadly turned to a life of crime as a juvenile, swears that Brian Riley is crashing at a house on Cornell Drive near the university. Duffy says he saw him there two nights ago."

Clayton tucked in his shirt. "How reliable is your snitch?"

Armijo poured Clayton a cup of coffee and handed it to him. "Duffy, bless his heart, provides very good intel because I have him on a short leash and he can't afford to screw up. If he pisses me off for any reason, I'll have his probation officer violate him on a commercial burglary beef. He'll go straight to the slammer and pull a dime."

Clayton took a sip of coffee, made a face, and put the cup on the bedside table. "This stuff is terrible."

"It's my super high-octane formula," Armijo explained as he threw Clayton his coat, "designed to get your motor running. Let's go. Bring your coffee with you. On the way, I'll tell you what else I learned from Duffy. It's all very interesting stuff."

Seated in Armijo's unit, Clayton drank his coffee and blinked against the harsh, cloudless sky, made slightly hazy by a low thin brown cloud of pollution that hung over the city. Albuquerque looked no better to him at midday than it did at night or early in the morning. Central Avenue still had a string of cheap motels near the Interstate, rows of small businesses in a hodgepodge of uninteresting buildings still bordered the boulevard all the way up the hill to the university, and the sounds of traffic on the busy street filled the air like the dull hum of a swarm of angry insects. In truth, Clayton didn't like cities much.

As Armijo drove, he filled Clayton in. Riley had told Duffy he'd gone into hiding because of something he'd learned that could get him killed.

"At first," Lee added, "Duffy thought it was just some paranoid, drug-induced bullshit Riley was laying on him. But Riley went on and on about how his father and stepmother had been murdered, and he was next in line unless he could stay out of sight."

"Maybe it was just paranoia," Clayton ventured.

"I put the same thought to Duffy myself and he strenuously disagreed. He said Riley told him he knew things about his step-mother that could get him killed."

"Did Riley say what it was he'd learned about his step-mother?"

Armijo shook his head and slowed as a driver pulled into traffic from a side street and swerved immediately into the left-hand lane. "Nope. Duffy and Riley. Doesn't that sounds like an old Irish vaudeville song-and dance-team?"

"And this conversation took place two nights ago?" Clayton asked, just a bit weary of Lee's wisecracking style.

"According to Duffy, that's a roger." A break in the traffic flow allowed Armijo to swing into the right lane. "Duffy also told me that Riley gave the guy he's crashing with money to let him hide out there until things cool down. He's been laying low since the night his father's murder made the evening news, and he hasn't once left the house."

"So if Riley is supposedly in hiding, how did this Duffy char-acter manage to connect with him?" Clayton asked.

Armijo signaled a right turn. "When he isn't busy burglarizing homes and businesses, Duffy peddles cannabis to a select group of people he knows and trusts. Brian Riley's host, Benjamin Beaner—I swear on a stack of Bibles that's his name—is one of Duffy's regular customers. Beaner called Duffy, placed an order, and asked him to deliver it. When Duffy arrived with product in hand, Beaner and Riley were already half-wasted. Duffy joined the party, and as the evening progressed Riley started talking."

"What do you know about Beaner?"

"I found one intel report on him," Lee replied. "Late thirties, bisexual, single, college dropout, heavy grass user with an off-the-charts IQ. Works as a salesclerk at a national chain home electronics and appliance store. In other words, he's a middle-aged, switch-hitting, pothead geek."

"Did Riley mention to Duffy or Beaner who he thinks is trying to kill him?"

"I thought you'd never ask," Armijo replied.

"Well?"

"Agents of a foreign government."

"What?"

Armijo eased to the curb in front of a cottage situated at the back side of a large, packed-dirt lot with one leafless, forlorn, thirty-foot-tall ash tree that overarched the driveway. Large cracked and partially broken limbs dangled dangerously from high branches above the roof of a beat-up silver Honda Civic.

"That's all I know." Armijo opened the car door. "Now lets go and see if any of it is true."

The officers approached slowly, eyeing the cottage as they crossed over the partially exposed, charred foundation of a structure—probably a house—that had burned. The cottage had a screened-in porch, but most of the screens were either missing or badly tattered. The front door, which had been partially painted dark green a long time ago, had a bumper sticker pasted on it that read "Free Tibet."

Clayton guessed the cottage had probably started life as either a garage, a shed, or an outbuilding for the main house that had once stood along a leafy lane, back in the days when the university was on the outskirts of town.

As he closed in on the front porch, he scanned the windows, looking for any sign of movement, while Lee Armijo kept his gaze locked on the door. They circled the cottage, found no rear exits, and returned to the front. Clayton knocked on the door and called out for Benjamin Beaner. When he heard movement inside, he knocked again.

"Yeah, what do you want?" a voice replied.

"I need to speak to Brian Riley."

"There's nobody here by that name."

"Are you Benjamin Beaner?" Clayton asked.

"Who wants to know?"

"Police. Open up."

The door opened a crack, and Clayton flashed his shield and Lincoln County Sheriff's Office photo ID. The door swung open to reveal a man with a sunken chest, round shoulders, a tuft of hair that dangled down from his chin, and pasty skin. He reeked of tobacco smoke mixed with the pungent aroma of marijuana.

"Benjamin Beaner?"

The man nodded. "If you're looking for Brian Riley, he's gone."

"When?" Lee Armijo asked.

Beaner shook his head. "I don't know. I woke up and he wasn't here. Took all his stuff with him."

"Exactly *when* did you wake up?" Armijo demanded.

"About seven this morning."

"Was Riley here last night?" Clayton asked.

"Yeah. He crashed before I did."

"Mind if we look around?" Armijo asked.

"You got a warrant?"

"Do you want to go to jail for felony pot possession?" Armijo countered.

Beaner swallowed hard. "Are you going to bust me anyway if I let you in?"

"We're not interested in arresting you, Mr. Beaner," Clayton answered.

Beaner stepped aside. "Look all you want."

The small front room was completely taken over by a home entertainment system consisting of a DVD player, a cable TV box, a stereo with large floor speakers, a wide-screen high-definition television, the latest video gaming system and a universal remote control. Two beat-up reclining leather chairs were positioned directly in front of the TV, within easy reach of a glass-top coffee table that held an ashtray filled with cigarette butts, a plastic bag about half full of marijuana, a water pipe, and several roach clips.

In front of the coffee table, no more than three feet from the screen, was one of those legless video rocking chairs gamers used to plug themselves into their artificial digital world. Clearly Beaner's private life was almost completely detached from anything real. The room, the dark eye of the TV screen, the absence of any personal touches reminded Clayton of fanciful and scary Ray Bradbury stories he'd read as a child. He asked Beaner where Riley had slept.

Beaner pointed to a small hallway and said, "Turn left."

The back room was filled with assorted boxes of salvaged electronics gear, a bookcase made out of stacked concrete blocks and unpainted pine boards, filled with technical manuals, a plywood worktable on sawhorses that held a laptop, scanner, printer, and digital camera, and a twin mattress on the floor that had been pushed up against a wall.

Clayton called Beaner into the room to ask him what, if anything, belonged to Brian Riley.

Beaner looked around and stroked the tuft of facial hair that hung from his chin. "I don't see anything here that's his."

"Nothing?" Clayton demanded.

"That's right."

"What did he come here with?"

"He had a backpack, a sleeping bag, a toilet kit that he kept in the bathroom, and the clothes he wore. That's it."

"And he gave you money to hide him?"

"A hundred dollars a night plus cash for food and extras, all of it in old money."

"What do you mean old money?" Armijo asked.

"There wasn't a bill less than ten years old that he gave me. Tens and twenties, and they hadn't been circulated much. I pay attention to things like that. I figured it was stolen and I asked him about it."

"What did he say?" Clayton asked.

"He said that he'd found it."

"Where?"

"I don't know. He dropped the subject. But he pulled a wad of cash out of his backpack to pay me for putting him up."

"Do you have any of those old bills?"

"No, I spent them fast in case they were counterfeit."

"I understand he told you he knew something about his stepmother that could put him in danger or get him killed," Clayton said. "Was he any more specific about it than that?"

"The night a friend dropped by, Brian said he'd found out something about his stepmother that was some pretty scary shit."

"Like what?" Armijo asked.

Beaner shook his head. "I don't know. He wouldn't talk about it other than to say she wasn't who she pretended to be."

Armijo stepped closer to Beaner. "Did he say how he knew this?"

"He mentioned finding some documents on his father's property."

"He used the word *property*, not house?" Clayton asked.

"Yeah."

Clayton flipped up the mattress, hoping Riley had left something behind. There were only dust balls on the wood floor and a spider that scurried away to safety. "Did he have a cell phone with him?"

"Not when he arrived. But he gave me cash to buy him one and sign up him for a prepaid calling plan at work under an alias."

"What name did he want you to use?"

"Jack Ryan," Beaner replied. "I've got his cell phone number if you want it."

"You bet we do," Armijo said.

Beaner took out his wallet and handed Armijo a slip of paper.

"I'll get the ball rolling on this," Lee said as he flipped open his cell phone and stepped into the front room.

"Stay put while I do a quick search," Clayton ordered Beaner. He shifted nervously from foot to foot as Clayton looked through the documents and papers on the plywood table, the content of the boxes, the material on the bookcase, and the junk in a small closet.

Clayton moved a box at the head of the mattress, picked up a paperback novel that had been hidden from view, fanned through the pages, and glanced at the synopsis on the back. It was a spy thriller featuring a CIA operative named Jack Ryan. "Is this Riley's book?" he asked.

"No, it's mine," Beaner replied. "He started reading it while he was here. That's where he got the alias he wanted me to use for the cell phone. He said that he liked the sound of the name and it was close enough to Riley that he'd remember it."

"Did he talk about hiding out from agents of a foreign government?"

"He mentioned that," Beaner replied. "But I didn't take it seriously."

"Why not?"

"Because it sounded made up, like something right out of that book you're holding in your hand."

Clayton hadn't read the novel. Maybe if he did, he'd get some insights into Riley. "Mind if I borrow it?"

"You can have it."

Lee Armijo stepped back into the room. "I've got an expedited search warrant in the hopper for the telephone records, and there's no toilet kit in the bathroom. Anything here?"

Clayton shook his head and returned his attention to Beaner. "Can you think of any reason Riley would leave so unexpectedly?"

"No."

"Do you have any idea as to where he might have gone?"

"No."

Clayton handed Beaner a business card. "If he returns, calls, or you hear about him through some other source, contact me immediately."

Beaner stuffed the card in his shirt pocket. "I don't think Brian is a bad person. I truly don't think he would hurt anybody. He's just a scared kid with an overactive imagination."

"Uh-huh," Armijo said. "Did you try to sleep with him?"

Beaner blushed and said nothing more.

Outside the cottage Armijo's cell phone rang. He glanced at the incoming phone number on the screen, put the phone to his ear, and said, "Talk to me."

He listened, grunted, hung up, and gave Clayton a totally disgusted look.

"What?"

"Captain Apodaca just informed me that one of his hotshot homicide detectives at the murder scene allowed a young man matching Brian Riley's description to drive off on the Harley motorcycle. Apparently, the young man told the detective that he lived at the apartment complex and needed his wheels to get to work. Since the bike hadn't been secured into evidence by the crime scene techs, the cop bought the story without batting an eye or thinking to check with anyone else. An APB has been issued."

"When did this happen?"

"Ten minutes ago. Every city, county, and state patrol officer in the greater Albuquerque area is looking for him."

"Well, at least Riley has surfaced," Clayton said as he climbed into Armijo's unit, although the stupidity of the mistake deflated his spirits.

Armijo grunted. "Yeah, but if he's on the run again it's because he found out that Minerva Stanley Robocker went and got herself executed. He's got to believe the killer is closing in on him."

"Let's get some protection here for Beaner before we leave," Clayton urged. "We don't need another person Brian Riley knows getting themselves unnecessarily killed."

Lee keyed the radio microphone and made the request. While the two men waited, they listened to radio traffic. Everyone on the streets riding any kind of motorcycle was being stopped. It didn't matter if they were on custom hogs, choppers with sidecars, dirt bikes, or motor scooters. If it had two or three wheels and an engine, it got stopped.

A squad car pulled up behind Armijo. He waved and drove off. "Now what?"

"It's back to Santa Fe for me," Clayton said. If Benjamin Beaner was to be believed, whatever Brian Riley found had been on the Cañoncito property Tim and Denise Riley owned. It consisted of a sizable piece of land, and only the double-wide, stable, horse trailer, and immediate surroundings had been searched. Unless Brian Riley was found and had started talking before

Clayton arrived in Cañoncito, he planned to comb every square inch of it if necessary.

"Get some sleep first," Lee said, covering a yawn with his hand. "You look like shit."

"Thanks a lot," Clayton replied.


During the hours Kerney had spent analyzing Denise Riley's letters to her sister, he'd filled a writing tablet with notes. When he'd reached the point where he was trying to decide if Denise's handwriting curlicues had changed over time, he decided to stop. He put the letters aside, stripped off the latex gloves he'd worn to handle the documents, and reviewed his findings.

Denise had indeed used repetitive phrases and stock comments throughout her letters. No matter where she'd roamed, all the men she'd hooked up with were outdoor type guys who loved sports. Almost universally, she would characterize them to Helen as "footloose and fun-loving—not ready to settle down." When she worked, her jobs were always "boring, but paid the rent." When she wrote about adapting to new customs, struggling to learn foreign language phrases, describing the people she encountered, recounting an excursion to a landmark destination, experiencing exotic cuisine, very little detail went with it. It was as though Denise had lifted her imagery, facts, and experiences from travel guides.

There were seventy-eight letters in total, some of them lengthy, many of them short, but only five letters had any cross-outs or strikeovers, and the total number of misspelled words could be counted on both hands.

Was Denise Riley one of the most exacting and error-free correspondents ever? It was possible, but Kerney doubted it. The era of letter-writing was long gone, a victim of computers, the Internet, and e-mail. Even if Denise was a throwback inclined to write leisurely letters to her older sister, surely once in a while a note home would have been dashed off in a scribbled hurry. There was none of that in the packet of correspondence.

Kerney suddenly realized that not once in any of her letters did Denise refer to sending home snapshots of the places she'd visited, the people she'd met, or the men she'd supposedly fallen in love with. He picked up the phone and dialed Helen Muiz's number. Ruben answered.

"How are things going?" he asked.

"I'll be honest with you, it's been rough," Ruben replied. "Just getting her up and dressed in the morning is turning into a major feat. I've talked her into letting me make an appointment for her to see a therapist."

"That's a wise thing for her to do. How are you holding up?"

"I'm hanging in. Do you need to speak to Helen?"

"Maybe you can answer my question. In Denise's letters home, did she ever enclose any photographs of the places she'd lived, her boyfriends, the excursions she'd made, or the tourist attractions she'd visited?"

"Never. She said she was too busy, felt that a camera made her look like a tourist and that she just wanted to blend in and experience the world rather than taking pictures of it."

"There's no explanation of that in her letters to Helen."

"Helen had a phone conversation with Denise about a year or two after she'd left Santa Fe. That's when the subject came up."

"Didn't you or Helen or the other family members think it odd that Denise wouldn't want to share a photograph or two of her world travels and adventures, the men she lived with, the new friends she'd made?"

"Of course, but you have to understand that Denise had a habit of completely shutting down on a subject once she decided she didn't want to deal with it anymore. It was one of her ways of establishing limits. Broaching a forbidden subject with her got you an icy stare or the cold shoulder. If it was a serious infraction, you could be completely frozen out of her life for months at a time until she decided to forgive you."

"And the family tolerated this behavior?"

"She could also be charming, loving, and irresistible, Kerney. She was the eccentric, uncontrollable kid sister who got to break all the rules."

"You've been a big help, Ruben," Kerney said. "Thanks."

"Is there anything you want me to tell Helen?"

"Just let her know that we're still looking for Brian Riley and I'm taking Denise's letters to the state crime lab for analysis."

"Okay."

"Ruben."

"What?"

"Don't forget to take care of yourself."

Ruben laughed. "Yeah, sure."

Kerney disconnected, put Denise's letters in a large, clear plastic evidence folder, and made the quick drive from police headquarters to the Department of Public Safety, the umbrella organization of the New Mexico State Police.

Once buzzed past reception, he first went to check in with his old friend, Chief Andy Baca, and found him behind his big desk signing paperwork. Andy looked up, grinned, and waved him in the direction of the couch that faced the desk.

"What's that in your hand?" Andy asked, sweeping the paperwork to one side.

Kerney sat on the couch and put the evidence envelope on the coffee table. "Letters from Denise Riley to her sister Helen that I'd like the Questioned Documents Unit to look at pronto."

Andy joined him on the couch. "You got it, amigo. Cop killings go to the front of the line at our crime lab, no questions asked. Now that there are two dead officers, everything else goes on the back burner."

"I know that, but a phone call from you while I'm on my way over there will surely add to their eagerness to be helpful."

"No problem." Andy eyed Kerney speculatively. "Do you really hope to break this case before you retire?"

Kerney nodded. "But it's looking less and less likely."

"And are you sure retiring is what you want to do? You've been in law enforcement your entire adult life. It's not that easy to walk away from something you enjoy doing. Believe me, I know."

Andy had retired from the state police as a captain, found it not to his liking, got himself elected as a county sheriff for two four-year terms, and had returned to Santa Fe after being appointed chief of the state police by the governor.

"I'm ready for a change," Kerney said.

"That's not the same thing as saying you're ready to stop being a cop."

"I'm going to find out what it's like to be an American living in London. We'll tour the continent as time allows, and when Sara is busy at work, I'll take Patrick fishing."

"You don't even like to fish."

"Don't take what I'm saying literally. I'm talking leisure time, recreational activities, sightseeing, expanding cultural horizons, soaking up European history."

Andy grunted and got to his feet. "Save me from grand tour of the continent rap. Connie called me a while ago to report that Sara has invited us to your house for dinner on Saturday night."

Kerney raised an eyebrow. Since coming home, Sara had showed little interest in food and virtually no interest in cooking. This was good news.

"You didn't know?"

"Nope, but I'm damn glad to hear it."

"She's coming along okay?"

Kerney laughed. "Seems the more I stay out of her hair the better she gets."

"Well, that's a no-brainer," Andy replied as Kerney headed for the door.

At the crime lab, Kerney met with the Questioned Documents expert and her assistant, who took the packet of letters and envelopes and immediately began recording the transfer of the evidence to the lab on an official form.

"Is there anything special we should be looking for?" Claire Paley asked.

In her fifties, Claire was rail-thin, wore bifocals that perched on the end of her small nose, had long dark hair pulled back in a bun that was always unraveling, and talked in a voice that was childlike in tone. As a result, she came across as a woman on the verge of becoming completely undone, but she was highly competent and extremely bright.

"Look at everything," Kerney replied. "From what I can tell, the victim used several types of stationery. If possible, identify the makers and check any watermarks against the FBI database. Also, I'd like to know if the stamps and cancellation marks are authentic, and there are a few strike-outs and cross-overs I'd like you to analyze. If you can read any impressions on the paper under the handwriting, that could be very helpful. Run a test on the inks used. I'm particularly interested in knowing the origin of the paper, envelopes, and ink. Are they of domestic or foreign manufacture?"

"What else?" Claire asked.

"I've included a recent sample of the victim's handwriting for comparison to help you determine if any of the letters were forged. To my untrained eye, it looks like the letters are all in the victim's cursive script, but that may not be so."

Claire's assistant handed her a letter and envelope that Kerney had placed in clear plastic sleeves, and she gave them both a long look.

"Excellent cursive writing," Claire said. "I'd bet that she was educated in Catholic schools."

"And you'd win," Kerney said. "How could you tell?"

"Because except for the Catholic schools, teaching cursive penmanship is fast becoming a lost art."

"You're probably right. But then so is letter-writing. Send everything to latent prints when you've finished. I'll drop off fingerprint cards to them on my way out."

"Chief Baca called to say you want results quickly."

"Burn the midnight oil, Claire. We need a break on this case. Two police officers and two civilians have been murdered in cold blood, an eighteen-year-old boy has gone missing and is on the run, and we've yet to nail down one substantial bit of evidence that can point us in the right direction."

"You've got it, Chief. After all, we can't have you looking like you're up shit's creek without a paddle," Claire said sweetly in her breathless twelve-year-old-girlish voice.

On the drive to Santa Fe, Clayton listened carefully to APD and state police radio traffic in the hope that Brian Riley would be taken into custody and thus make the search of the Cañoncito property unnecessary. But by the time he climbed La Bajada Hill, Riley was still at large.

Although the sky in Clayton's rearview mirror was a crisp, cold, clear winter blue, facing him was a ground-hugging storm that blanketed Santa Fe, hid the mountains, and swept wind-driven snow across the Interstate, slowing traffic to a crawl. He switched on his overhead emergency lights, headlights, and warning flashers, and kept moving, passing motorists stalled on the side of the highway and a jackknifed semi that had wound up on its side in the median.

Clayton stopped to check on the trucker. He made sure the man was unhurt, determined that the load was not hazardous—

the driver was hauling kitchen appliances—set out flares behind
the trailer, and called regional dispatch to send assistance.

Clayton bundled the trucker in a blanket and sat with him in
his unit with the heat cranked up, waiting for the state police and
a wrecker to arrive.

"I'm sure glad you came along," the trucker, a man named
Bailey Mobley, said.

"Yeah." Through the swirling snow and dark gray squall
clouds Clayton could see the first flicker of blue sky. The storm
was moving fast, traveling southwesterly, but it was leaving behind a good six inches of heavy, wet snow on the pavement, perhaps more closer to the mountains. He wondered if the road to
Cañoncito would be passable.

He thought about asking Ramona Pino to bring her detectives
and meet him at the Riley double-wide for a ground search, but
decided the place was probably under deep snow, which made
the chances of finding anything in the current conditions remote
at best.

Bailey Mobley said something that Clayton didn't catch.
"What was that?" he asked.

"Can I smoke in your squad car?" Mobley asked, showing a
pack of cigarettes.

"No, you can't."

Mobley smiled sourly, got out of the unit, closed the door,
pulled the blanket over his head, turned his back to the wind,
and lit up.

The radio squawked. A patrol officer was en route, ETA five
minutes. Through the windshield, Clayton could see that the
sliver of blue sky had turned into a swath and the branches of the
trees at the side of the highway were no longer being whipped by
gale-force wind gusts.

Except for the little sleep he'd caught earlier, Clayton had been up for at least thirty hours, and the idea of delaying a search of the Rileys' property and getting a good night's rest was very appealing. He'd almost talked himself into going straight to Kerney's ranch and crashing in the guest quarters, when it occurred to him that having been scared out of Albuquerque, Brian Riley might well be on his way back to the double-wide.

Granted, there was nothing Clayton knew that pointed to that possibility, but conversely there was nothing that argued against it. As a precaution, it only made sense to look for him at the double-wide. He should have thought of it a whole lot sooner, and being tired wasn't an excuse for his lapse of smarts.

He glanced out the windshield. Traffic was moving slowly on the highway, vehicles throwing up gobs of icy spray from the slushy snow. Up ahead Clayton could see the approaching emergency lights of a state police cruiser. It brought to mind the deer that had crashed into his unit and the image of Paul Hewitt and Tim Riley hurrying to him to see if he'd been injured. It seemed as though all that had happened months, not days, ago.

Just as the state cop rolled to a stop, Bailey Mobley opened the passenger door to the unit and stuck his head inside, his breath reeking of tobacco smoke. He shook Clayton's hand and gave him the wadded-up blanket. "Thanks again."

"Glad you weren't hurt, Mr. Mobley," Clayton replied as he got out of his unit and walked with the trucker to meet the state cop.

After introducing himself and turning Mobley over to the state cop, he asked how the roads were northeast of the city.

"Where do you need to get to?" the officer asked.

"The lower Cañoncito area."

"It's probably snowpacked but manageable in your four-by-four. But the Interstate is closed in both directions just north of there at Glorieta Pass."

"How long has it been closed?" Clayton asked.

"Two hours."

"Any motorcyclists waiting to get through?" Clayton asked. He gave the officer a description of Brian Riley and his Harley.

"We're all looking for him," the officer replied. "Let me ask." He keyed his handheld and asked the uniforms at the roadblock if anyone matching the description of Riley and his Harley had been spotted waiting for the highway to be reopened. The reply came back negative.

Clayton thanked the officer and drove on. The clouds had lifted over Santa Fe to reveal foothills and mountaintops covered in a white blanket of snow. Against the backdrop of a blue sky, the frosted radio and microwave transmission towers on the high peaks looked like man-made stalagmites poking toward the heavens.

Tire tracks on the road to Cañoncito told Clayton that a good foot of snow was on the ground but motorists were getting in and out. He kept his unit in low gear with the four-wheel drive engaged and steered gently through the curves as a precaution against any hidden ice patches. The western sun turned the snow-covered mesa behind the settlement into a massive monolith, and the houses along the dirt lane that led to Tim Riley's driveway were thickly blanketed with snow. Horses pawing the ground in the adjacent corrals exhaled billows of steam that sparkled and then dissipated in the frigid air.

The snow-covered driveway to the Riley property showed no sign of fresh passage, either by vehicle or by foot. Clayton turned in and drove toward the double-wide with his driver-side window open, listening intently for any sound above the rumble of his engine that might signal someone was nearby. He was halfway up the driveway when the distinctive roar of a motorcycle engine came to life and cut through the air. He shifted quickly, floored the unit, and almost crashed into the Harley bearing down on him. The rider veered off the driveway and gunned his machine up a slope toward the base of the mesa behind the double-wide.

Clayton geared down and followed, slaloming around trees, the tires of his unit digging through deep snowbanks. He plowed into a hidden boulder and high-ended the vehicle. He threw the unit into reverse, the rear tires burning rubber on the frozen ground, and realized that he was hopelessly stuck. He bailed out of the unit, grabbed the wadded-up blanket the trucker had used, wrapped it over his shoulders, and started following the motorcycle on foot. Up ahead he could hear the whine of the engine. He ran toward it, and through a break in the tree cover he saw the rider unsuccessfully trying to force his machine up a steep rock-face incline, once, twice, three times.

From a good fifty feet away, Clayton yelled at the cyclist to stop. The man turned, and Clayton for the first time got a good look at Brian Riley in the flesh. The boy's expression was wide-eyed, frozen with fear.

"Police," Clayton shouted, throwing off the blanket. "Don't run. I'm here to help you."

The boy spun the Harley around, spraying an arc of snow behind the rear tire, revved the engine, and headed down the slope away from Clayton, zigzagging through trees, ducking over the handlebars to avoid low branches.

Clayton followed on foot, scrambling down a rock-strewn slope, quickly losing hope that he'd catch up with Riley as the sound of the Harley's engine began to fade in the distance. He broke free of the trees at the base of the mesa and followed anyway at a fast jog.

Up ahead he could see the railroad tracks that cut through the narrow valley and followed the course of a shallow streambed. The railroad right-of-way was fenced, but at a track siding where new railroad ties were stacked, a gate had been left open. Running into a stiff breeze that turned his ears and nose painfully cold, Clayton followed the path the motorcycle had taken across the railroad tracks and through another open gate. When he could no longer hear the sound of the Harley's engine, he slowed to a walk and listened. Riley was long gone.

As he walked on, he tried to call the Santa Fe S.O. on his cell phone, but the call kept getting dropped. He jumped a fence, walked in the ruts of a snow-covered lane, approached the first house he came to, knocked at the door, and got no response. Two houses farther on, he encountered an elderly Hispanic man breaking the ice in a water trough at a horse corral. He showed the man's shield and asked if he could borrow the man's phone.

The old man gave him a thorough once-over before speaking. "Was that you yelling in the woods?" he asked.

Clayton nodded.

"Were you chasing that motorcycle rider that just passed by?" the old man asked.

Clayton nodded again.

"On foot?" the man asked incredulously.

Clayton nodded for the third time.

"That's loco."

"Can I borrow your telephone?"

"Come inside," the man said, leading the way to a back door.

The toasty warm kitchen of the old man's house smelled of freshly baked bread and had framed pictures of saints and a hand-embroidered copy of the Lord's Prayer on the walls. Using an old wall-mounted, rotary-dial phone straight out of the 1950s, Clayton called Don Mielke at the Santa Fe S.O. and reported his sighting of Brian Riley.

"I'll put out an APB and BOLO immediately," Mielke said.

"I crashed my unit. I need a tow truck and a ride."

"What's your twenty?"

Clayton covered the telephone mouthpiece and asked the elderly man for his name.

"Francisco Ramirez," the old man replied.

"I'm at Francisco Ramirez's house," Clayton said. He gave Mielke directions and added, "Look for a Cattle Growers sign on the garage that's opposite the house."

"Ten-four."

"And ask Ramona Pino to meet me at the Riley crime scene," Clayton added.

"Are you on to something?" Mielke asked.

"Riley came back here for some reason. I want to take a look around the property to see if I can find out why."

"What do you expect to find with a foot of snow or more on the ground?"

"Tracks," Clayton replied. "Tracks that might lead me somewhere."

"I'm coming out there," Mielke said.

"Come along," Clayton replied. "Bring a couple of deputies with you. We might as well do another full search of the double-wide, horse barn, corral, and horse trailer. Tell them to dress warmly."

"Whatever you're looking for, Riley may have already taken with him."

"Yeah," Clayton said, "and that would be par for my day. But let's look anyway."

He disconnected. If he'd just passed by the jackknifed semi on the Interstate and reported it to dispatch, he might now have Brian Riley in custody and be finding out what had caused the murder of two police officers and two civilians. But failing to render aid and assistance to Bailey Mobley would have been the wrong thing to do.

Clayton sighed in frustration. So far, the only good to come from his marathon effort to find Brian Riley was that he'd crashed the Lincoln County S.O. unit, which meant he wouldn't have Tim Riley's ghost hanging around him anymore. That was a burden lifted, but only a minor one.

He joined Francisco Ramirez at the kitchen table and looked over at the stove, where a coffeepot was slowly percolating over a low flame. "Is that coffee I smell, Señor Ramirez?"

"*Sí*, and from the way you look I believe you need some."

"I look that bad?"

Francisco Ramirez pointed to Clayton's forehead. "You've been bleeding."

Clayton touched his head. At the hairline he felt a thick glob of congealed blood. He couldn't remember bumping into anything. "Mind if I clean up?"

Francisco pointed to the passageway. "Go ahead, Sergeant. I bake my own bread and have two loaves in the oven. Would you like some with your coffee when you return?"

Clayton's stomach rumbled in hunger. "That would be great."


After getting away from the cop, Brian Riley ground the Harley to a stop on the paved road that led to Santa Fe and considered his options. If he drove to town on the frontage road or tried to get on the Interstate, chances were good the police would swarm all over him. That was if the guy who had chased him really was a cop.

Brian decided he couldn't risk finding out. He turned left and took a country road that climbed the mesa, wound through woodland and pastures, and hooked up with a highway miles south of Santa Fe. At the top of the hill, the pavement turned to dirt, and Brian had to downshift the Harley to power his way through wet snow two feet deep.

A few miles down the road, where the forest gave way to

rangeland, Brian paused. Up ahead he could see snowdrifts piled four feet high against the fences. If he made it to the highway south of Santa Fe, it would be a long, cold ride, and he wasn't sure he could do it without warmer clothes and maybe some food and water to carry with him.

Last year when he'd stayed with his father and stepmother, Tim had let him use the truck to explore the mesa, and Denise had let him ride one of the horses along some of the lightly traveled Forest Service roads. On this stretch of the country road there was a good deal of privately owned land. On horseback Tim had investigated some of the ranches that were hidden away and posted to keep trespassers out. If he remembered correctly, there was one such ranch house deep in the woods where the rangeland ended.

He rode on, fighting to keep the Harley upright as the tires sought traction through the drifts. He found the turnoff and kept going through the virgin snow. His dad had told him the small ranches were summer operations only, and so far there was no sign of any recent traffic on the ranch road. The last rays of a weak sun were at his back and the forest had dimmed to dusk when the small ranch house, closed up and dark, came into view.

Brian skidded to a stop near the steps to the front porch and got off the Harley, his muscles aching from the exertion of riding the bike through the deep snow. He took a long look around before knocking on the porch door. An old truck parked by the barn was covered with snow, the sliding barn doors were padlocked, and there were no animal tracks in the empty corral.

He looked carefully at the house. In the gathering dusk he couldn't see anything behind the windows. The porch door was locked. He thought about using his elbow to break the glass and decided against it. He found a wrench in the glove box of the old truck and used it to smash the glass.

Once inside, Brian realized how really cold he was. He stumbled over a chair and ottoman, found a lamp on a side table, and turned it on. The front room served as a kitchen, dining, and sitting area. It had a wood cookstove next to a kitchen sink that got water from a hand pump. The place looked like something straight out of the old two-reel Western movies that were sometimes shown on late night television.

In a wall cupboard above an empty refrigerator that had been turned off for the winter, Brian found a good stock of canned and packaged foods. He went to the kindling box next to the cookstove and got a fire started before looking around the rest of the house. There was no telephone or television, but a tabletop radio sat on a shelf next to a stack of *New Mexico Stockman* magazines.

An old but serviceable heavy barn coat with a good pair of insulated gloves stuffed in the pockets hung on a wall peg in the small back bedroom. In a rickety handmade chest of drawers next to a twin bed on a cast iron frame were some rolled-up socks and several tattered wool sweaters. Underneath the sweaters Brian found a pistol in a holster. It was a loaded Smith & Wesson revolver. He put the holstered gun in a bundle made up of the barn coat, the gloves, a pair of socks, and a heavy sweater and carried it into the front room, which had started to warm up. In front of the cookstove he stripped down to his underwear, hung his wet jeans, shirt, and jacket over the two wooden chairs near the small kitchen table, put his shoes close to the stove, and dressed in the dry socks and the wool sweater with the barn coat draped over his shoulders.

At the sink he used the hand pump to fill a pot with water and put it on top of the wood stove to boil. In the food cupboard he found a package of macaroni and cheese, a jar of instant coffee, and some restaurant-size sugar packets. In another cupboard there were mugs, plates, several pots, and some eating utensils.

As soon as the water boiled, Brian cooked the macaroni, mixed in the cheese sauce, and wolfed it down, sipping heavily sugared coffee with each bite. When he finished, he put the dirty dishes in the sink and looked out the window. Snow pelted against the glass. He could hear the wind howling, and the sky was a sheet of solid leaden gray.

It was no time to be traveling. He added some wood to the cookstove, mixed up another cup of instant coffee, and settled into the overstuffed chair. If he hadn't gotten up early at Beaner's and turned on the television, he wondered what would have happened to him. It had been a shock to see his Harley in the parking lot of Stanley's apartment building as a TV reporter talked about the double homicide. In that instant, he knew Stanley was dead and he was next, so he packed and bolted.

What Brian didn't know for sure was why somebody wanted him dead, or why Tim, Denise, and Stanley had been killed. Inspired by the spy novel at Beaner's, he'd told him and his dealer friend Duffy that he was being chased by foreign spies. But who was it really?

He'd found the money by accident in an old well house on his father's property where he liked to go to smoke dope in the evenings when Tim and Denise were home and keeping an eye on him. It was in a locked briefcase hidden under some boards behind a rusted water pump.

After breaking the case open, he had stared openmouthed at the stacks of U.S. dollars, a pouch containing gold coins, and three passports issued by foreign governments to Denise under different names.

He had inspected the old coins but had taken only the fifty thousand U.S. dollars. Counting on the snowstorm for cover, he'd come back today to see if the briefcase was still in its hiding place, to get the coins. But it was gone, which meant someone was killing anyone who might have known about it.

But why murder Denise? After all, the foreign passports in the briefcase had been issued to her under false names, which meant she'd probably hidden it in the well house in the first place. Was she some kind of government agent his dad had met when he was in the air force? Had he been killed because he knew about her past or had helped her do something illegal? And why had Stanley and a police officer been murdered? How did the killer even find out about Stanley?

Brian checked his clothing. His jeans and shirt were dry enough to wear. He dressed in front of the stove, thinking he'd spend the night and then figure out what to do after the storm passed. He still had almost five thousand dollars left from the fifty and that could get him to Mexico, where he could hide out.

He sat back down in the easy chair, with the holstered pistol in his lap. The old house was creaky and drafty, and there were mice scurrying in the walls. He was half-asleep when he heard the sound of footsteps on the porch. He raised his head, opened his eyes, and saw a man standing in the doorway holding a rifle.

Brian fumbled to release the strap that secured the revolver to the holster, and as he yanked the pistol free the man pointed the rifle and shot him between the eyes.

# Chapter Ten

The bullet from Clifford Talbott's bolt-action rifle splattered blood and brains against the back of the easy chair. The perfectly centered dark red hole above the dead man's eyes made him look like a fallen Cyclops.

With shaky hands, Talbott lowered his Remington, walked to the kitchen sink, put the rifle on the counter, and promptly threw up.

During a lifetime of hunting, Talbott had killed untold numbers of varmints, a dozen or more coyotes, brought down his fair share of buck deer in season, bagged an occasional turkey, and had once taken a trophy-size elk, but he'd never before shot and killed a person, much less even pointed a gun at anybody.

He stayed bent over the sink for a long moment with his back to the dead man, smelling the stink of his vomit as he washed it down the drain with the hand pump, wishing he could just as easily wash away the last five minutes of his life.

Thirty-five years ago, Clifford Talbott had inherited the ranch from his father. Since then, in early March of every year, no matter what the weather, he drove up from his home in Moriarty, a town just south of the Santa Fe County line, to air the place out, make necessary repairs, and get it shipshape and ready for a small herd of cattle that he would buy at a spring auction, fatten up over the summer, and sell in the fall.

Most years he broke even on the effort, once in a while he lost money, and some years he made a small profit. But running livestock on the ranch kept his property taxes low and allowed him to renew his Forest Service grazing permit, which was hard to come by and valuable.

He looked out the window over the sink. On the outside sill an inch or more of white stuff had piled up against the glass. If he'd stayed home and waited for the storm to blow over like his wife had asked him to, he wouldn't be standing in the ranch house his father had built with the still-warm body of a man he'd just shot and killed.

Finally, he turned. The dead man—a boy probably no older than Talbott's teenage grandson—still clutched the pistol. Clifford recognized the handgun as his old S&W Model 10 revolver, which he'd left behind in the bedroom chest of drawers.

He glanced away from the body. The police needed to be told, but there was no way to call them unless he got back in his truck and drove to Cañoncito, where he should be able to either get a signal for his cell phone or borrow a phone from someone in the village.

Talbott's wife was a big fan of television detective shows, so Clifford had learned that it was best not to touch anything at a crime scene. He left the Remington rifle on the kitchen counter, banked the woodstove to lower the fire, and went to his truck, wading through a good foot and a half of snow past the motor-cycle parked near the porch.

He'd made it to the ranch in four-wheel drive, but it had been slow going. With wet snow still coming down, he decided to put chains on the tires before starting out. He drove the truck into the barn, turned on the single bare lightbulb that dangled from a roof joist, and got to work, his hands still shaking from what he had done.

He got the chains snapped on and started for Cañoncito. Blowing snow cut his visibility down to less than ten feet, and the truck headlights couldn't penetrate enough to give him a fix on the road. He reduced his speed to a slow and steady five miles an hour and used the vague outline of the fence line bordering the county road to keep himself on track. The bad driving conditions worsened his already jangled nerves. He sat bolt upright, gripping the steering wheel with all his strength, looking for any obstruction up ahead.

An hour passed before he began the descent into the narrow canyon that sheltered Cañoncito. He rounded the last curve where the pavement started. Soon the train tracks and the streambed came into view, and Clifford let out a sigh of relief, which turned into a lump in his throat when he spotted a police car with flashing emergency lights blocking access to a side road.

He slowed to a stop behind the vehicle and flashed his headlights. A deputy sheriff got out and walked to the truck.

"This road is closed, sir," the deputy said after Clifford lowered his window. "If you live on it, I'll need to see some ID before I can let you through."

"I don't live here," Clifford said, wondering how to tell an officer of the law that he'd just killed a person.

The deputy pointed toward the paved road that crossed the streambed and the railroad tracks. "Then you'll have to move on."

"No, you don't understand," Clifford said. "I need you or another police officer to go with me to my ranch up on the mesa."

"Is there someone in need of immediate emergency assistance?" the deputy asked.

Clifford shook his head, took a deep breath, and worked out what he needed to say before speaking. "I'm trying to tell you that a man broke into my house, started a fire in the stove, cooked and ate some of my food, and tried to shoot me when I showed up. I killed him."

The deputy's friendly expression vanished and his hand found the pistol grip of his .45. "When did this happen?"

"Just now," Clifford said.

The deputy drew his weapon and opened the driver's door to Clifford's vehicle. "Keep your hands where I can see them. You say you killed this person?"

Clifford raised his hands above his head. "Yes, with my hunting rifle, right between the eyes."

"Where's the weapon?"

"I left it at the ranch."

"Do you have any other weapons on your person or in the truck?"

"No."

"Step out of the vehicle," the deputy ordered.

Clifford climbed down from the cab of his truck. "Are you arresting me?"

"Open your jacket and turn around."

Clifford did as he was told. The deputy patted him down for weapons, cuffed him, took his wallet, and put him in the backseat of the police car behind a protective cage. He relayed Clifford's driver's license information to a dispatcher, asked for a records check, and then turned in his seat and read Clifford his rights.

Clifford said he understood them, didn't need a lawyer, and would answer any questions.

"This person you shot, did you know him?" The deputy held a tiny tape recorder in his hand.

"No, I never saw him before."

"In your own words, tell me exactly what happened."

"I drove to my ranch and when I got there I saw that somebody had smashed the glass to the porch door and the lights were on inside the house. I took my rifle off the rear window rack of my truck and went to see who it was. I was sort of thinking that maybe somebody had broken in to get out of the cold. In this kind of weather it didn't make much sense to think that somebody had driven to such an out-of-the-way place to rob me."

"Go on."

"There was a motorcycle parked outside next to the porch, so I called out a couple of times and even went back and sounded my truck horn hoping to get the attention of whoever was inside. But the wind was howling so bad I guess he didn't hear me."

"A motorcycle was parked outside?" the deputy asked with heightened interest. "Do you know what kind?"

"I didn't pay it no mind. Anyway, I went inside and here was this young kid, no more than eighteen or nineteen. He had my old barn coat wrapped around his shoulders and was sitting in my easy chair with my Smith and Wesson pistol that I keep in a bedroom dresser pointed at me. He raised the pistol as if to shoot me and I shot him first."

"Do you remember the make of the motorcycle?" the deputy asked.

"I don't pay any attention to those contraptions," Clifford said with a shake of his head.

"What did you do after you shot him?"

"I put chains on my truck tires and drove straight here so I could call the police. Then I saw you and stopped. I didn't touch anything at the ranch, except to throw up in the sink and damp down the fire. I just left that boy sitting there, dead in my chair."

Clifford choked up and paused to collect himself, but his voice broke anyway. "In my mind's eye it's a terrible thing to see."

"Now, just relax, Mr. Talbott," the deputy said soothingly. He turned away, keyed his radio microphone, and spoke to someone in code.

"Bring him to my twenty now," a voice on the radio replied when the deputy had finished.

"Ten-four."

"Will I have to go to jail?" Clifford asked as the deputy drove down the snowpacked dirt road. The thought scared him. Although he was still strong and healthy, he was seventy years old and the only gangbangers, criminals, and drug addicts he'd ever seen were on television news shows or on TV dramas.

The deputy nodded. "At the very least you'll be transported to the jail and booked."

"Is that necessary?"

"Yes, it is. If the facts jibe with the statement you gave me, you may only be held overnight. But if the facts don't agree, you'll need to go before a judge and ask for bail."

"I shot only in self-defense."

"That may well be," the deputy said. "But I took you into custody, cuffed you, and read you your rights. That constitutes an arrest and I can't undo it. You will be booked."

"What are my chances that I'll be let go?"

"I can't say for certain, but the rule of law says that a person has a right to defend himself when his home has been invaded and he has reason to believe his life is in danger. If your story holds up, your chances may be good. But first, you'll be questioned, officers will be sent to the crime scene, evidence will be gathered, and the district attorney and medical investigator will be called in."

Clifford sighed. "Can I call my wife in Moriarty?"

"No, sir, that will have to wait." The deputy slowed to a stop at the end of a long lane where police vehicles were parked in front of a manufactured home with a wooden deck.


Don Mielke followed the yellow crime scene tape that Clayton Istee had strung from the side of the double-wide where Brian Riley had left footprints in the snow to an abandoned well house where the footprints ended. There he found Istee and

Ramona Pino working by the light of battery-powered flood lamps, rigging a canvas tarp over the partially caved-in roof of the well house.

"There's someone you need to talk to right now," Mielke said when Clayton had finished tying off a rope to the trunk of a nearby tree.

"Who's that?" Clayton asked.

"A rancher by the name of Clifford Talbott may have shot and killed Brian Riley. He's in custody at the double-wide."

Clayton stopped in his tracks. "You're kidding."

Mielke shook his head. "Nope."

"If it's true, it sucks," Ramona said.

"Tell me about it," Mielke replied sourly.

Clayton looked at Ramona. "Can you get started here without me?"

"Sure," Ramona answered.

Clayton picked up the end of the last rope that needed to be tied off, walked to the tree behind the well house, threw the rope over a low branch, and knotted it. Unless the storm turned heavy again, the tarp would do a fairly adequate job of protecting the well house from further snowfall. He looked at Mielke. "Let's go."

Mielke paused as Clayton started toward the double-wide. "Do you want me to send someone help to excavate the snow inside that structure?" he asked Ramona.

"No, thanks," she replied. "There's only room inside for one person at a time."

Mielke turned away and left Pino to her task, which was to first carefully clear out the snow inside the well house, looking for physical evidence along the way. Once the snow was removed, every inch of the structure would be examined, probed, dusted for prints, and if necessary dismantled, in an attempt to find anything that could explain why Brian Riley came back to it during a blinding snowstorm while every cop in the state was looking for him.

Walking through knee-deep snow took effort, and by the time Mielke caught up with Clayton he was short of breath.

"Tell me what you know," Clayton said as Mielke came abreast of him.

"Give me a minute," Mielke replied, gasping for air as Clayton moved effortlessly through the wet, heavy snow without breaking a sweat. He'd read somewhere that during the Indian Wars, Apaches had been known to run fifty miles a day through the blistering summer heat of the Southwestern deserts without stopping for food or water. Watching Istee made him a believer.

As he struggled to keep up with Clayton, Mielke filled him in on Talbott's statement. When they reached the double-wide, the arresting deputy told them that the old man had identified Brian Riley from a driver's license photograph.

Clayton's expression turned sour. "Where is he?"

"In the backseat of my unit," the deputy replied.

"Bring him inside."

The deputy fetched Talbott, removed his handcuffs, and sat him at the kitchen table across from Mielke and Clayton, who gave the man the once-over. No more than five feet eight, Clifford Talbott had thick, stubby fingers, a well-formed upper body, a short neck, and a full head of curly gray hair. He sat with his head bowed and had a morose expression on his face.

"Tell us what happened," Clayton said.

Talbott put his hands in his lap and looked up. "I've done that twice already, and all it does is makes me feel worse about shooting that boy."

"*I* need you to tell your story one more time," Clayton replied. "What you have to say to me might help solve several recent murders."

Talbott's eyes widened. "That boy killed people?"

"I didn't say that," Clayton answered, "and I can't talk about ongoing homicide investigations. Now, please, tell me with as much detail as you can what happened at your ranch."

Once again, Clifford recounted the events that had led to the fatal shooting of Brian Riley. When Talbott finished, Clayton asked if the two had exchanged any words.

"Nary a one," Clifford replied.

"Did you see anything in the room that may have belonged to Riley?"

"I don't recall anything."

"Think hard," Clayton urged.

Talbott brought his hands up from his lap to the table and studied them for a moment. "At the foot of my easy chair there was a backpack. Blue, I think. One of those smaller ones you see high school and college students lugging around."

Clayton smiled. "That's good, Mr. Talbott. Anything else?"

Clifford shook his head. "That's it, I'm afraid. Now am I going to go to jail?"

"We'll keep you here," Mielke answered, "until we can get to your cabin, take a look around, and see if what you've told us can be verified."

"You're going to have a tough time getting to my ranch," Clifford replied. "I came down the mesa in four-wheel drive with chains on the tires and almost didn't make it."

Mielke stood up. "We'll get there all right. The county has a road grader and a snowplow on the way, and I'm borrowing two Arctic Cat snowmobiles from Search and Rescue."

As he rose, Clayton gave Mielke an approving glance. Calling for special equipment had been a smart move. He stepped around the table to Talbott and placed his hand on the man's shoulder. He may have killed Brian Riley, but in Clayton's mind Clifford Talbott wasn't a murderer.

"Stay with the deputy, Mr. Talbott. If you think of anything else you may have forgotten to tell us, let the deputy know about it."

"I'll do it," Clifford said with great seriousness.

On the deck to the double-wide Clayton stood with Mielke as the snow swirled around them. It was hard to tell how much of it was wind-driven off the fresh accumulation on the ground and how much was falling from the sky.

"I'll handle the crime scene at the ranch," Mielke said.

"Good deal."

"Our mobile command center will be here in a few minutes," he added. "There's a drop-down bunk bed in it. Get some sleep before *you* drop dead. I'll wake you if anything important turns up."

"I need to call Sheriff Hewitt and Chief Kerney."

"Already done. Chief Kerney is on his way, but it make take him a while. All the highways are dangerous and there are white-out conditions in some places."

"Where's your boss?" Clayton asked.

Mielke looked up at the sky. "Monitoring the situation from home."

"That's great."

"Are you being sarcastic?"

"No, I am not."

Mielke kept looking at the night sky. "I didn't think so." He knew Clayton had been going almost nonstop since the crack of dawn yesterday. "Take a catnap in the mobile command center."

Although Clayton had no plans to go to sleep, getting off his feet for a spell sounded like a good idea. "I think I will. Send someone to get me when Chief Kerney arrives."

"Sure thing," Mielke replied, lying through his teeth.


Kerney wrestled his truck slowly down his ranch road, hoping the highway had been plowed and sanded, only to find it snowpacked and covered in places by drifts that were almost axle-deep. He pushed on, wipers thudding against the accumulation of wet snow on the windshield, heater blasting away to clear the fog off the side windows. In all his years in Santa Fe, he'd never seen a winter storm of such magnitude. It had to be a fifty-, maybe even a hundred-year event.

Where the highway connected to the Interstate, he turned onto the freshly plowed and sanded frontage road and made his way without delay to Cañoncito. At the turnoff to the Riley double-wide, he talked briefly with the deputy at the roadblock. The deputy told him that a grader and a snowplow were halfway down the country road to the crime scene with Major Mielke and one of his investigators following behind on borrowed Arctic Cat snowmobiles, that Clifford Talbott, the confessed killer of Brian Riley, was at the residence under watch, that Ramona Pino was excavating the well house, and Clayton Istee was catching twenty winks in the S.O. mobile command center.

At the double-wide Kerney sat down across the kitchen table from Clifford Talbott. He knew Talbott from several spring and fall works, the semiannual cattle roundups that both men had participated in at ranches on the Galisteo Basin. In the vast stretches of rural New Mexico, there remained a long-standing tradition for ranchers, cowboys, and their families to congregate twice a year at the various spreads to gather, brand, and sort out livestock to be sold at auction, held over for breeding, or kept for private sale to other stockmen.

Talbott's small ranch bordered the basin, and he had always been a neighbor to count on when it came to lending a hand. Last fall, Kerney had worked a long, dust-choked day with Talbott branding and tagging calves at one of the largest ranches on the basin. Talbott had been cheerful and talkative, and had pulled his share of the weight when it came to getting the work done. Kerney had enjoyed his company.

"How are you holding up?" Kerney asked.

"I don't know," Talbott replied, looking rather hangdog. "I sure didn't set out to kill that boy, Kerney. If he hadn't raised that pistol at me, I never would have fired. They say I have to go to jail. I don't know what's going to happen to me after that."

"It will all get worked out."

Talbott looked around the room and glanced at the deputy who'd positioned himself by the front door. "Why are they keeping me here? Whose place is this, anyway?"

"Just be patient," Kerney replied.

Talbott shook his head. "The idea of jail scares the bejesus out of me, Kerney. I've been asking, but they won't even let me call a lawyer, my wife, my minister, or my son over in Tucumcari."

"How long have you been held here?" Kerney asked.

"It's going on two hours since I told the deputy what happened."

Kerney did a quick mental calculation. Under normal circumstances, Talbott would have been booked and processed at the county detention center and allowed his phone call by now.

"Who do you want me to call for you?" he asked.

"My wife, Enid."

"Won't telling her what happened upset her?"

"She'll be upset some, but she's a strong gal. Just tell her to trust in the Lord, stay put at home close to the phone, and to call our minister."

"Give me the phone number."

Talbott broke into a relieved smile and rattled off his number. Outside on the deck, where the winds had quieted down and light flakes in a clearing night sky were floating lazily to the ground, Kerney made the call. Enid Talbott answered after the first ring. Kerney identified himself, told her there had been a shooting at the family's ranch, and her husband was unharmed but a police investigation was under way.

"What happened?" Enid Talbott asked breathlessly.

"I'm not at liberty to say, Mrs. Talbott. Your husband would like you to stay at home and not attempt to come to Santa Fe. Do as he asks, ma'am, the highways are treacherous. He also wants you to call your minister and tell him about the shooting. Does he have a special reason to ask you to do that?"

"Probably because our minister is also the chaplin for the Moriarty Police Department and he might be able to find out more about what's going on."

"I see."

"Is Clifford in trouble?"

"That's a possibility, Mrs. Talbott."

"Is someone dead?"

"An investigator from the Santa Fe Sheriff's Office will be in touch with you as soon as they know more about the situation."

"Can't *you* tell me more?" Enid Talbott pleaded.

"I'm sorry, I cannot."

After advising Enid Talbott to call a friend to keep her company, Kerney disconnected. He walked to the barn, where Detective Matt Chacon was in the tack room working under the overhead glare of a bare lightbulb. From the doorway Kerney watched Matt use a pry bar to loosen a slat from the wall and poke his hand inside to feel around.

"Find anything?" Kerney asked.

Matt turned around. "Nothing yet, Chief. But the nails holding this board in place were of a different type and looked newer, so I thought I better check to see if something was stashed inside the wall."

Kerney nodded. "Good thinking, Sergeant."

Detective Matt Chacon blinked in surprise. "Excuse me?"

Kerney smiled. "I'm giving you a heads-up. You're about to be promoted."

Matt cracked a big, boyish grin. "Unbelievable."

"It's well deserved, Matt. As of next week, you're the new Property Crimes Unit supervisor." Kerney paused. "The sky is clearing and the temperature is dropping fast. Don't stay out in the cold too long, Sergeant Chacon."

Matt nodded and kept grinning. "Yes, sir. Thank you, sir."

Kerney returned to the double-wide and followed the crime scene tape to the well house. Sergeant Ramona Pino was crawling out of the structure on her hands and knees. Her nose and cheeks were bright red from the cold, and the winter coveralls she wore were soaking wet.

"How's it going, Sergeant?"

Ramona stood under the jerry-rigged canopy, brushed some snow off her coveralls, and shook her head. "It's too early to tell, Chief. I'm still excavating snow."

"That's enough for tonight, Sergeant. This can wait until morning. I want you to head back to the double-wide and get yourself dried off and warmed up."

"I can keep going, Chief."

"A half-frozen detective sergeant is of no use to me." Kerney flipped open his cell phone and asked for a deputy to be sent to his twenty to protect the crime scene. "Head out, Sergeant. I'll stay here until the deputy arrives."

The sound of footsteps breaking through the frozen crust of the snow drew Kerney's attention. Clayton stepped under the canopy into the light. He looked worn down, and in spite of the cold his face had little color to it.

"I thought you were getting some rest," Kerney said.

"Can't sleep." In truth, in spite of trying to force himself to stay awake, Clayton had fallen asleep, only to have a spooky dream startle him back into consciousness. In it, Tim Riley, wearing a kerchief headband, knee-high buckskin boots, and a painted leather war shirt, chanted a death song.

Why had he dreamt that Tim Riley was an Apache warrior singing a song no white eyes should know? And why had there been a faceless women in the dream laughing soundlessly as Riley sang?

Clayton knew that if he couldn't shake off Riley's ghost he would have to have a ghost medicine ceremony performed after he got back to the Rez. He turned on his flashlight, walked to the well house, bent low, looked inside, and glanced back at Ramona. "I'll take a turn."

Kerney gave Clayton a measured look. "No, you will not. We'll pick this up in the morning. Go back to the double-wide with Sergeant Pino."

Too tired to argue, Clayton yawned, shrugged, turned on his heel, and trudged away.

Kerney gestured at Ramona to follow. When both officers disappeared in the darkness, he took a peek inside the well house. There was maybe a foot of snow left to remove before any close inspection could be made. Parts of an old well motor were partially exposed under the intact section of roof at the back of the structure, and there was a rusted section of pipe leaning against a half-rotted wall. Clearly the well had been abandoned years ago.

Kerney couldn't even hazard a good guess about what had once been secreted away in the dilapidated, abandoned structure. But whatever it was, apparently it had become a catalyst for murder. Counting Brian Riley and Denise's unborn child, six dead so far. He wondered if there would be more.

The wind picked up and felt like a raw, icy slap against his face. It was a hell of a night to be outside for any reason at all, including murder.

At Clifford Talbott's ranch, Don Mielke climbed off the Arctic Cat and told the snowplow driver and road-grader operator to stay with their equipment. The two men huddled together in the cab of the snowplow to stay warm. Stiff from the cold, Mielke gestured to his senior investigator, Tony Morales, to join him.

Morales killed the engine to his snowmobile and grabbed his equipment bag. After a quick look at the license plate on the Harley to confirm that the motorcycle belonged to Brian Riley, and a glance at the broken porch door glass, the two men drew their sidearms and cautiously entered the ranch house. The corpse in the easy chair was clearly dead, so they did a fast sweep of the premises before returning to the front room.

The slug from a hunting rifle, which was on the kitchen counter just where Talbott said he'd left it, can do lethal damage to a target several hundred yards away. From a range of less than ten feet, the results were lethal and god-awful. The entry wound above Brian Riley's eyes from the round of Talbott's bolt-action Remington .30–06 was almost perfectly cylindrical. But the exit wound in the back of his head was an explosion of blood, brains, and bone that had penetrated and saturated the upholstery of the easy chair and blown a pulse of blood splatter onto the far wall.

Riley's bowels had released at the time of death, and the stench of Talbott's vomit still lingered, so the room smelled as bad as it looked.

Mielke gave the body a careful once-over while Morales took photographs. Riley's hand was wrapped around the pistol grip of the revolver, and an empty, handmade leather-tooled holster was in his lap. He was wearing a heavy wool sweater at least two sizes too big and had an old faded barn coat draped over his shoulders. On the floor to his right, next to a leg of the chair, was a backpack.

Mielke left the backpack untouched and made a thorough search of the small house. In the bedroom, dresser drawers had been pulled out and left open. In the kitchen cabinets, dust on the shelves had been disturbed. A dirty plate, a gummy fork, and a pot with the remains of gooey macaroni and cheese stuck to the sides sat on the counter. In the bottom of the trash bucket was the empty macaroni and cheese box. A pot of water that had boiled down to almost nothing sat on the woodstove, and an empty coffee mug was on the lamp table next to the easy chair.

On the front porch Mielke found an adjustable wrench that Riley had likely used to break the glass to the door. Back inside, Tony Morales was busy bagging and tagging the cookware, plate, utensils, and trash.

"Have you finished photographing the body?" he asked.

Morales nodded.

He handed Morales the wrench to bag and tag, went to Riley's body, took the Smith & Wesson revolver out of the dead boy's hand, and opened the cylinder. The handgun was fully loaded. Mielke held it up for Morales to see.

"I think this is just what it appears to be, Major," Morales said. "Straightforward self-defense."

"Apparently so." Mielke reached down, picked up the backpack, opened it, dumped the contents—which looked to be only clothing—on the floor. He searched through the smaller side pockets, found a large envelope containing currency, put the envelope aside, and pawed through the wadded-up, dirty, smelly clothing looking for anything in the pockets. All he found was a pack of matches advertising a nightclub in downtown Albuquerque and a plastic bag with a small amount of grass. He dropped the empty backpack on top of the pile of dirty clothes.

"Nada?" Morales asked.

"Nada." Mielke flipped open his cell phone. Although Talbott had told him it wouldn't work, he tried to call out anyway, but there was no signal. He keyed his handheld, got dead air on the S.O. frequency, and switched through the remaining police and emergency channels with the same results.

"Are we cut off from radio contact?" Morales asked.

"That's affirmative." The room had cooled down quite a bit since their arrival. Mielke checked the woodstove, opened the vent to increase the airflow, and added some wood to the bed of hot embers. "You're going to have to stay here while I go back and report in. If the medical investigator is there, I'll send him to you right away. Meanwhile, dust for prints. Make sure you get the handgun, the rifle, and the wrench."

"Ten-four, Major."

Morales had used both a digital camera and a 35mm Pentax to photograph the crime scene. Mielke asked Morales for the digital camera so Kerney and Clayton could see what the crime scene looked like. With the camera safely zipped into an inside pocket of his parka, he stepped over to the kitchen cabinet that contained foodstuffs, reached to the back of the top shelf, pulled out a full pint bottle of whiskey he'd spotted earlier, unscrewed the top, and took a swallow. It felt good and warm going down. He held the bottle out to Morales. "Go ahead, we've earned it."

Morales hesitated, took the bottle from Mielke's hand, tilted it to his lips, and let the liquid run down his throat, wondering if the major would be taking the whiskey bottle with him. On more than one occasion he'd watched Mielke down eight shots in a row at the FOP and get totally stinking drunk.

Morales held the bottle out to Mielke.

Mielke shook his head as he went to the door. "Clean off the fingerprints and put it back in the cupboard. I'll be back as soon as I can."

After returning to the double-wide with Ramona Pino, Clayton forced himself to stay awake. He wanted direct confirmation from Don Mielke that the dead man in Clifford Talbott's ranch house was truly Brian Riley.

In the mobile command vehicle, he talked with Ramona for a while until she left to go home and get some sleep. Then he spent some time with Kerney filling him in on how close he'd come to finding Riley in Albuquerque, and how an Albuquerque cop had let Riley waltz right into the Minerva Stanley Robocker crime scene and drive away on the Harley.

Kerney, in turn, told Clayton about his analysis of the letters Denise Riley had written to her sister during the years she'd supposedly lived far away from Santa Fe, at times in foreign countries.

"When will you hear something?" Clayton asked.

"Tomorrow, hopefully." Kerney looked at his wristwatch. "But maybe not. With all this snowfall, except for essential personnel, the governor will probably shut down all state offices. I imagine the mayor and the county commission will do the same."

Clayton suddenly remembered he'd high-ended the Lincoln County S.O. unit on a boulder and had asked Mielke to send a tow truck to free it. "Do you know the status of the vehicle I was driving?" He wasn't about to claim Riley's assigned S.O. 4×4 as his own.

"It's at the county yard in Santa Fe," Kerney said, "and not going anywhere for a while. It has a broken front axle, a leaking radiator, two flat front tires, and a bent wheel. Paul Hewitt told me you ran into a deer recently and put your marked unit in the shop. Seems you're rather hard on your assigned vehicles."

"That deer ran into *me*. Can I borrow a P.D. vehicle?"

Kerney thought it over. "I've got a clunker in the headquarters parking lot that you can use."

"Thanks a lot," Clayton retorted, unable to keep a sarcastic tone out of his voice.

Kerney smiled pleasantly and was about to respond when a knock at the command vehicle door interrupted their exchange. The door opened to reveal the arrival of the medical investigator, an MD named Mark Trask who worked full-time for the state health department and did occasional on-call work for the Office of the Medical Investigator, headquartered in Albuquerque.

"Do you have a body for me to inspect?" Trask asked, stomping his boots on the carpet to shake off some clinging snow. Mark weighed in at a hefty two hundred and fifty pounds on a five-six frame, so the RV shook slightly underfoot.

"Not here," Kerney said.

Trask flipped back the hood of his parka. His gray walrus mustache was wet with condensation and his eyes were tearing from the cold. "Then where might I find the deceased, Chief?"

"About five miles up on top of the mesa," Kerney replied.

"Ah, and how am I to get there in this blizzard?"

"We're in the process of securing appropriate transportation for you," Kerney answered.

"Such as?"

"It could be a road grader, a snowplow, or as a passenger on a snowmobile."

"Wonderful," Trask said with a grimace, eyeing Clayton. "And who do we have here?"

Kerney said. "Sergeant Istee, this is Dr. Mark Trask."

Trask reached out and firmly shook Clayton's hand. "Pleased to meet you. Have either of you viewed the remains of the deceased?"

"No," Kerney replied. "Don Mielke and one of his investigators are there now. We're waiting for a report."

Feeling as though he could fall asleep on his feet, Clayton was about to step outside and suck down some cold air when the door opened again and a man stepped inside. Tall with an angular face, he quickly took off his coat and nodded at Kerney and Trask before turning his attention to Clayton.

"We haven't met. I'm Kirt Latimer, ADA."

"Sergeant Clayton Istee, Lincoln County S.O."

"Don Mielke told me on the phone this might be a case of justifiable homicide. Is that correct?"

"It's likely." Kerney turned to the built-in desk and picked up a palm-size tape recorder and several microcassette tapes, and handed them to Latimer. "Tape one is Clifford Talbott's voluntary statement made immediately after he was taken into custody. Tape two is an in-depth interview with Talbott conducted soon after his arrest."

Latimer juggled the cassette tapes in his hand. "But nothing of the suspect's story has yet to be confirmed."

"We're waiting on Don Mielke," Clayton said, "who is at the crime scene with one of his investigators."

"What can you tell me about Talbott?"

"I'll answer that," Kerney said. "He's a seventy-something white male, married, with one adult son, who lives in Moriarty. He has two grandchildren, a boy and a girl, I think, and was a state livestock inspector for thirty-five years before he retired. He owns a small ranch on the mesa that he inherited from his father and runs a herd of cattle on it during the spring and summer months."

"How do you know all that?" Clayton asked.

"Because I've met Clifford Talbott several times before," Kerney replied.

"Do you think he's a cold-blooded killer?" Latimer inquired.

"Cold-blooded, no. But that's only one of the fifty-seven varieties of killers I've met over the years."

Conversation ended when Latimer started playing the tape recording of Talbott's confession, and Clayton used the moment to put on his coat and step outside the command center. He took a deep breath and listened for the wind, but all was still and quiet. Heavy snow not only buried everything in a white blanket, it made the world miraculously fall silent for a time. It was a soundlessness like no other and always served to remind Clayton of how needlessly noisy life had become.

The momentary stillness passed with the faint but gradually

growing sound of an engine, and soon Clayton could discern the full-throated, barely muffled growl of a snowmobile coming down the long driveway to the Riley double-wide. He watched as Mielke brought it to a stop next to the cluster of police vehicles parked in front of the deck to the double-wide.

Clayton walked through deep snow to greet Mielke. He waited to speak until Mielke removed his goggles, flipped back the hood of his parka, and took off his ski mask. "How did it look?" he asked.

"It appears to be just the way Talbott said it would be, and I don't think anything was staged."

"Can you confirm that Brian Riley is the deceased?"

"There's no doubt about it. I saw his body. I searched his backpack and personal items and only found money and a small quantity of grass, nothing else." Mielke unzipped his parka, reached inside, brought out a digital camera, and nodded toward the command center RV. "Who's here?"

"Mark Trask, a medical investigator, and ADA Latimer are inside with Chief Kerney."

"Good." He waved the camera at Clayton. "I've got photographs of the crime scene we can download to a computer."

"Let's go take a look."

Inside the mobile command center, Mielke downloaded directly to a computer software program that ran the photographs as a slide show. The four men clustered around Mielke in front of the monitor as he talked them through his preliminary investigation at the scene.

"Personally," Mielke said, "I think that if Talbott hadn't entered his house with his rifle, Riley would have shot him."

"I believe I'll declare the subject dead based on your graphic photographs and go home to a snifter of brandy," Trask said.

"You have to personally inspect the body, Mark," Latimer replied.

Trask sighed dramatically. "I know, but I'm just not a cold-weather person. Riding on the back of a snowmobile in a blizzard holds no appeal."

"I've got a grader and a snowplow working on the country road from here to Talbott's ranch," Mielke said. "We should be able to travel by four-by-four to the crime scene within the hour. If we can't get an ambulance up there, we'll bring the body out the same way."

Trask smiled. "That sounds much more agreeable."

Mielke eyed Latimer. "Does this give you enough to make a decision on how to proceed?"

"I'll meet with him, but I'm not willing to decline to prosecute until your investigation is complete. At best, I'll think about filing an involuntary manslaughter charge, but I want him held overnight and brought before a magistrate judge for a preliminary hearing first thing in the morning. If everything continues to check out by then, I may agree to a reasonable bond."

"With this storm, the courts may be closed tomorrow," Mielke said.

"I'll find a judge."

Mielke turned to Kerney. "Do you have a question, Chief?"

"Is there any reason to believe that Talbott shot Riley, got his Smith and Wesson revolver from the bedroom, and put it in the dead boy's hand?"

Mielke used the mouse to scroll through the sequence of photographs taken of Riley's body. "As you can see, nothing looks staged. Tony Morales, my senior investigator, is dusting for prints. If we find Riley's fingerprints on the bedroom dresser where Talbott kept his revolver, that will be fairly conclusive evidence that the weapon wasn't planted on his body."

Kerney nodded. "That makes sense." He turned to Clayton. "Is there anything you'd like to add, Sergeant?"

"If anyone has any viable suspects in the murders of Deputy

Tim Riley, his wife Denise, Minerva Stanley Robocker, and APD Officer Judy Connors, I'd love to know who they are."

A tight-lipped silence greeted Clayton's frustration.

"We'll get the investigation back on track tomorrow," Kerney promised.

Latimer, Trask, and Mielke nodded in agreement and left the command center.

"Let's call it a night," Kerney said.

"I'll sleep here in the command center," Clayton replied.

"That's unacceptable. You're coming home with me."

"Can we even get to your place?"

"I'll just bet we can."

Driving home with three feet of fresh snow on the ground wasn't the smartest decision Kerney ever made, but he managed to pull it off without getting stuck, although it took almost two hours to travel the fifteen or so miles from Cañoncito to his ranch.

Sara had all the outside lights on, and most of the inside lights were burning brightly as well, so during the slow ascent up the ranch road from the canyon, the house was an inviting beacon in the night.

Kerney parked, breathed a sigh of relief, and looked over at Clayton, who'd fallen asleep ten minutes into the drive, with his head resting against his wadded-up coat. He hadn't moved a muscle since. Kerney shook Clayton hard to wake him.

Slowly Clayton opened his eyes. "That was speedy," he said, talking through a yawn.

"Not really. You want something to eat? There's some left-over green chili stew in the refrigerator."

"No, thanks. I think I'll take a shower, call Grace, and go to bed."

"Okay." Kerney killed the engine.

Clayton didn't move.

"What is it?" Kerney asked.

"I'm flat out of ideas on how to catch this killer."

"We haven't exhausted all possible leads yet. Denise's letters could give us something, and maybe the well house will yield some evidence. Sergeant Pino will be out there first thing in the morning."

"Tell her to be very careful working in that snow," Clayton said. "Moisture can easily destroy latent fingerprints and make it almost impossible to find any trace evidence."

"Sergeant Pino is up to the task, Clayton."

Clayton smiled and put his hand on the door handle. "Yeah, you're right."

Inside, Clayton made his excuses to Sara and went immediately to the guest quarters. In the kitchen, Kerney joined Sara for a cup of tea. A partially destroyed gut from a drug dealer's bullet had pretty much done away with Kerney's coffee-drinking days.

Sara reached out and touched Kerney's cheek. "I was starting to get worried about you."

"It was slow going, but we made it. Clayton needs sleep. I ordered him off duty but that didn't seem to work. So I decided that I didn't want him staying anywhere else but here tonight."

Sara's eyes danced. "That sounds remarkably like what a concerned parent would do."

"That's a good thing, right?"

"A very good thing. Jack Burke called to say he would be out at first light plowing his roads with his grader. He said if you're not in a fired-up hurry to get to work early, he'd have ours cleared by eight o'clock."

Jack was Kerney's closest neighbor, friend, and the man who'd sold him two sections of ranchland. He owned an old Highway

Department surplus road grader that he used to keep his ranch roads in good condition. "Bless him." He took Sara's hand. "You seem in a good mood."

"I'm loving this storm. It reminds me of Montana winters on the ranch when we would be snowbound for a week. There were days when nothing moved, when even my father was forced to stay inside until the sky cleared and the winds died down. Those days were magic for me and my brother. The land an unbroken white blanket. The mountains frosted cones. The ranch house cozy and warm. Me in the kitchen with my mother learning how to make biscuits from scratch."

"Most people nowadays will never have those kind of memories."

Sara squeezed Kerney's hand. "Well, we do."

Kerney raised his wife's hand to his lips. The Sara he loved was back, at least for a while. There would be rough spots to come, but it was heartening to see her eyes dance and hear that lovely country lilt creep into her voice. "Let's keep making those memories," he said.

# ChapterEleven

Overnight the tail end of the blizzard backed into northern New Mexico and dumped an additional six inches of snow on Santa Fe County. At dawn Kerney broke his way through the frozen crust of deep snow to the barn and spent the better part of an hour cleaning out stalls and feeding the horses and Patrick's pony.

Kerney had kept the stock inside the barn for protection during the storm, and they were restless and in need of exercise. One by one he turned them loose in the corrals, and they pawed, kicked, pranced, stuck their muzzles into the snow, and high-stepped through the drifts near the fence line. Patrick's pony, Pablito, bucked his way around the perimeter fence, whinnying as he went.

Kerney watched their spirited antics for a few minutes before deciding to leave them outside until after breakfast. As he trudged back to the house, the depth of the snow made him doubt that Jack Burke would have the ranch road plowed by eight o'clock as he had promised. In fact, Kerney doubted that much of anything would be moving in northern New Mexico for at least another day.

He shucked off his coat and boots in the mudroom, sat at the kitchen table, downed a big glass of orange juice, and listened for sounds of movement from Sara, Patrick, or Clayton. All was quiet. He called the regional dispatch center and asked for a report on road conditions.

"It's a big mess, Chief," the dispatcher said. "The Interstate is shut down, none of the major city arterials have been plowed or sanded, there are six-foot snowdrifts on some of the county roads, and we've got people calling 911 to report that they are stuck in their driveways and would I please send someone to help. There are motorists in ditches, none of the tow truck operators are moving, officers can't make it to work, and those who have are attempting to transport emergency medical personnel to the hospital or rescue stranded motorists along the Interstate."

"Put me through to the shift commander."

"Deputy Chief Otero is ten-eighty-one if you want to talk to him."

Somehow Larry had made it to police headquarters. "Ask him to stand by for my phone call," Kerney said.

"Ten-four."

He called and talked to Otero, who told him that the graveyard shift had been held over to pull a double, and only about half of the first shift had reported for duty.

"I've told all commanders to respond to emergency calls, only if we can even get to those locations," Larry added, "and I've authorized all nonessential civilian personnel to take a snow day."

"Very good."

"Also, the state police report that the governor is going to declare a state of emergency. He's calling out the National Guard to assist."

"That will help a lot."

"Sergeant Pino and Detective Chacon are on their way to the Cañoncito crime scene. Pino wants to know if you have contact with Sergeant Istee."

"Tell her affirmative and to proceed without us. We'll be at her twenty later in the morning. Speaking of Sergeant Istee, he needs to borrow a vehicle. What do we have on the lot?"

"If he can get here, there's an unmarked Crown Vic with a rebuilt motor he can use."

"I'll let him know," Kerney said. "Thanks, Larry."

"I'm here if you need me," Otero said before disconnecting.

Kerney checked the pantry and refrigerator to see what he could whip up for breakfast. He had no idea how long Clayton would sleep, so he decided he would make blueberry pancakes— one of Patrick's all-time favorite meals—and keep a batch warming in the oven for Clayton.

He put the teakettle on the stove, got the coffeepot started for Sara, and was halfway through his prep when Patrick came into the kitchen still wearing his pajamas and holding his copy of *Herman and Poppy Go Singing in the Hills*, a storybook of the friendship between a horse and a pony.

"Good morning, scout." Kerney picked up his son and gave him a smooch. "It's blueberry pancakes for breakfast."

"Yummy." Patrick grinned and threw his arms around Kerney's neck. "Mom says it's a snow day and everybody has to stay home."

"Some of us can't, sport." Kerney lowered Patrick to the floor. "But the time is coming when I won't have to go to work anymore."

"And you won't be a police chief anymore," Patrick added.

"That's right," Kerney said, wondering how *that* was going to feel.

He poured Patrick a glass of orange juice and sat him at the kitchen table. Between sips of his juice, Patrick read the fantastic adventures of Herman and Poppy aloud. Only Sara's arrival temporarily interrupted the telling of the tale. Clayton followed along soon after, looking a whole lot better after a good night's sleep.

Kerney put the finishing touches on breakfast and served it up while Patrick regaled the table with the part of the story where Poppy the pony goes missing and Herman the horse goes looking for his friend.

Clayton said it was one of the best stories he'd ever heard.

Patrick replied there was one that was even better and hurried off to his room. He returned with his all-time favorite book, a dog-eared copy of *Pablito the Pony*, and promptly started reading it to Clayton.

After breakfast, all hands pitched in to clear the table and stack the dishwasher. Chores done, the foursome went to the barn to put the horses back in their stalls. On their return to the house, Jack Burke and his road grader came into view. From the front courtyard they watched as he cut a swath in the snow wide enough for one car to get through and cleared the driveway to the ranch house.

At Sara's insistence, Jack came inside for a cup of coffee. Patrick promptly climbed onto Jack's lap as he sat at the kitchen table and asked if he could have a ride on the road grader. With Sara's permission, Jack agreed to give him a short ride to the lip of the canyon and back.

"Can I drive it?" Patrick asked.

"You sure can," Jack said, getting a nod from Kerney.

Patrick's eyes lit up. He jumped off Jack's lap, ran to the mudroom, returned with his boots and cold weather gear in hand, and started getting ready to go back outside.

"Guess I'd better hurry up and finish this coffee," Jack said with a grin.

"We have to go as well," Kerney said, gesturing toward Clayton. "Thanks for plowing our road."

"No need for thanks," Jack replied. "I like driving that big old grader about as much as Patrick does."

Bundled up and ready to go, three men and one excited little boy trooped out into the fierce glare of sunlight bouncing off the thick layer of snow.

In the truck, Kerney lowered the visor, honked the horn, waved at Patrick and Jack, and started down the road. Even with the plowing Jack had done, it was slow going. Kerney made the turn onto the highway, looked at Clayton, and grinned.

"What?" Clayton asked.

"I was just thinking that you look a hell of a lot better once you get a good night's sleep."

Clayton smiled slightly. "Too bad it didn't make me any smarter. Maybe then I'd have some ideas of what we should do to solve the murders."

"Sometimes the solution is in the little details."

Clayton nodded. He'd slept hard until just before he woke, when the dream of Tim Riley dressed as an Apache warrior and the faceless, laughing woman had returned. What did it mean? Why couldn't he shake free of Riley's ghost? Today he'd worn black jeans and a black wool sweater to protect himself from ghost sickness. But maybe it was too late.

"Are you okay?" Kerney asked, noting the dark expression on Clayton's face.

"Yeah, I'm fine," Clayton replied, forcing a smile, trying to make himself believe it.


At the Cañoncito double-wide Ramona Pino and Matt Chacon found an empty fifty-five-gallon oil drum in the stables and rolled it over the snow to the well house. At the woodshed they gathered up and carried armloads of kindling and firewood until they had enough to keep a good fire going for several hours. Matt got the fire started with blank paper from a writing tablet, and soon the warmth from the drum had noticeably raised the temperature under the improvised canopy that had been put up hastily during yesterday's storm to protect the area from additional moisture contamination. But the canopy kept the smoke from rising, and after deciding the extra warmth wasn't worth smoke-filled lungs and watery eyes, the two detectives cut it down.

Once the smoke had dissipated, Ramona crawled into the well house and turned on the battery-powered camping lantern. The partial roof on the structure and the temporary canopy had helped to keep deep snow from covering the dirt floor, but with a probe she could tell there was still a good twelve inches to dig through.

With the lantern instead of a flashlight and the morning sunlight streaming through the damaged roof, illumination inside the well house was much improved. Ramona did a careful visual inspection of all the surfaces that might have been touched by Brian Riley or anyone else who'd entered the structure, paying particular attention to the door, walls, and the metal parts of the old well motor and pipes that were exposed.

A good investigator knew that a person coming in contact with anything could leave a trace. Knowing what to look for could turn up a critical piece of evidence. It could be a hair, a fiber, a drop of blood, a mark left by a tool, a fingerprint, a footprint, or a toothpick with dried saliva on it. Cases had been solved and murderers convicted based on plant life, insects, and soil samples found at crime scenes.

On the rough-cut boards to the door there were what looked like some short dark hairs, quite possibly from rodents, stuck to the wood. It would be up to the lab to decide if the hairs were human or not. Using tweezers, Ramona removed each hair and bagged it separately.

She dusted for prints on likely surfaces and lifted several good ones from the metal door latch, the old motor, and one of the broken roof joists that hung down five feet above the dirt floor.

The snow accumulation behind the motor had an uneven

indentation that Ramona closely examined. There were several scoop marks in the snow, made possibly by gloved hands. Brian Riley had come here yesterday looking for something, and this looked to be the likely spot.

Using a small trowel, Ramona began removing the snow by scraping away a thin layer at a time. When her trowel scratched something solid, she brushed the snow away to expose some wooden boards frozen to the dirt floor. Gently she pried the frost-covered boards loose and inspected them. There looked to be the outline of fingerprints on one of them. If so, when the frost on the board melted, the prints would mostly likely vanish.

Ramona quickly dusted the impressions, photographed the prints, and then examined the shallow pit the wooden slats had hidden. The earth had been disturbed, as though something had been dug out. A rectangular, dimpled outline around the edge of the pit suggested the object had been about the size of a briefcase.

Ramona photographed the pit, and the flash from her camera reflected off something shiny at one corner that was almost completely covered in dirt. She tried to pick it up with tweezers but couldn't pull it free. Using the trowel, she pried it loose, slipped it off the trowel into a clear plastic bag, and zipped it closed. It was a gold coin, a 1974, one-troy-ounce South African Krugerrand. She put it in her coat pocket along with the other evidence she'd collected and went outside.

"Is it my turn?" Matt Chacon asked, standing next to the fire in the oil drum, looking warm and dry.

"Look at this." Ramona handed Matt the bagged coin.

"A one-ounce Krugerrand. First produced in 1970. The obverse depicts Paul Kruger, the first president of the South African Republic, and the reverse shows the springbok, the national animal. During the apartheid years in South Africa, Krugerrands were banned from the United States."

"I didn't know you were a numismatist." The heat from the fire felt wonderful. Ramona edged closer to the oil drum.

"Hardly that. I earned a coin collection merit badge in Boy Scouts."

"I'm impressed. So how much is it worth?"

"If I remember correctly, Krugerrands contain exact amounts of gold, so the value of each coin is equivalent to the current market price of gold."

"Which is?" Ramona asked.

"You've got me. The price of gold can change daily. It's somewhere over five hundred dollars an ounce, I'd guess. Maybe way over." Matt laughed. "I wish the pennies in my Lincoln collection were worth that much. I'd probably get seventy-five bucks for all of them, max. I like to think of the collection as my emergency cash fund. That's pretty sad, isn't it? Do you think there are any more Krugerrands in there?"

"I don't know," Ramona said, "but it does raise my curiosity to know what else might have been hidden here and why."

"I'll take a look. Finders keepers, right?"

"Get real, Detective," Ramona replied with a smile.

Matt gave the coin back to Ramona and ducked inside the well house.

Using one of the tarps that had served as part of the canopy, Ramona assembled her collected evidence, tagged everything, and filled out the evidence log. She'd just finished up when Matt emerged from the well house holding another bagged coin for her to see. It was contained in a clear plastic sleeve, which had some letters and numbers on it in permanent ink.

"It was buried just a little bit deeper in the pit," he said. "This one is a twenty-dollar U.S. gold piece. It's called a Saint-Gaudens after the man who designed it. These are highly collectible and usually sell way above the value of the gold content."

"What do the numbers and letters on the plastic sleeve mean?" Ramona asked.

"They have nothing to do with the grading of the quality of the coin, which looks to be uncirculated to me."

"Uncirculated is good?"

"About the best there is. It's one step down from brilliant uncirculated. I'm thinking the numbers and letters represent an inventory designation given to the coin by either the owner or a dealer who sold it."

"So give me a guess on its value."

"It could be thousands," Matt replied. "It depends on rarity and condition."

"From the evidence Don Mielke collected at Clifford Talbott's ranch house, Brian Riley was down to his last five thousand dollars in cash," Ramona said. "Do you think he may have come back here for the coins?"

"Maybe, but there were no gold coins listed in the evidence inventory from the ranch house."

"Riley could have hidden the coins in the house before Talbott arrived and shot him. Ask Mielke to send an investigator out there to look."

Matt keyed his handheld and made the request just as Chief Kerney and Sergeant Istee came into sight.

"Good morning," Kerney said as he entered the small clearing. He handed each detective a thermal mug of coffee that had been freshly brewed in the mobile command vehicle. "Bring us up to speed."

Coffee in hand, Ramona talked about their morning finds and showed them the two coins. "It will probably take all day for Detective Chacon and me to finish up here," she added.

"Not if the four of us take shifts," Clayton said.

"That's a good idea," Kerney said. He turned to Ramona.

"Why don't you and Matt head back to the S.O. command vehicle and see what you can find out about any open or cold cases involving stolen gold coins while we take a turn inside the well house. Take the fingerprint evidence with you and run it through any computer database you can think of while you're there."

"Will do," Matt said.

"Have you told her?" Kerney asked Matt with a nod in Ramona's direction.

"Told me what?" Ramona asked.

"No, I haven't," Matt answered.

"Shall I?"

"Go ahead, Chief."

"Sergeant Pino, meet Sergeant Chacon, effective the first of next week. You're losing him to the Property Crimes Unit."

"And you didn't tell me?" Before Matt could answer, she swung around to face Kerney. "Do I get to pick his replacement?"

Kerney nodded, laughed, and slapped Matt on the back. "See how soon you'll be forgotten?"

Grinning from ear to ear, Matt faked a sad head shake.

As the two left the clearing, Ramona continued chewing out Matt for not being forthcoming.

"I'll take the first shift," Clayton said.

"There could be footprints in the frozen ground underneath the hard-packed snow in front of the entrance," Kerney said. "I'll start on that."

"That's a good idea."

Kerney threw some wood onto the fire and picked up a small shovel. "Let's get to it."

The two men worked steadily for an hour without uncovering anything of value. There were no footprints under the packed-down snow in front of the well house door, and the buckets of snow Clayton had removed from inside the well house and melted over the fire contained no trace evidence visible to the naked eye.

As they warmed themselves by the fire, Clayton asked if anyone had inspected the *exterior* of the well house for evidence.

"Not that I know of," Kerney replied.

After a careful but futile up-and-down look at the exterior walls, they returned to the fire burning in the oil drum.

Clayton threw another log on it. "We've been assuming that Riley followed a path to the well house when he came here yesterday. What if he didn't? What if it wasn't a path to begin with and he simply went cross-country."

Kerney looked back through the trees in the direction of the double-wide. "If he did go cross-country, he took a fairly direct route from the residence to the well house."

"This well house hasn't been used in years," Clayton replied. "It was abandoned long before Tim Riley bought the land and moved his double-wide onto the property. Maybe there's an old path. That's where we have the best shot at finding any footprint evidence."

Kerney made a three-sixty scan. The clearing and the well house were in a slight depression on the downslope of a mesa. Below, through a break in the trees, he could see the narrow canyon floor where the railroad tracks followed the creekbed. He looked up at the mesa. Near the top, a quartet of deep arroyos converged into one and snaked down to join with the creek within fifty feet of where he stood.

"What are you thinking?" Clayton asked.

"I'm thinking this well was drilled here to tap into the groundwater supplied by that nearby arroyo. In its time, it would have been a more reliable source of water than the creek. I'm betting it once served a homestead that probably sat below us on the canyon floor."

"The old electric motor inside the well house is stamped with the maker's name and a patent date of 1936," Clayton said.

"I doubt that rural electrification would have reached Cañoncito before then."

Clayton looked at the treetops. "I don't see any electric lines or poles running up here."

"Scavenged long ago," Kerney suggested.

Clayton walked to the edge of the clearing, squatted down, and gazed through the trees at the canyon. "There's a snow-covered mound on the flat just to the left that doesn't fit with the topography. It's just behind a fence. That could be the rubble from the old homestead."

Kerney joined Clayton. "Just eyeballing it, I'd say that mound falls easily within Riley's property boundaries."

Clayton stood, broke off a small dead branch from a piñon tree, walked to a point ten feet east of the tracks through the snow, and marked an X next to a large juniper tree. "The original path is here."

"You're sure of that?" Kerney asked.

"Yep. Coming up from the canyon this is the easiest, most direct route. New growth obscures it in places now, but this is the path. Riley couldn't see it because of all the snow, so he just made a beeline straight to the well house."

"Let's find out if you're right."

Kerney got two shovels and handed one to Clayton. They removed most of the snow quickly, slowing the pace when they reached the last few inches, and then set aside the shovels and brushed away the last of the powder with gloved hands. At the edge of the two-foot-long trench they'd dug there was a heel print clearly visible in the frozen ground. They cleared away more snow until the entire print was visible.

"It could be Brian Riley's shoe print from an earlier visit," Kerney said.

Clayton hunkered down for a closer look.

He'd found partial shoe prints on the porch to Tim Riley's rented cabin in Capitan, and the print in front of his eyes looked identical. "Did Brian Riley have small, narrow feet?"

"I don't know."

"This is an impression of a boot that is no more than a narrow size eight. That's small for a man, plus it looks a hell of a lot like the partial impression I found at the Capitan crime scene."

"Can you make a definitive comparison?" Kerney asked.

"I took photographs of them. They're in my briefcase in your truck."

Kerney called Ramona and asked her to bring Clayton's briefcase to the well house.

"Will do, Chief," Ramona replied.

"Also, where is Brian Riley's body right now?" Kerney asked.

"It's being held at a local mortuary until tomorrow, when it will be sent down to the OMI in Albuquerque for an official autopsy."

"Send an officer to the mortuary ASAP. I want to know what shoes or boots Riley was wearing at the time of his death, and what the size is. Have the officer check Riley's personal effects to see if he had any other footwear, take pictures of the soles of all left-foot shoes, and send them to me at my cell phone number."

"Ten-four, Chief. Anything else?"

"What's happening on your end?"

"No fingerprint hits so far, and there are no open or cold cases we can find in the national data banks that match the gold coins we uncovered. Sergeant Chacon is querying Interpol and a number of law enforcement agencies in foreign countries."

"Very good. See you in a few."

While they waited for Ramona to arrive, Clayton photographed the impression, removed what loose material he could from around it, and then used Ramona's casting kit to build a form. He mixed up a batch of plaster using melted snow, sprayed oil on the form so the material wouldn't bind to it, and poured the mixture into it.

"It should set up in a few minutes," he said as he got to his feet.

Ramona appeared in the clearing. They joined her at the oil barrel, where the fire had burned down almost to embers. As Clayton searched through his briefcase for the photographs, Kerney threw more wood into the barrel and stirred the flames to life with a stick.

"We have a match," Clayton said, handing the photograph to Kerney.

Kerney threw the stick into the fire, looked at the photograph, nodded, and handed it back.

"And if the impression turns out to be from Brian Riley's shoe, that puts him at the Capitan crime scene," Ramona said, "which makes him a very dead prime suspect."

Clayton waved off the possibility with his hand. "You can't convince me that Brian Riley was a natural-born psychopath who killed his father, his stepmother, a police officer, and a young woman who had befriended him, for no apparent reason other than the enjoyment of it."

"He returned to the Robocker crime scene, concealed his identity, and ran from the police," Ramona countered.

"Okay, let's assume for the sake of argument that he is the killer," Clayton said. "He's down to his last five thousand dollars and needs a lot more money than that if he's going to disappear for a very long time. So he lies about his identity to a cop at the Robocker crime scene, jumps on his motorcycle, and drives here through a gathering blizzard to get the gold coins hidden in the well house."

"That makes sense," Ramona said.

"Up to a point it does. But if the coins were here yesterday when Riley came for them, the only logical place they would be today is at the Talbott ranch house. Have the deputies searched it?"

Ramona nodded. "From top to bottom and there wasn't one gold coin to be found."

"So if it wasn't the coins that drew him back here, what did?" Kerney asked.

In response, Clayton shrugged his shoulders and Ramona shook her head.

Kerney's cell phone rang. The incoming call was from the officer who had been sent to the mortuary to take digital photographs of Riley's shoes. He looked at the screen for a moment and then passed the phone to Clayton.

"They aren't a match with the footprint," Clayton said.

"So we're back to zero suspects," Ramona said.

"Not necessarily," Clayton replied. "We need to find someone connected to Tim or Denise Riley who wears men's narrow size eight shoes."

"Oh, goodie," Ramona replied in her sweetest voice. "That *narrows* down the field considerably."

Kerney laughed in spite of himself. "Let's get back to work," he said.

Halfway through Kerney's shift inside the well house, Matt Chacon arrived with news about the coins.

"The Saint-Gaudens is from a ten-year-old heist of an art dealer's personal collection in Brisbane, Australia. The entire collection, a hundred coins worth over two million in Australian dollars, was taken out of a safe in his house. A Brisbane police detective is faxing the case file to us."

"Any suspects?" Clayton asked.

"None," Matt replied.

"Exactly when did the robbery take place?" Kerney asked.

Matt checked his notes and read off the dates.

"If I'm not mistaken, that's when Denise Riley was allegedly living in Australia. What about the Krugerrand?"

"There is nothing unusual enough about the coin to help connect it to a specific robbery," Matt replied, "so I queried Interpol again and asked for a list of all unsolved heists of large quantities of coins that included Krugerrands. I made a similar request of law enforcement agencies in the Asian rim countries and the Australian Federal Police."

Kerney nodded in approval.

"One more thing, Chief. I examined the plastic sleeve used to protect the Saint-Gaudens. There's an indistinct but recognizable partial thumbprint on the inside of the flap. I powdered it, and it could be a match to a thumbprint Sergeant Pino lifted from inside the well house, but that's just a guess. However, it doesn't appear to belong to Brian Riley, Tim Riley, or Denise Riley. It's going to take a special lab technique to get results that will allow us to make a definitive comparison."

"Okay," Kerney said.

"Let's hope the thumbprint can identify a male subject who wears a size eight narrow shoe," Ramona said.

"Is that who we're looking for?" Matt asked. "Those are some really tiny feet." Matt had met or seen somebody recently with feet like that, but couldn't remember who or where. "Would he be small in height as well?"

"Not necessarily," Clayton answered.

Kerney's phone rang. It was Claire Paley, the questioned documents expert with the state crime lab.

"I didn't expect you to be at work today," Kerney said.

"You wanted quick results," Claire said in her lilting, girlish voice. "Besides, I was born and raised in northern Minnesota. Three feet of snow is hardly enough to keep me from getting to work."

"What kind of results do you have for me?"

"Come to my office and I'll show you," Claire answered. She disconnected before Kerney could question her in detail.


Kerney and Clayton left Matt Chacon and Ramona Pino behind to finish up at the well house and made the slow drive to the state crime lab on barely passable roads and streets. The cold, harsh light from a yellow sun blurred the rolling hills beneath the mountains. On the mountaintops, strong breezes whipped snow into the clear blue sky, creating the illusion of undulating clouds. In the city, long shadows cascaded across deep, untrammeled snow cover that created an oddly different landscape, empty of people and movement. Trees bowed under the weight of snow, branches almost touching the ground. So much snow had fallen that streets and sidewalks were invisible. Traffic lights at deserted intersections blinked and changed colors in sequence along empty thoroughfares.

Large drifts had softened the shape of buildings, hiding much of the boxy ugliness of the businesses along Cerrillos Road, the main route through town. Where major roads had been plowed, only one lane in each direction was passable, and the mounds of snow pushed to the curbs climbed halfway up the lampposts and street signs. In the parking lots only the telltale humps scattered here and there gave evidence of those few cars that had been abandoned by their owners during the storm.

For the moment, it was a world almost without motorized vehicles or the constant background noise of engines. Kerney liked the look of it a lot, but he was glad to be driving his truck to the crime lab and not hoofing it down Cerrillos Road.

At the Department of Public Safety, the parking lot was empty except for a Subaru with a Minnesota Vikings bumper sticker that sat near the public entrance. They found the front entrance unlocked, but no one was on duty at the reception area to sign them in and pass them through the electronically controlled interior door.

Kerney called Claire on his cell phone, and she came and got them. As they walked down the hall, he introduced her to Clayton and asked what she'd discovered.

"That depends on whether or not what I've found makes any sense to you," Claire said as they entered the lab. She led Kerney and Clayton to a large worktable where some of Denise's letters were arranged, protected in clear plastic sleeves.

"First, my analysis of the handwriting conclusively shows that all the letters were written by Denise." Claire peered at Kerney over the bifocals perched on her nose. "Secondly, you wanted to know if the foreign stamps and cancellation marks on the envelopes are real. They are. Then, as you asked, I looked carefully at the paper and watermarks, and found they are of both domestic and foreign manufacture, the highest quality paper being Canadian in origin. The inks used were easily identified by the chemical footprint added by the manufacturers."

Claire glanced from Kerney to Clayton. "You do know that the manufacturers change the chemical composition each year, which makes dating the substance a relatively easy task."

"Of course," Kerney replied.

"So, by comparing the dates in the letters with the paper watermarks and the ink used in composition, I can say without a doubt that they were all written in the year in which they were mailed. However, it is not possible to narrow down the actual composition of the letters to anything less than a twelve-month time frame."

Claire paused for questions.

Kerney knew from experience that Claire was very precise in her presentation of facts, and it was best not to rush her. Besides, she'd braved the elements to get this work done, and he owed her big-time. "We're with you so far," he said.

"Good. I examined the cross-overs and obliterations, and they all fell within the category of misspellings or poor word usage." Claire pointed at the letters on the table. "You wanted me to identify and decipher, if possible, any impressions of handwriting on the paper. The letters before you are the only documents I found with that kind of indentation. Four of them show signatures in Denise Riley's handwriting. The names used are Diane Plumley, Debra Stokes, Dorothy Travis, and Mrs. John Coleman."

"All in Denise's handwriting," Clayton said.

"That's correct." Claire pointed a finger at the letter closest to her on the table. "This document, however, contains more decipherable information than just a signature. Again, it was written in Denise Riley's hand. The return address on the envelope and salutation shows that it was mailed to Helen Muiz by Denise Riley from Brisbane, Australia. The indented writing in the letter is a short thank-you note to a Jann and Jeffery McCafferty for a lovely dinner party. Not every word is readable, but it's dated September 17 and signed 'Dot,' which of course could be short for Dorothy."

"Excellent work, Claire," Kerney said.

"Thank you." Claire patted an errant strand of hair back into place. "But is it helpful information? Do any of these aliases Denise used years ago have a bearing on your case? And who are Jann and Jeffery McCafferty?"

"We don't know yet," Clayton said. "But every factual detail helps."

Claire looked decidedly piqued by Clayton's response. "How unforthcoming you are, Sergeant."

"We do know that the State Department has no record of having issued a passport in Denise Riley's maiden name," Kerney said quickly. "The aliases you've found may very well help us clear that up."

Claire smiled warmly. "Good. I've made photocopies for you of the indented handwriting I was able to discern under oblique light." Claire handed Kerney a manila envelope. "I was going to forward the letters to our fingerprint specialist today, but he's not at work because of the snow."

"What if I send Detective Matt Chacon here to work with you on that?" Kerney asked. Matt Chacon had started his law enforcement career as a civilian fingerprint and tool-mark specialist in the state crime lab, before becoming a police officer with the Santa Fe P.D., and in addition to being a questioned documents expert, Claire was also certified as a forensic fingerprint specialist.

"Under your supervision of course," he added.

Claire hesitated, frowned, and thought it over.

"I'll clear it with Chief Baca," Kerney added.

Claire's expression brightened. "Well, it is your case evidence, and since I'm here now I might as well stay for a while and work with Matt."

"You're a sweetheart, Claire," Kerney said.

Claire adjusted her eyeglasses in a failed attempt to hide a blush.

After Kerney called Andy Baca, who gave the green light for Matt Chacon to work in the lab, Clayton called Matt, filled him in on the plan, and asked him to get to the state crime lab pronto.

Clayton disconnected. "Matt is on his way."

Claire walked the men to the reception area, where Kerney paused at the door and thanked her again.

"I'm going to miss you when you retire Chief Kerney," she said in her tiny, breathless voice.

"I'll miss you too, Claire," Kerney said, holding her hand in his. When he released her hand, she turned quickly and hurried away.

Outside Clayton chuckled. "You made her blush twice. I didn't know you were such a ladies' man."

"Get real."

"I can't get over that little-girl voice of hers. It's just doesn't fit with who she is, what she does, and the way she looks."

"Claire's a force to be reckoned with in more ways than one. State police agents have used her to catch Internet sexual predators. If a pedophile wants to talk directly by telephone to the fictitious underage female he's solicited in the phony chat room the department runs, Claire acts as bait. I understand she has a flair for the theatrical and does a great Lolita. She's helped to put a few really bad scumbags in the slammer for a long time."

"Isn't that something."

"Yes, she is," Kerney said as they piled in the truck. "Let's start running down Denise Riley's aliases, and see if we can find out who Jann and Jeffery McCafferty are."

"Okay."

Kerney cranked the engine and turned to Clayton. "I don't know why Claire found you so unforthcoming. I thought 'every factual detail helps' was a perfectly reasonable response. Much in keeping with my thought earlier in the day that sometimes the solution to a crime is in the little details."

Clayton groaned. "Don't try to bust my chops. That's conduct unbecoming a parent."

Kerney laughed, let the clutch out, and slowly drove out of the slippery parking lot. "Tit for tat," he said.

Matt Chacon's years of experience as a fingerprint technician had taught him that the best detection techniques depended on the nature of the surface to be examined, the presence of any contaminants such as blood or fluid, whether or not the surface was wet or dry, and the likely age of the prints.

Since he would be dealing with dry stationery that had been kept out of direct sunlight for a number of years and quite possibly handled by several of the victim's family members, Matt decided to start with a simple visual inspection of the documents. In the crime lab, he sat on a stool across from Claire Paley at a large examination table. Wearing gloves and using tweezers, they removed each piece of paper and envelope from its protective plastic sleeve and studied it under white light. The few latents revealed by the white light were immediately documented and recorded, but they would have to use ultraviolet light to bring out the invisible prints.

Matt looked across the table at Claire. "When we finish the visual, we'll put everything under ultraviolet. Do we have an autopsy fingerprint card for Denise Riley?"

"Yes," Claire said, "plus Chief Kerney provided fingerprint cards for Helen Muiz, her husband, and other members of her family."

"If nothing else, the chief is very thorough," Matt said gloomily. Many officers in the department, Matt included, weren't happy with the idea of losing Kerney as their top cop. He'd restored professionalism and pride to an organization that had been badly mismanaged by his predecessor.

An hour into the ultraviolet scan, Matt looked at the stack of untouched documents enclosed in clear plastic sleeves. With the number of latents that were showing up on each piece of stationery, he estimated it would take several days to finish the job. He called a halt to the process.

"There's no way we can get through all of this in less than two or three days," he said.

"I agree," Claire said. "What do you suggest?"

"There's a barely visible latent on a protective clear plastic coin sleeve that might match up with a print from a fixed surface at the crime scene. But since it's on a nonporous surface, we need to enhance it."

Claire rose from her stool. "Let's get started. We'll use laser light first, and if that doesn't work, there are a couple of other techniques we can try."

Clayton sat at a small conference table in Kerney's office at police headquarters, paging through the cold case file of the coin collection robbery that the Brisbane P.D. had faxed.

Across the table, Kerney was on the phone talking to federal officials at government agencies. Since arriving at headquarters, he'd been asking every relevant bureau within the State Department, Justice Department, and Homeland Security to do an expedited computer database search on Denise Riley's aliases.

Clayton waited for Kerney to hang up and then quickly said, "The victim of the coin collection theft was, or is, Andrew Edgerton."

Kerney raised an eyebrow. "Meaning?"

"The last entry in the case file is two years old, and Mr. Edgerton was not in good health at that time. If he is still alive, he'll turn seventy-nine on May 18."

"What was the date of the theft again?"

Clayton flipped back to the face sheet and read off the date.

Kerney had made the copies of the letters Denise had sent to Helen Muiz before taking the originals to Claire Paley. He went to his desk, fanned through them, and found Denise's Australian correspondence.

"Denise was in Australia at the time of the heist," he said. "Does the case file give a phone number for Andrew Edgerton?"

"It does."

"Read it off to me."

"What time is it in Australia?" Clayton asked.

"I don't know," Kerney replied. "If it's the middle of the night and Edgerton is dead, it won't matter that I might have disturbed him. If he's still alive, maybe he'll be happy I woke him up and reminded him of the fact. Give me the number."

Clayton read it off. Kerney wrote it down, looked up the international calling code for Australia in the phone book, dialed the number on his desk phone, and motioned to Clayton to turn on the speaker phone that sat in the center of the conference table.

Kerney looked at his watch. It was three o'clock in the afternoon, which meant it was sometime tomorrow morning in Australia. He listened for the call to go through, and when he heard the distinctive ringtone, he hung up the handset and joined Clayton at the conference table.

A man with an elderly voice answered the call and Kerney asked if he was speaking to Andrew Edgerton.

"That's right."

Kerney introduced himself as the Santa Fe, New Mexico, police chief, told Edgerton that Sergeant Clayton Istee was also on the line, and asked if Edgerton would mind talking about the theft of his coin collection.

"Have you found the collection?" Edgerton asked. "Did the thieves take it to the United States?"

"We only found one coin," Kerney replied, "so I can't tell you if the coins were smuggled into the country."

"Which one did you find?"

Kerney described the Saint-Gaudens in detail.

"A very nice gold coin," Edgerton said. "Probably worth a lot more now than what the insurance company reimbursed me. Don't send it to me. The insurance company owns it now."

"I understand that, Mr. Edgerton. Would you mind if we ask you some questions about the robbery?"

"Go ahead, but I'll tell you right now I've been over all of this a dozen times or more and it hasn't done a bit of good."

Kerney and Clayton took turns asking Edgerton questions, and his answers were consistent with the facts recorded in the case file. The night of the robbery, Edgerton, a widower, had locked all the doors and windows to his house, armed his home security system, and gone to bed around ten-thirty. Just after midnight, a masked, armed man woke him and ordered him to open the safe in the downstairs library. Edgerton did as he was told and the robber cleaned out the contents, which consisted solely of the coin collection. The robber tied Edgerton up using duct tape and left by a rear door.

"There were two of them," Edgerton said. "I'm sure of it. When the thief with the gun was leaving my house, I heard a car engine start up. He had a wheelman."

Clayton smiled at Edgerton's use of crime story slang. "But you didn't see the driver."

"No, and as I said, I didn't really see the man with the gun. He was masked."

"In your statement you said he was slender in build and about five-eight or five-nine in height," Kerney said.

"That's right. But he was wearing one of those ski masks so I didn't get to see the color of his hair or any of his features."

"His eyes?" Kerney asked.

"I was too scared to notice."

"What did he sound like?" Kerney asked.

"An average bloke," Edgerton replied.

"Australian?"

"That's right."

"Had there been any other recent robberies in your neighborhood?" Clayton asked.

"No. The police who investigated told me that I'd been targeted because of my coin collection. They talked to everyone who knew about it, and that wasn't very many people as I tend to keep my affairs to myself."

"A wise thing to do," Clayton said. "Did anything out of the ordinary occur in your neighborhood prior to the robbery?"

"Out of the ordinary?"

"Door-to-door salesmen coming around, large parties that might have attracted strangers to the neighborhood, people asking for donations to worthy causes."

"I can't recall anything like that."

"Mr. Edgerton," Kerney said, consulting the list of names that Claire Paley had deciphered from Denise Riley's letters. "I'd like to read you some names and have you tell me if you either know the person, or if the name sounds familiar."

"Go ahead."

"Diane Plumley."

"No."

"Debra Stokes."

"No."

"Dorothy Travis."

"No."

"Anyone who might have used Dot as a nickname."

"No."

"How about a Mrs. John Coleman?"

"I don't know anyone named Coleman."

"Jann and Jeffery McCafferty?"

"Jeff and Jann are friends, although I don't see them very often now that they live in Sydney. Jeff's a senior vice president of a bank."

"How did you make their acquaintance?" Clayton asked.

"At church. I've know them for twenty-five years or more. In fact, Jeff got me started collecting coins as an investment. He's a serious numismatist."

Clayton zeroed in on Edgerton's interactions with the

McCaffertys around the time of the robbery. Edgerton had lost his wife to a stroke six months before the theft. To bolster his spirits, the McCaffertys had made him a frequent guest at their dinner parties. Mostly the guest list consisted of bankers and their spouses, but sometimes Jeff threw a beer and pizza party for his serious coin collector friends.

"Think back, Mr. Edgerton," Kerney prodded. "A few weeks before the robbery, do you remember meeting an American woman at one of the McCaffertys' dinner parties? She would have been Hispanic looking, attractive, in her early thirties, slender and petite, with dark hair."

"I can't recall meeting an American woman like that," Edgerton replied. "But there was a very interesting couple from Belize Jeff had met at a Brisbane coin show. Belize used to be British Honduras, you know. Part of the Commonwealth. He was a Brit and she was half-English and half-Hispanic. However, I don't recall their names."

"Can you describe the man?"

"No, it was years ago and I only met him and his lady friend that once."

"Thank you," Kerney said. "You've been very helpful."

A smiling Matt Chacon stood in the open doorway. Kerney waved and pointed to an empty chair. Matt entered and sat.

"I hope you catch the bugger who stuck that gun in my face and stole my property," Edgerton said.

Kerney promised to do his best, said good-bye, disconnected, and turned his attention to Chacon. "Why the smile?"

"Because the thumbprint on the plastic coin sleeve belongs to one Archie Pattison, a citizen of the United Kingdom. He is also known as John Culley, Denise Riley's employer."

"By chance does Mr. Pattison have any ties to what was once known as British Honduras?" Clayton asked.

Matt looked surprised. "Yes, he does. He was born there.

When British Honduras became the independent country of Belize, he retained his British citizenship and emigrated to London. He served in the Royal Marines and disappeared from sight after his discharge."

"What else do you know about Mr. Pattison, aka John Culley?" Kerney asked.

"Other than he's in this country as a permanent resident under a false identity with a forged passport, that's it for now," Matt replied. "What do you know about him, Chief?"

Kerney stood. "Culley and Denise Riley, posing as a married couple, probably pulled off that coin heist in Australia. Let's go pay Culley a visit. Where's Sergeant Pino? She needs to be in on this."

"She's on her way here," Matt replied.

Kerney headed for the door with Clayton and Matt at his heels. "Tell her to meet us at Culley's house."

"Roger that, Chief," Matt replied.

# Chapter Twelve

John Culley lived on a hill off a dirt lane near Acequia Madre. The area hadn't yet become completely gentrified, but the upscale Santa Fe–style estates already outnumbered the tiny, dilapidated casitas with peeling paint, rickety doors, and tumbledown concrete block walls owned by the *plebe*.

The deep snow and heavy drifts on the unplowed side streets made the trip to Culley's road a thirty-minute adventure. The three officers arrived at the bottom of the hill to find Ramona Pino parked and waiting in her unmarked unit. They stood with her in front of her vehicle and gazed at the steep, impassable lane.

"Did anyone remember to bring snowshoes?" Ramona asked.

Kerney looked down at his petite sergeant and smiled. "I don't think it's quite over your head. We'll pull you to safety if it is. How far up the hill does Culley live?"

"I don't know," Matt replied. "I only met with him at his place of business."

"I'll break trail," Clayton said.

"Lead on," Kerney agreed.

They started out in single file behind Clayton, with Ramona and Matt bringing up the rear.

"Do we even know if Culley is at home?" Ramona asked Matt.

"Nope. On a day like this with everything shut down, the chief thought it best to make an unannounced visit so as not to raise any suspicions."

"So what's the plan when we get there?"

"We surround the house, while Chief Kerney and Sergeant Istee knock at the front door and introduce themselves."

"That should work."

Up ahead, Clayton and Kerney paused to look at street numbers on some mailboxes that were poking up above the snow level at curbside.

Ramona was happy to take a break. Trying to keep up with her long-legged companions had turned into quite a chore. "Do you think Culley was the father of Denise Riley's unborn child?" she asked.

Matt gulped down some cold air that freeze-dried his throat. "I had the distinct impression that he was gay. But maybe he's bi."

"There was no mention in your notes that you talked to Culley's alleged lover."

"Never did," Matt said. His legs were aching from pulling each foot free from the deep snow and plunging on. "At the time of my interview, Culley was a source of information, not a suspect."

Ramona's breath iced up in the air. "Maybe Culley's housemate, lover, or whatever you want to call him, is a beard."

"Could be. Do you think Culley killed her because she was pregnant or because she had appropriated some of their ill-gotten gains without his knowledge?"

Ramona's nose was runny. She wiped it with a tissue. "Rage is one possible motive. Greed, jealousy are others."

"Maybe Culley, his lover, and Denise Riley were a ménage à trois."

"That's an interesting notion." She stuffed the tissue in a coat pocket.

Twenty feet ahead, Kerney and Clayton stood at the front of a driveway where two vehicles sat under a carport. Neither the walkway to the house nor the driveway showed any sign of foot or vehicle traffic. There were lights on inside the residence.

Using hand signals, Kerney motioned for Ramona to cover the front of the house and Matt to take the back.

"I doubt Culley is going to try make a getaway under these conditions," Matt said as he checked his semiautomatic and returned it to its holster.

"You're such a spoilsport, Chacon," Ramona said as he moved off.

Culley's house was one of those old adobe casitas that had been renovated, expanded, and made into a seven-figure property. It had a squat profile, rounded parapets, recessed windows in the double adobe walls, two chimneys spewing piñon smoke into the cold sky, a wide flagstone portal, and a tall, hand-carved antique Mexican front door.

Kerney rang the doorbell and brushed snow off his soaked pant legs with a gloved hand while he waited. Clayton stood to one side of the door stomping his feet to loosen snow from his boots. He had his hand in his jacket pocket, gripping his semi-automatic.

The door opened to reveal a slender, middle-aged man wearing a crewneck wool sweater, fleece sweatpants, and bedroom slippers. He had rather tiny feet. Size eight, Clayton guessed.

"John Culley?" Kerney asked.

"Yes, indeed." Culley glanced from Kerney to Clayton with what appeared to be amused interest. "Surely you're not new neighbors, unless someone has moved away from the lane within the last twenty-four hours."

"Surely, we're not, Mr. Culley." Kerney stepped through the

doorway before Culley could react. "Or should I call you Archie Pattison?"

Culley's lighthearted expression vanished. "You're cops?"

"Indeed we are. Is there anyone in the house besides you?"

"My partner is in the library."

"Anyone else?"

"No."

"Very good. Where is the library?"

"Why do you ask?"

"The library, Culley," Kerney demanded.

"Straight through the living room and turn left at the hallway."

Kerney nodded to Clayton, who went to round up Culley's partner.

"Why are you barging in here?" Culley asked.

"We're arresting you on five counts of murder one." The death of Denise's unborn child counted as a separate homicide. Kerney spun Culley around, pushed him up against a wall, cuffed his hands at the small of his back, and recited the Miranda rights.

"That's absurd."

"Why don't you tell me why you killed them, Culley? You're going to prison anyway for illegal entry, false identity, and whatever else the feds decide to throw at you."

Culley's eyes narrowed. "I have nothing to say to you, and I want to call a lawyer."

"All in good time." Kerney used his handheld to call Ramona and Matt into the house. When they arrived, he turned Culley over to them and went to find Clayton, who was talking to a nervous man in the library.

"This is Proctor Whitley," Clayton said.

Whitley looked to be about Culley's age. He was stout and had a long narrow chin that quivered slightly.

"Are you going to arrest him?" Kerney asked.

"Whatever for?" the man asked in a quaking voice.

Clayton shrugged. "He says he wants to cooperate."

"Okay, see what he has to say. Matt and Ramona will work with you. I'll tell them to get started on a search warrant."

"Where are you going?"

"Culley doesn't want to give up his Miranda rights, so I'm taking him to jail. Check in with me when you're done here."

"Will do."

At the front alcove, Kerney told Culley he was going to jail and pushed him out the door.

"There's three feet of snow out here," Culley said. "At least let me put my shoes on and get a coat."

"It's not that far down the hill," Kerney said as he yanked Culley off the portal face-first into the deep snow. "You'll make it just fine."

During the drive to the county detention center on Highway 14 outside of town, Culley didn't say a word. He didn't even bitch about being forced to walk through the snow in his bedroom slippers without a coat. He sat silently in the backseat shivering and staring out the window with a blank look on his face.

At the jail, Kerney asked Culley if he wanted to change his mind and talk without an attorney present. Culley gave Kerney a scornful look and shook his head. Kerney put him in a holding cell and went to do the paperwork. Just as he was finishing up, Sid Larranaga, the district attorney, sat down next to him.

"I didn't expect to see you here," Kerney said.

Sid removed his hat and ran a hand through his slicked-back hair. "This is your last major case before you retire, and I want to make sure you get it right."

Kerney smiled. Sid had publicly announced that he would not stand for reelection two years hence, and there was talk among the local politicos that he planned to run for state attorney general instead. The Culley case, if won, would be a feather in his cap as a true crime fighter.

"That's awfully good of you, Sid. Do my people have a search warrant?"

"They do. Judge Cooke just phoned it in. Is your murder suspect going to cooperate and make a full, voluntary confession?"

"Not a chance. This guy is a cool customer."

Sal took off his coat and hung it on the back of his chair. "Okay, beyond probable cause, tell me what you've got."

Kerney ran it down, and by the time he was finishing up, Larranaga didn't look happy.

"You're telling me you don't have a clear-cut motive, there's nothing yet to tie Culley to the double homicide in Albuquerque, and the evidence gathered in Capitan and Cañoncito only puts him at the crime scenes but doesn't prove he killed Deputy Riley and his wife."

"That's right," Kerney replied.

Sal looked gloomy. "Sometimes I wish I had become a defense attorney. So far all you've got that I can walk into a courtroom with right now is a case against a felon wanted on a fugitive warrant for a heist in Australia who's been living the good life in the old U.S. of A. under an alias with a forged passport and screwing his now deceased, recently murdered secretary while pretending to be gay."

"Don't be such a pessimist, Sal," Kerney said. "You know as well as I do that the really important work comes after an arrest."

Sal grunted. "Three weeks from now when you're retired and sitting under the portal in a rocking chair on your ranch, I'll remember that. I swear, Kerney, if this case does go to trial on the murder one charges, I'm going to subpoena you to testify even if it means you have to come back here from London or wherever the hell you'll be living at the time."

Kerney laughed. "I'll be glad to oblige. How long do you think it will be before Culley can talk face-to-face with a lawyer?"

"With the way the roads are, I doubt anybody's going to be willing to make the trip out here from town until late tomorrow morning. Why do you ask?"

"I'd hate to see him go into the general population if there's a chance that his lawyer can get out here sooner rather than later."

Larranaga raised an eyebrow. Kerney wanted Culley kept overnight in a holding cell, which came handsomely equipped with a concrete slab to sleep on, a washbasin, a crapper, and a glaringly bright ceiling light that was never turned off. It was unorthodox treatment to say the least, but certainly well deserved for a scumbag who had five murder counts against him, including two cops.

"Has Culley made his phone call?" Sid asked.

"Not yet. He'll be processed and dressed out first."

"Once he does make that call, I certainly wouldn't want him to be denied quick access to legal counsel," Sid said. "I'll ask the shift supervisor to keep him in the holding cell until his lawyer arrives."

"Excellent. Also, I need a search warrant to draw a blood sample from Culley, so the lab can determine whether or not he was the father of Denise Riley's unborn child."

"The fetus has been preserved?"

"It has."

"That won't be a problem," Sal said.

"Have you made a decision on Clifford Talbott?"

"I'm ruling it a justified homicide. Kirt Latimer will cut him loose tomorrow."

"Would you mind if I told him he's off the hook?" Kerney asked.

"You know him personally, right?" Sid stood and stuck an arm into a coat sleeve.

"I know him casually, but he strikes me as a good man."

"Go ahead and tell him. I'll have Kirt give his wife a call so she can arrange to pick him up. I'd like you and all your principal investigators to meet with me in my office at eight A.M., so we can go over everything we've got so far."

"That's not a problem."

Larranaga gave Kerney a sad shake of his head. "It's not going to be the same without you, Kerney."

Kerney got to his feet and slapped Larranaga on the back. "Now, don't go and get all teary-eyed on me, Sid."

Sid faked a sniffle and wiped away an imaginary tear. "I'll see you in the morning, Chief."

Kerney nodded, gathered up his paperwork, and dropped the booking forms off to the correctional officer at the intake station. Before he asked for Clifford Talbott to be brought to an interview room to meet with him, Kerney stopped by the holding cell to tell Culley that he'd be spending the night lying on a cold slab, which was exactly where he belonged.


After advising a very relieved Clifford Talbott that he would not be prosecuted for the shooting death of Brian Riley, Kerney returned to the Culley residence. During his absence, Clayton, Ramona, and Matt Chacon had executed the search warrant and called in Don Mielke, several of his S.O. investigators, and three city detectives to help collect evidence.

In the kitchen, which had been designated as the evidence collection area, Kerney looked over what had already been discovered. An empty battered briefcase with traces of soil on it, most likely from the well house, sat on the kitchen table. Next to it were a number of gold coins in clear plastic sleeves, and passports from the United Kingdom, Canada, and Belize bearing Denise Riley's photograph and the names of Diane Plumley, Debra Stokes, and Dorothy Travis—the aliases used by Denise that had been uncovered by Claire Paley, the questioned document expert.

Kerney gave the gold coins a careful once-over. Some were Krugerrands, and according to the Brisbane P.D. coin heist case file, none of the stolen Edgerton coins had been Krugerrands. He asked the young sheriff's investigator who'd been assigned the responsibility of receiving, logging, and guarding evidence if the Krugerrands had been found with the other coins.

The cop consulted the form on his clipboard and nodded affirmatively.

Also on the table was a Beretta over/under twenty-gauge shotgun with gold engraving and a high-grade walnut stock worth at least six to eight thousand dollars. Kerney wondered if it had been the weapon used to kill Deputy Riley.

"Have other guns been found?" he asked.

"Not yet, Chief," the investigator said. "But that sweet Beretta twenty-gauge you're looking at showed up as stolen from a gun heist in Montreal, Canada, over twelve years ago. Twenty-three sporting weapons and rare antique rifles were taken out of a private residence while the owners were vacationing in Mexico. Total value of the haul at the time of the burglary was 1.2 million in Canadian dollars. Major Mielke has requested a copy of the case file from the Montreal police."

"Do we have any indication that Culley may be connected to the robbery?"

"Not yet, but Detective Chacon is working on it."

"Well, if Culley did pull the heist, I can understand why he kept the shotgun," Kerney said. "It's a beauty. Is there any evidence the gun has been recently used?"

The cop shook his head. "It's been thoroughly cleaned and oiled, but Sergeant Istee says it wasn't used to kill Deputy Riley."

"Why does he say that?"

"Because a twelve-gauge was used in that shooting."

On the countertop next to the sink was a pair of men's light-weight hiking boots with a tread that matched the shoe impression Clayton had found on the trail to the well house. There was soil embedded in the heel which a forensic geologist might be able to match to the soil at the well house. The size label stitched inside the tongue showed that the books were indeed a size eight narrow.

Next to the hiking boots was an closed accordion document file. Kerney asked the young S.O. investigator what was inside.

"Financial papers, Chief. Sergeant Pino said she would have a detective go through them after the house search is completed."

Kerney looked at what had been gathered so far. It was all good, damning circumstantial evidence, but hardly the stuff an ironclad multiple murder conviction was made of. In his head, he could hear Sid Larranaga saying the same thing at the meeting tomorrow morning.

Clayton entered the kitchen carrying a Glock 9mm handgun in a clear plastic bag.

"Is that the same caliber used in the Robocker-Connors homicides?" Kerney asked hopefully.

"Negative." Clayton handed the weapon to the young officer, who began logging it in as evidence. "According to the autopsy reports, the bullets that killed Robocker and Officer Connors came from a thirty-eight. Probably a throwaway. Did Culley confess or make a statement?"

"He said he wanted a lawyer and clammed up. The DA has asked to meet with us tomorrow morning, and he'll be waiting to hear that we've got hard evidence he can use to guarantee a conviction."

"I'd like that too, but so far it isn't happening. I called Detective Armijo at APD and gave him information about Culley's vehicle. He's gathering video from the surveillance cameras at Robocker's apartment complex and a nearby traffic camera used to catch drivers who run red lights. Hopefully, we'll be able to put Culley in his vehicle at or near the crime scene."

"What did Proctor Whitley have to say?"

"Whitley's gay, Culley's bi, and Denise Riley, who was also bi, was Culley's lover. Whitley swears he didn't know Denise was pregnant. He did say that Culley went out of town to attend some insurance training seminars just before and after Deputy Riley's murder and the double homicide in Albuquerque. We still don't know if he's an accomplice in Culley's past crimes or involved in any of the homicides."

"If Culley ever starts talking, it will be interesting to see what kind of alibi he comes up," Kerney said. "So you're telling me that Tim Riley was the poor sap Denise Riley married to make her straight, Catholic siblings believe that she'd given up her wild ways and settled down."

"That's what I'm telling you."

"I've asked the DA to get a search warrant to draw a blood sample from Culley."

"Culley had to be the one who got Denise pregnant," Clayton said. "That's the only way this makes any sense. I think Denise Riley made a decision to leave Tim Riley, talked him into taking the Lincoln County S.O. job, and had no intention of moving with him. Maybe she was even planning to leave Santa Fe and disappear. I also think she decided to have the baby rather than abort, and when Culley demanded that she abort it, she decided to end her relationship with him. Maternal instincts can be very powerful."

"There was a strong sexual element to the staging of Denise's murder in Cañoncito," Kerney said. "And it was his least well-organized killing. It was if he was angry, not thinking clearly, and wanted to degrade her. But why bushwhack Deputy Riley, hunt down Brian Riley, and kill Robocker and Connors along the way?"

"Paranoia makes sense," Clayton replied. "Maybe Culley started worrying that Denise had spilled the beans to her husband and stepson about him, their criminal past together, and their intimate relationship. Maybe he figured Brian could have told Robocker, so to protect himself Culley took her out. Officer Connors just happened to get in the way."

"I want to know everything there is to know about John Culley, aka Archie Pattison," Kerney said. "I want Sid Larranaga armed with enough information about Culley to convince a jury that the man had the necessary knowledge and expertise to commit these crimes. And I want Proctor Whitley put through an intense interrogation. Either he washes clean in all past or present cases or we book him on every felony we can think of that applies. Have Sergeant Pino take him into custody, remove him from the premises to police headquarters, and start the process now. Tell her we need to squeeze every bit of pertinent information we can out of him pronto."

Clayton gave Kerney a quizzical look. "We've got a lot of time to work this case before it goes to trial. Why the big hurry?"

"Because *I'm* running out of time and I want this case as far along as possible on the day I retire." Kerney turned and started for the door.

"Fair enough. Where are you going now?"

"To tell Helen Muiz that we've caught her sister's killer. I'll be back."

In the days remaining until his retirement, Kerney put in long hours overseeing the progress of the investigation. While it was clear he would leave without handing Sal Larranaga the clear-cut proof needed to guarantee Culley's conviction as a mass murderer, the circumstantial evidence that the team had amassed against Culley was overwhelming.

Detective Lee Armijo's review of videotapes from surveillance and traffic cameras clearly put Culley in the vicinity of the Robocker-Connors murders on the day before the crime. A deep background check of Archie Pattison, aka John Culley, revealed that not only had he served in the Royal Marines, he'd been trained in an elite force that carried out special covert ops.

In the years following his military service, Culley had traveled the world, financing his extravagant lifestyle by pulling off well-planned robberies. Both the Brisbane coin heist and the Montreal weapons caper had been conclusively pinned on Culley and Denise Riley, and based on evidence seized at Culley's house, the duo were primary suspects in a half-dozen more cold cases spanning three continents.

Arrest warrants for Culley had been issued by police departments of three foreign countries, and various federal agencies had slapped heavy felony charges against him for violating a number of immigration laws and criminal statues. But Kerney figured once Culley was convicted on the murder one counts, most of the pending cases would be dropped.

Ramona Pino's interrogation of Proctor Whitley revealed the man was not an accomplice to any of Culley's crimes. He agreed to cooperate fully and gave specific information about several heated arguments he'd overheard where Culley had demanded that Denise get an abortion. Because it went straight to the issue of Culley's motive, Sid Larranaga loved it. Sid was also very happy when the paternity test results confirmed that Culley had been the father of Denise's unborn child.

Even with his hectic work schedule, Kerney got to savor some special moments. In a ceremony at the Lincoln County Courthouse, with Sara, Patrick, Wendell, and Hannah standing at his side, he watched Grace and Sheriff Paul Hewitt pin lieutenant bars on Clayton's collar. That same week, back in Santa Fe, he pinned lieutenant bars on Ramona Pino and announced that the mayor had appointed Larry Otero, Kerney's second in command, to be the next chief of the department.

There were somber moments too. Kerney attended the burial of Deputy Tim Riley at the Santa Fe National Cemetery, a memorial service in Albuquerque for Officer Judy Connors, and Denise Riley's funeral, all within the span of a few days.

Devastated by Denise's murder and the revelations of her secret past, Helen Muiz chose not to return to work prior to her official retirement date. She sent her husband Ruben to clean out her office, and while he was there he told Kerney that he was taking Helen to Italy to visit the Vatican and that the archbishop was attempting to secure an audience for her with the pope.

Because he was still spending most of his time away from home on the case, Clayton talked Grace into taking some time off from work, letting the kids miss a few days of school, and joining him in Santa Fe. They stayed with Kerney, Sara, and Patrick in the guest quarters at the ranch, and for five days the house was a beehive of activity filled with the sound of children slamming doors, running in and out, giggling and laughing, arguing about what games to play, drawing pictures and coloring at the kitchen table, and asking any adult within earshot to let them go horseback riding again and again and again.

Having Clayton and his family as houseguests clearly emboldened Sara's spirits. When their guests left to go back home, she told Kerney it had been the best five days since her return from Iraq.

"I could see that," he said.

"It was my most fun time *ever*," Patrick said.

"I could see that too," he said. "Maybe you need a brother or a sister."

"A little brother," Patrick announced, "not another grown-up one like Clayton."

"What about a little sister?" Sara asked.

Patrick thought about it for a moment. "That would be okay."

Sara reached down, scooped him up, and nuzzled his cheek. "We'll see what we can do."


There is a ceremonial mesa on the Mescalero Apache Reservation that gives a clear south-southwest view of White Sands, the Tularosa Basin, and the San Andres Mountains beyond, seventy-five miles distant. The day after Lieutenant Clayton Istee had wrapped up the Tim Riley homicide investigation, he tiptoed out of the house at three-thirty in the morning while his wife and children slept, and went to the mesa.

Although the dream of Tim Riley singing the Death Song hadn't reoccurred, it had become fixed in Clayton's mind and he needed to shake it off permanently. In the darkness of the night with the Big Dipper overhead, he took two large rocks, placed one at the north compass point and the other at the west, which was the direction the dead always took during their beginning passage. Between the two rocks Clayton buried a photograph of Tim Riley in uniform that he'd taken from the Cañoncito double-wide and then bracketed the photograph with smaller stones to symbolically separate the image from the living world. Finished, he stood back, tossed a handful of dirt into the center of the circle, said a few words about Tim Riley, and left for home.

In four days, he would return to the mesa and remove all traces of the burial ritual. As he drove down the mesa, he could already feel himself letting go of Tim Riley. Or was Riley's ghost letting go of him?

## ABOUT THE AUTHOR

Michael McGarrity is the author of the Anthony Award–nominated *Tularosa*, as well as *Mexican Hat, Serpent Gate, Hermit's Peak, The Judas Judge, Under the Color of Law, The Big Gamble, Everyone Dies, Slow Kill*, and *Nothing but Trouble*. A former deputy sheriff for Santa Fe County, he established the first Sex Crimes Unit for the department. He has also served as an instructor at the New Mexico Law Enforcement Academy and as an investigator for the New Mexico Public Defender's Office. He lives in Santa Fe.